PRAISE AND AWARDS FOR *DISSOLUTION OF PEACE*
BOOK 1 OF *THE SERENITY SAGA*

"Lots of action, good emotional points and I love the landscape… I left my soft chair and became a love-crossed, beautiful captain of a starship."
— Scifi Book Review

"Recommendation: read this if you feel like re-visiting the Golden Age of Sci-Fi."
— The British Fantasy Society

"This book was a fantastic science fiction thrill ride… This book could very easily become a memorable sci-fi series comparable to Star Trek."
— Bookworm Babblings

"Tension. Betrayal. Love. Lust. Politics. Action. This story has it all."
— Robert D. Marion, Author *Danger Close*

Dissolution of Peace

The Serenity Saga: Book 1

Richard Flores IV

Dissolution of Peace

Fourth Edition

Copyright © 2023 Richard Flores IV

Original Copyright © 2012 Richard Flores IV

Book Layout by Richard Flores IV

Cover Art by Neil Jackson

Published by Richard Flores IV Auburn, Washington

www.floresfactor.com

ISBN: 0615706851
ISBN-13: 978-0615706856

FOR CINCO, JANGO, AND KIRK

Keep dreaming big and never let go of those dreams.

"It isn't enough to talk about peace. One must believe in it. And it isn't enough to believe in it. One must work at it."

- Eleanor Roosevelt

Ranks of the Earth Military by Branch

Enlisted

	Army	Navy	Air Force	Security Forces
E1	Private	Crewman Recruit	Airman Basic	Officer Recruit
E2	Private	Crewman Apprentice	Airman	Officer Trainee
E3	Private First Class	Crewman	Airman First Class	Officer Second Class
E4	Corporal or Specialist	Petty Officer Third Class	Senior Airman	Officer First Class
E5	Sergeant	Petty Officer Second Class	Staff Sergeant	Corporal Second Class
E6	Staff Sergeant	Petty Officer First Class	Technical Sergeant	Corporal First Class
E7	Sergeant First Class	Chief Petty Officer	Master Sergeant	Sergeant First Class
E8	First Sergeant	Senior Chief Petty Officer	First Sergeant	First Sergeant
E9	Sergeant Major	Master Chief Petty Officer	Chief Master Sergeant	First Sergeant

Officers

	Army	Navy	Air Force	Security Forces
O1	Second Lieutenant	Ensign	Second Lieutenant	Second Lieutenant
O2	First Lieutenant	Lieutenant Junior Grade	First Lieutenant	First Lieutenant
O3	Captain	Lieutenant	Captain	Captain
O4	Major	Lieutenant Commander	Major	Major
O5	Lieutenant Colonel	Commander	Lieutenant Colonel	Assistant Chief
O6	Colonel	Captain	Colonel	Chief
O7	Brigadier General	Rear Admiral Lower	Brigadier General	Brigadier General
O8	Major General	Rear Admiral Upper	Major General	Major General
O9	Lieutenant General	Vice Admiral	Lieutenant General	Lieutenant General
O10	General	Admiral	General	General

CHAPTER 1

Janice Kanter was mesmerized by the size of the warship as it blocked the view of the stars through the window of the runabout. She knew the ship was big, but to see the size of it now, even at this distance, was awe-inspiring. The Navy had nicknamed these warships "flying bricks" because of their shape and size. The name was accurate; it appeared to be a giant grey brick floating in space.

As the runabout circled the warship awaiting clearance to land, the details became more apparent. The flight deck could be seen below the engines. The hull was speckled with cannon slots. How many guns did a ship in a peaceful navy need? The bridge dome was to the top front, large letters read "E.S.S. Australia."

The approach to the flight deck reminded her of her hatred for space flight. She looked away from the window to the crewman sitting next to her. He turned away quickly. She wasn't sure if he was checking her out or staring because of her uniform. It was probably the latter.

She was the only one wearing it on the runabout filled with Navy Crewmen. Her dark grey uniform, with its black accents, contrasted with the tan Navy uniforms. It was more than a simple difference that caught their eye. It was what the uniform symbolized: Law Enforcement.

She smiled at the crewman when he turned to glance at her again. A stray hair contrasted with the Earth on her arm patch and she dusted it off. The image of the planet, spread out like an atlas, was the only color on the dark uniform. Its blues and greens highlighted by the black background of the circle patch. The word "Security" along the top and "Forces" on the bottom labeled her. The crewman turned away again.

"Do you ever get used to space flight?" Janice said to the man. "I hate it."

"I don't know. This is my first assignment." He smiled only out of pleasantries. "They tell me you don't even notice you're moving on a ship that size."

"I hope so." Janice turned back to the window. She could see the rapidly growing size of the flight deck. The sheer size of the opening made her feel as if she was being swallowed by a beast. She sunk into her seat, realizing they were landing.

Being in space was bad enough. She really hoped she could get used to it. The reality was she just didn't like this assignment. She had only gone to Protective Services training because it was made clear to her that she couldn't promote without a specialty assignment. She planned for a six month assignment protecting some Governor. Not a military assignment and certainly not a space assignment. It would be at least a year before she could go back to patrol.

The shuttle surged forward as it hit the deck. She swallowed hard to hide her reaction. As soon as the light turned on she unhooked her restraints and made her way to the ramp in the middle of the shuttle. She was glad all her belongings were sent up ahead of her. She was halfway down the ramp before it contacted the deck.

Janice started making her way to the back of the flight deck, when someone yelled at her. She turned around quickly to see a man in the same uniform as her, pointing her way.

"Hey, get over here." His stern face made Janice pause. "Yes, you. Where are you going? You're holding up the rest of the people."

"What?" Janice walked over.

"Everyone boarding the ship has to be checked in." He made no effort to hide his annoyance. He pulled out a small device no bigger than the palm of his hand, a chip scanner.

"Even us?" Janice moved her hair from the back of her neck.

"This must be your first military assignment." The man's face softened and there was a bit less aggrevation in his tone. He scanned the back of her neck and read over the screen. "Everyone is checked in and out, no matter what branch or how long their stay will be. Anyway, your orders check out. Corporal Carlson has asked you to meet him over there."

Janice surveyed the area he gestured to. At the far side of the bay stood a man in a dress uniform, which really just included a tie. That was her new partner. A Corporal even; Janice wished she'd read the orders better.

As she approached him, he put out his hand. She shook it firmly. "You must be Corporal Carlson. You didn't have to meet me here."

"'Mike' is fine. And I just came back from a couple weeks' shore leave."

He turned. "Follow me. It's much quieter once we get off the flight deck."

Carlson was a tall man, even with Janice's height. Dark black hair was trimmed within regulations but was hardly the typical high and tight that most wore. He was thin, but just a hint of muscle could be seen on his arms. He wasn't all that attractive, but he wasn't ugly, either.

As they stepped through the doorway, Carlson spoke. "There, much better. Welcome to the Australia. She is a good ship and the Captain is a good person to work for. Better than most Captains to protect. Or so I have been told."

"Youngest Commanding Officer in the fleet, too." Janice moved up next to Carlson.

"Ah, so you did read some of the file then." Carlson seemed to be judging Janice with his eyes, she was sure it was because she was new to this. She only nodded in response. "Good. She's smart and deserves to be in command."

The interior of the ship's walls were a nondescript blue, much like a cubical. Screens were near every major junction and the lighting was really good. Janice had worried that working in space would be dark and depressing; this was the opposite.

She noticed a lot of people moving around; a lot more than she thought she would see on a naval ship. The crew compliments must have been large. That information was probably listed in the orders she'd barely read.

"You didn't have to get dressed up for me," Janice broke the silence. When Carlson gave her a puzzled look, she flashed a quick smirk to show she was kidding.

Carlson turned and studied the floor in front of him. "I attended an officer's funeral today. I arrived back on the ship in the runabout before yours."

"Oh," Janice studied Carlson's reaction. "If I may ask, was it your old partner?"

"No." Was that a trace of anger she saw in his eyes? Carlson changed the subject. "You were quite the star at the academy. Top marksman with the L-pistol, third with the rifle. Top in your class in academics and second best in physical fitness."

Janice really wished she had read up on Carlson more; hell, she wished she had read anything about him. Why was he talking about her time at the academy anyway? That was years ago. "Yeah."

"Yet, you barely passed the Protective Services training. Fourth from the bottom."

Janice didn't like having that pointed out to her. She could have, and should have, done better. "And now you're stuck with me."

"I picked you." Carlson looked her over again. "I asked for records, not names or descriptions."

"And why do you want the fourth from the bottom?"

"There are two reasons most people join Protective Services. They either want to protect the Prime Minister," Carlson stopped at a hallway. "Or they just want an easy specialty so they can return to patrol and promote."

"You think you got me figured out then, is that it?" Janice spoke with a controlled tone. Who was this Corporal to analyze her records and make a judgment about her? And why did it bother her that he was right?

"I am not sure about that," Carlson said. He activated a screen at the intersection. "This screen will show you a map of the ship. Your stuff should be in your quarters. Our first shift is tomorrow night, third watch. See you then."

Janice watched him walk away. Space work, a smart-ass Corporal for a partner, and graveyard work. This was going to be a long year.

Chapter 2

A twinge of pain shot through Captain Christina Serenity's left hip. Maybe she shouldn't have persuaded the Doctor to clear her for duty. But, she wasn't about to spend any longer in that hospital bed surrounded by her two "bodyguards" and thinking about what happened to her. She had a ship to run.

Besides, the longer she sat in bed, the more the Admiral would think of ways to replace her. An injury would be the perfect justification and she wasn't about to give him the satisfaction. So, she lied about the pain. And they listed her fit for duty.

She sat down at the desk of her ready room, right off the bridge, when there was a knock at the door. One of the Protective Services officers opened it. Lieutenant Commander Zimmerman was standing there waiting to be acknowledged.

"Come in. Sit down." Serenity turned to the officers. "Wait outside."

Once they left, Zimmerman—who was still standing—spoke. "How are you feeling, Ma'am?"

"No need to be so formal, Zach. And for God's sake, please sit down." Serenity waited for him to sit on the couch before she sat at her desk. "I'm doing fine. Just glad to be back up and moving around. Sickbay can get confining."

"What about having the Protection detail following you?"

"I've always been used to that." Zimmerman just stared at her; he wasn't accepting that answer. Serenity let out a sigh. "They are a reminder of what happened, and reminders are the last thing I need. But I tell myself that they didn't do it, one man did. So, it is tough but nothing to worry about." She gauged Zimmerman's body language. "And that stays between us. They are part of the job, and that's the last thing I need getting back to the Admiral."

"Of course. You can trust me." Zimmerman wore his trademark big grin, his white teeth gleaming. "You don't think the Admiral would do that?"

"The Admiral has made it no secret that he doesn't like young Captains commanding ships. He already talked Captain Trinity into a desk job with false promises of a promotion. But this is where I wanted to be. This was always my goal." The Admiral had hoped to put her on a lousy ship, but she had managed to fight for what was rightfully hers: The first available command, the Australia. "So yes, I think the second he has an excuse to move me, he will."

"Age shouldn't be a factor." Zimmerman was right, it shouldn't be. He was fifteen years older than Serenity but never once treated her as anything less than Captain. "But, I am sure you are right. Admirals are more involved in politics than leadership."

"Are we prepared for the Peace Day ceremonies? The Admiral will be contacting me soon about my return to duty, and I would like to have something to tell him on the status of our ship."

"The last of the new crewmen are aboard. They look forward to this so they have been eager to help prepare."

"You enlist in the Earth Navy to see space, not just Earth orbit. The only upside to being here is participating in the Peace Day festivities. Just another way the Admiral has—" A buzz came from her desk transmitter. She pressed the blinking button on the screen. "Yes."

"Admiral McCorvick for you, Ma'am."

"Put it to my desk." Serenity gestured to Zimmerman to stay. She waited for the screen in her desk to show the Admiral's face. "Admiral McCorvick, I've been expecting your call."

"It's good to see you're back to duty. The Doctors were surprised by how quick you recovered." McCorvick then looked up at Serenity.

"Thank you, Sir. I am just glad to be able to remain in command."

"I see." McCorvick went back to reviewing papers in front of him. "I have new orders for your ship. You are to head for the Earth-Martian border and relieve the E.S.S. Everett on border patrol duties. These orders are effective immediately."

"What?" Serenity stopped to control herself. "For the last month you have been telling our crew to prepare for the Peace Day events. The crew was looking forward to this, Sir."

"In all fairness, Captain, I haven't told you anything in three weeks. You were out. I was waiting for you to return."

"You couldn't tell Zimmerman?" Serenity took another breath to hide the pain creeping into her left hip again.

"These kinds of outbursts are exactly the issue I have with you, Captain. The needs of the Navy change and you serve the Navy's needs."

"Surely, the Navy has better needs of a warship than border patrol. Hell, the Everest is a destroyer for crying out loud." Serenity's voice had become louder, but she was careful not to yell. "The crew expects to host the festivities in three days, this isn't fair to them."

"Fair?" McCorvick hit his desk. "Your lack of experience is showing again. I feel a Captain with more familiarity with military combat operations should be there."

"We've been at peace for well over a hundred years. There is not a Captain in this Navy that has any more experience with combat than me because not one of them has fired a shot in anger." The pain in her hip was so bad she fought to hide it with her irritation. "Our ship has intercepted more drug runners and smugglers than the last three ships on this assignment combined. That should testify to my—"

"Enough, Captain. The Everest will handle the Near-Earth assignments now. Get under way, your official orders should be on your screen."

The instructions came up on the screen. Serenity glanced over them. There was no need to push her luck with the Admiral over the matter. "We will leave within the hour, Sir. If that is all, I have matters to attend to."

"That is all."

Chapter 3

Carlson hadn't said much to his new partner over the first two shifts. It had made the last two nights long. He could pull rank and move to another shift, but he liked the nights. Carlson wasn't intentionally ignoring Janice, but she didn't say much and frankly he didn't expect her to last long. She didn't seem to take it seriously; it was exactly why he picked her.

But she was quickly proving him wrong. The first night, she studied the Captain's file and the files on the bridge crew. Last night, it was the bridge layout and protocols. Even now she continued to study; this time, it appeared to be the ship's layout.

Janice hadn't been what Carlson expected from day one. She was a beautiful woman, which had been a surprise in itself. She had dark brown hair that might go down past her shoulders if it were worn down. She had an athletic figure that her uniform showed well. She was tall, only a few inches shorter than he. And the few times Carlson had seen her smile, it was radiant.

Janice glanced up from her pad at Carlson; he was caught looking at her. "Next, you're going to read my file."

She showed that smile again, "I did that before our first shift together."

"Oh." Carlson was surprised. Janice had clearly decided to be more prepared for this assignment than he had expected.

"You pissed me off when you knew so much about me, but I knew nothing about you." Janice set the pad down on the table between them. "I'm not about to be shown up again."

So he had been the one to kick-start her interest in her job. "Why did you skate by in Protective Services School? Clearly, you could have aced it if you'd put in some effort."

"You had it right," Janice shrugged. "I was just looking for an easy specialty to promote."

That had likely been what pissed her off. But Carlson had counted on her dropping out quick. "So why the sudden interest?"

"If I have to be here a year, I may as well do it right. Especially if I am going to be partnered with you. Seems you got the job down to a science." Janice smirked, this time his cheeks flushed a bit. Was she flirting with him?

"I guess. I just do the job, even when it's hard." Carlson turned his attention to the ground. It had recently been really hard.

"Your file doesn't say much about your past partner."

Carlson hadn't known they removed it from his files, or at the very least put it under higher clearance. He thought for a moment, not sure how to address it.

A red light clicked on above the entrance to the quarters. A few seconds later, the klaxon sounded. Janice jumped. Carlson was relieved to avoid the issue. "It's General Quarters. Stand up."

"That doesn't sound good."

"It's usually noth—" Carlson stopped mid-sentence when the Captain came out of her room.

Serenity glanced at them both as she walked out. "Transport crossed the border outside shipping lanes, and it's not responding to our transmissions." She gave Janice a good looking over, top to bottom. This would be her first time seeing her. "You know your bridge rules, officer?"

"I am learning them, but I know to shut up and stay out of the way. That is, unless I have to outrank you," Janice said, just a touch of attitude leaking out. Carlson cleared his throat. "Oh, Ma'am."

Serenity smirked at Janice, turned, and walked out of her quarters; Carlson and Janice right on her heels.

* * *

"Tell me what's going on," Serenity said as soon as she walked on to the bridge. She went straight for her seat in the middle of the circular room. Carlson gestured for Kanter to stand to the right behind her chair while he took his spot on the left.

"There is no response to any of our transmissions on all known frequencies," the ensign said. Carlson recognized her. Her name was Willard, if he remembered correctly. "We requested destination and identification, then the ship changed course."

"Back to Martian Space?" Serenity didn't look up from her reports.

"No, Ma'am. Intercept course," Willard said. "Moving slowly. No identification beacon. It appears to be a standard shipping transport."

"Can we get more information?"

"If we move to intercept we can be in range for better scans in five minutes."

"Broadcast a message, all frequencies." Serenity waited for the signal from Willard, "This is Captain Christina Serenity of the E.S.S. Australia. Identify yourselves, or we will be forced to intercept your vessel." Serenity waited for a response; when there was none she signaled for the channel to be closed. "Move to intercept. Ready a boarding party. Can we detect any damage or signs of distress?"

"Some signs of damage, it appears old. The ship markings have been removed. It appears to have a really thick hull, twice as thick as usual. No weapons detected."

"All stop, hard left, expose the right side cannons, have them acquire the target, but don't fire. Dispatch a fighter wing to move in on them."

Carlson didn't like the sound of this, but he couldn't really figure out why. Janice had her hand rested on her L-pistol. He nudged her and pointed to his own weapon. Her face had a puzzled expression, but she moved her hand.

* * *

Fern jumped off the transport and began to climb the ramp into his fighter. The fighters were warming up, and the rest of his squadron awaited his take off. Fern strapped on his helmet; his four other fighters, their damage, and the pilot's health appeared in his right eyepiece. The squadron received clearance and left the docking bays.

Fern targeted the vessel and reported in. "Alpha group moving to intercept target as ordered."

"Alpha Leader, Australia Control. The Captain orders you to avoid hostile action, unless necessary."

Fern noticed the transport ship picking up speed, but still heading for the Australia. Alpha Group conducted a fly-by of the vessel. The other ships moved into the four corners of the transport. Fern repeatedly hailed the vessel. His scanners reported back additional information on the ship.

"Australia Control, the ship is an old troop transport with heavy armor, and two-hundred plus persons on board. Vessel is increasing speed."

"Message received."

Fern heard the transmission coming in from the bridge. "Unidentified vessel you are on a collision course, if you do not alter course we will engage."

The transport altered course and began to pass the Australia. The fighter group stayed on it as it went past the massive warship. Fern let out a sigh of relief to see it keep moving. The transport turned left quickly, the fighters peeled off just in time to avoid a collision. The unidentified ship tripled speed and headed for a collision course with the Australia's two docking bays.

"Unidentified Vessel, stand down and prepare to be boarded. Continuing with your course will be considered a hostile act." The transmission from the bridge repeated.

"Alpha Leader this is Australia Control, disable that transport." Fern checked his radar and noticed ten more contacts crossing into Earth Space. "Alpha Group, engage target."

He fired the fighter's twin lasers at the bridge of the transport. "Australia Control, ten contacts entering Earth Space. Martian Vessel on collision course with the docking bays. Scramble additional fighter groups."

Fern made another firing pass on the transport. He was unable to keep up with the ship at the speed it was traveling. The Australia's heavy cannons fired on the Martian ship. Fern broke off his pass.

His group brought their fighter about, only to watch the Martian vessel smash into the docking bays.

* * *

The bridge shook violently. Carlson caught himself on the Captain's chair. Reports were being called out from every station.

"Collision at the Flight deck, the transport is wedged in tight. Life support is holding in that area."

"The ship has been boarded by unknown hostiles. Security Forces teams are responding," Major Kingsworth, the Security Forces Commander, reported.

"Seal the bridge, move the other Protection teams to the access points," Carlson called out. The Major gave him a dirty look but did what he said.

"Radar shows ten Martian Fighters approaching. Two Martian Warships are on the border, but holding."

Serenity stood up. "Send the distress call. Move the fighters in close, there won't be more support. Can we identify those Martian Warships?"

"No Ma'am. Still trying to get data on them."

"Open a channel," Serenity said. "This is the Captain of the E.S.S. Australia. Stand down your fighters. Their actions are considered hostile. Repeat, stand down your fighters."

"Captain, the fighters are circling us outside of cannon range," Willard said.

"The Security Forces teams have engaged the unknown attackers on the flight deck." Kingsworth keyed a few more buttons. "They are not dressed in any uniform, but they are far from inexperienced. Casualties seem limited at this point."

"Notify sickbay so they can prepare. Find a safe place to have medical teams stand by," Serenity called out. "What do they seem to be after?"

"Captain, aft cannons went offline," the weapons officer shouted.

The ship rattled slightly. "The fighters have engaged, they seem to be concentrating fire on the rear sections of the ship."

"Have Alpha Group engage them," Serenity called out over the sound of the ship's cannons. "Try to reroute the systems to keep them from getting access."

"They are powering down another series of cannons, Captain."

"Notify engineering that I will be locking them out of the systems. Their codes have been compromised." Serenity keyed something into her chair. "My codes are not responding! How did they lock me out?" Serenity looked back at Carlson. He just shrugged. She turned to the Major. "Get them off my ship now." She spun back to the engineer. "Cut power to the flight deck. All systems except life support."

"Captain, we are losing fighters."

"They have us locked out of the systems. I'd have to cut power to the whole deck. Based on what I am seeing they are trying to get access to the bridge lockdown controls," the engineer said.

"They'd have to cross the ship to get to here." Serenity paused and addressed Carlson again. "Any direct routes?"

"They could try air ducts, but they would still have to cross the ship."

Serenity turned back to the Engineering Officer. "Are there any air duct access points near the enemy?"

"One, but it doesn't access the bridge."

"Major."

"We'll check it out, Ma'am," Kingsworth said. "We have cut their numbers by two thirds. We should have control over the flight deck soon."

"Captain, we are losing fighters, we have two left," the weapons officer said.

"Have them do their best." Serenity turned to Willard, "Who is responding to our distress call?"

"We've had multiple responses, Ma'am. The Carrier Atlantic should be here any moment."

"Update the Atlantic of our status." Serenity said. "No response from the Martian warships?"

"None."

"Captain, all two hundred enemies have been killed. None captured," Kingsworth said.

"Get an engineering team down there to restore the systems." Serenity said. "The fighters?"

"They are withdrawing to the Martian Warships. The Atlantic is arriving on long range now. They are dispatching their full complement of fighters," Willard replied. "The Martian warships are making maneuvers that imply they are preparing to withdraw."

Carlson let out a sigh of relief.

"We all feel that way, Corporal." Serenity said with a smirk. She turned back to her bridge crew. "Go to ready stations. I want full reports within the hour. And someone get that transport out of my hull."

Chapter 4

Janice couldn't sleep after her shift. She really hadn't adjusted to the night work. But, really it was a matter of everything that had gone on the night before.

She hadn't expected that much excitement from working on a ship. This was supposed to be peacetime, these things were not supposed to happen. A nameless, faceless enemy had attacked an Earth warship.

Her adrenaline was still flowing, and the only way she was going to calm down was to walk around, so she had been wandering the ship for the last hour.

The news media was going to have a field day over this. The media laws wouldn't allow them to broadcast any speculation, but once the Australia arrived at space dock all bets were off. Janice knew the routine. They would only report that the ship arrived damaged. But that is all it would take for the public to start asking questions. Within hours the Navy or the Prime Minister would be forced to make an official statement.

Politics wasn't Janice's thing, but when you work for the government you learn the game. It was worse when you were in Security Forces, which was by far the largest branch of the Military. When you had to police the world, police the military, and staff the prison, that was a lot of personnel. The Navy was a distant second, but still had a significantly larger staffing level than the Army or Air Force. There just wasn't much need for a standing army when there was peace and the only threats would come from space.

Janice wasn't really sure where she was. She didn't know the ship well outside of the maps, and Carlson wasn't being much of a host. His file was about all Janice knew of him.

He has served on the Australia for most of his time in Security Forces, has been in Protective Services for about three years. He had the same partner since he'd been on board. Roger Mathews. There was nothing on him. His file was restricted to a clearance above Janice's. That was odd enough. But, there was nothing in the record about why they were suddenly not partners anymore. Janice was beginning to think it had been Mathews's funeral Carlson attended when she arrived.

Janice found a bar on deck 6. She knew there was one up near the shops, but not down here. It would be something different than the mess hall. She went in. It was a lot like the bars of Earth, only cleaner. Dimly lit with dark paint, and soft music playing. There were pool tables and booths around the room; to the left was the long bar. Sitting there, alone, was Mike.

Janice took a seat next to him. He'd seen her as soon as she got close. He was certainly on his toes. She motioned the bartender over and ordered a drink. "Can't sleep, either?"

"I haven't even tried." Carlson's voice was quiet. "That was a first for everyone on this ship."

She studied him for a moment. "So you come here often?" Carlson gave a chuckle. "Actually, I do. It's quieter here."

"I didn't even know it was here."

"I used to patrol this deck before I went to Protective Services."

* * *

Serenity waited as the Admiral poured through the reports. He insisted she remain on the transmission until he had reviewed it. He hadn't said much yet.

"Why didn't you continue to intercept?" The Admiral barely moved when he spoke. He continued to read the tablet in front of him.

"When I was told the ship had no markings, I was concerned the ship may not be what it appeared. I felt exposing the most weapons to the transport was more intimidating," Serenity explained.

"You were right. It wasn't what it appeared to be." Serenity was shocked to hear this from the Admiral. Had he really just said she was right? The Admiral sat back, making eye contact with her. "Well done, Captain. You did better than I would have expected."

"Th- thank you, Sir." Serenity stuttered a bit, surprised even still.

The Admiral continued over her reports. He asked a few more questions, mostly about the attacking force. She referred him to Major Kingsworth's report. He asked about the transport, but the technicians were still evaluating the systems and computers.

"Alright, I will submit this to the Prime Minister." He set the tablet down. "Do you have a few more moments?"

"Of course, Sir." Serenity had been in the transmission for thirty minutes—what were two more?

"This is off the record. I am not supposed to release this to anyone. But you need to know." Admiral McCorvick's eyes met Serenity's again. This time his eyes were cold and stern. "I know we don't get along, but I know you have enough sense of duty to be trusted."

"Yes, Sir." Serenity wondered if this information he was about to share was the reason he was being so kind. Perhaps it was some sort of set-up.

"I received word that Roger Mathews escaped New Alcatraz," Admiral McCorvick's voice was dry, almost hoarse.

"Escaped? That's impossible." Serenity was feeling the pain in her hip again. She trembled slightly, but took controlled breaths to steady herself. New Alcatraz was on the Moon. It was the first of Earth's terra-forming projects. Two large domes contained the atmosphere needed for survival. One dome holds Moon City, the other, New Alcatraz. Escape meant getting past all the shuttle screens, or trying to pass through the miles of unprotected space between the domes. No one had ever escaped alive.

"They haven't found his body on the Moon's surface, and I can't relay any details. But he has escaped and you can presume he is alive."

"Sir, Protective Services should be made aware."

"That is up to Security Forces. For now, General Valentine insists it stay under wraps. But, I really felt you needed to know."

Serenity realized the trap she had been put into. If this information leaked out at all, the Admiral would lose his position and face jail time. But, that wasn't the worst of it. He could well have something on her now, leverage to get her to transfer to that desk job. Well played, Admiral. "Thank you, Sir. It will stay between us."

"Good. I will give you new orders when you come in for repairs."

The transmission ended. Roger Mathews was out and free. Would he dare try to get back on this ship and come after her again? It seemed unlikely, even impossible. But escape from New Alcatraz was supposed to be impossible too.

* * *

Janice and Carlson had talked for twenty minutes. Carlson couldn't help himself. He was a talker by nature. It had finally occurred to him that perhaps giving Janice the cold shoulder wasn't the best tactic to deal with his own issues.

It had been his hope not to have to get close to any of his partners again. He always knew that wasn't practical. He could be friendly without becoming friends.

"So, you never did answer me on that partner of yours," Janice nudged him gently.

"We don't talk about my last partner." Mike slammed his glass down on the bar. Rage seemed to boil up from deep inside him. Alcohol was only aiding the release of suppressed anger, fear, and pain. He turned away from Janice, embarrassed.

Janice took him by the shoulder and pulled him around to face her. She had anger in her eyes, but it was controlled. "Listen to me, asshole. I came here dreading this assignment, only to be angered by a smart-ass Corporal who had me figured out pretty good.

"I spent the next week trying to learn about you, this ship, and what my job will be. You've rewarded me by saying a handful of words to me. The people of this ship seem to think you are great, but you've been nothing but a dick to me."

Janice still clung to Carlson's shoulder. His anger started to slip away. With it no longer available to mask his feelings, tears swelled up his eyes. She released him and he turned to face his drink. He felt her hand on his back.

After several moments, Janice spoke. "Sorry, it's just I can't find anything on the guy. It's all been restricted and..."

"Roger Mathews is a traitor." Carlson's own words surprised him. It actually felt good to say it. He took a huge breath. "He attempted to kill the Captain. Shot another officer, who later died, and worst of all, managed to avoid the needle."

Carlson stood up. He felt renewed to speak to someone about it, but exhausted. He walked out of the bar without saying a word, leaving Janice alone.

Chapter 5

Roger **Mathews** looked at the screen as the transmission with his contact loaded. There was a certain amount of anonymity associated with these transmissions. The encryption process alone took some time. He set up his privacy screen image—a simple color pattern was enough for him—and engaged the voice disguiser. If anyone happened to get around the encryption, they wouldn't be able to see who was talking or recognize the voice.

He brushed off his Red uniform shirt—a ridiculous color for a Navy uniform; but these damn Martians were so proud of their red planet. They painted the ships red, they wore red uniforms, and he was surprised there was no requirement for red underwear.

An image appeared. The familiar pre-Unification painting *The Son of Man* filled the image screen with the apple hiding the face of a man in a hat. His contact always used this picture. Which was interesting, considering the contact's voice morphed into something that led him to believe it belonged to a female. Names were never used, that was obviously foolish. So there really was no way of knowing for sure.

"Are you there?" the voice said.

"I am here." Mathews paused, "Is this important? You shouldn't be risking contacting me here."

"Important? Of course it is important. You failed, and you failed miserably." The voice disguiser had trouble with the rapid raise in volume. "And how many civilians died? She was your target, not all those other people you killed."

"You told me you wanted her dead. I told you I would do it my way." Mathews took a drink of water. Killing Serenity was not necessary to accomplish his own plans.

"Well, she isn't dead, is she?"

"Not yet."

"You've already failed twice. After the first time, I got you out of the death penalty and I got you out of the inescapable prison. Then I got you the right connection on the red planet. I've taken a lot of risks for you. I deserve some insights here."

Mathews hated the fact that this contact obviously knew who he was, but he knew nothing about her, or him. It had bothered him from the beginning, but the amount of money he was getting was worth it. And this person wasn't in as much control as they thought they were, either. "You're not the only one to take risks. I gave up a job. I am a traitor to Earth. Twice over now, I might add. I have nothing now, except what you paid me which was frozen by the Earth Government after my arrest." There was a bit of embellishment in the fact, but as long as this contact thought Mathews was down on his luck, it would work to his favor.

"You told me you could handle this."

"And I told you not to underestimate her ability to command. She surprised me with some maneuvers that resulted in a boarding landing nowhere near the bridge. Security Forces are just too well trained to get to her from that far away." A hint of pride slipped from Mathews's voice. "I told you I would kill her, and I will."

"And how do you plan to do it this time? This last attempt may well propel Earth into some type of military action."

Good, Mathews thought. "I have a man on the inside working to solve this problem one on one."

"You couldn't do it yourself and you were close to her all the time. How do you expect someone else to handle this?"

"Simple, I had to do it with Carlson around. This person won't. And that is all I am prepared to share."

"But—"

Mathews ended the transmission. He wasn't worried about angering his contact. In fact, he could care less. Mathews had far more money and power now than his contact could possibly know. The only reason he still pursued this assignment was because, for now, attacking Captain Christina Serenity went along with his current plans.

Chapter 6

Carlson liked working nights because it kept him off the bridge. But the day crew wasn't coming in, so he and Janice had no choice but to hold over. There was one positive note: Carlson got to actually see Serenity.

He really hadn't seen her much since he sat with her in sickbay for a week. She seemed to be moving better and he was pleased she had healed so fast. She was going to bed before Carlson even got on shift. That was new. Carlson wasn't sure if she was avoiding him or it was just part of her recovery.

Serenity was the most beautiful woman Carlson knew. He would never tell her that. That would be a certain transfer and reassignment. She could not have any romantic interest from crew members. She'd have to report it as soon as he spoke the words. Serenity would do it too. She was loyal to Earth and loved her position too much.

And Carlson loved his assignment too much to say anything. There was only one person Carlson ever confessed this to, and he turned out to be a traitor. Luckily, he was in New Alcatraz and no one would believe him if he said anything.

Serenity was sitting at her desk now. Her blonde hair shimmered with the overhead lighting of her ready room. She was short, but the way she carried herself made her seem taller. Her curves were well defined in her well-tailored Navy uniform.

She looked up and he glanced away all too aware he had been staring at her. He glanced back at her and she smiled at him. He smiled back.

"Corporal."

Even with the formality, her voice made his heart skip a beat. "Ma'am?"

"How are you holding up?"

"Well…" Carlson turned to Janice for a moment. "As good as can be expected."

Serenity nodded and went back to her work for a moment. She stopped again and stood up. "Officer Kanter, would you give us a moment?"

Janice seemed puzzled and waited for a response. He nodded to her and she walked out onto the bridge. Serenity took a seat on the couch. She patted the seat next to her gesturing for Carlson to sit.

That would be uncomfortable for Carlson. "If it is all the same, I'll stand, Ma'am."

"It's not all the same. Sit down, Carlson."

Carlson took the seat as far away as he could, while still sitting on the couch. He felt silly for being so awkward about this. It was as if he was a teenager sitting next to his crush for the first time.

"Mike, relax. This isn't formal."

With the authority out of her voice, Carlson found it soothing. He nodded and took a deep breath to try to show he was relaxed. He wasn't.

"I understand you spent a lot of time with me in sickbay when I was still unconscious." She turned away from him.

This was it, she knew something now. She was going to let him know she was reporting her suspicions. At least he didn't get a transfer order without an explanation. "I felt responsible for what happened. I had to make sure it was made right."

"It wasn't your fault, Mike." She scooted over next to him, resting a hand on his shoulder. A calming touch, but it had little effect on Carlson's nerves.

"I shouldn't have left the area. It's against protocol for a reason. A mistake I won't make twice." Carlson slumped a bit forward but quickly sat back upright.

"Well, I want you to know that I don't blame you." Serenity patted his shoulder. "You deserve the medal you got, even if you don't think so. I'd be dead if you hadn't been there for me. And, I wanted to thank you for your emotional support during my recovery. I may not have been awake to know about it, but I am sure it must have been helpful."

Serenity stopped as the door opened, Janice stuck her head in. She stared at them for several moments.

"Is there something you need, Officer?" Serenity said as she stood up.

Carlson quickly jumped up to his feet.

"Sorry to interrupt, Ma'am. I have a crewman who wishes to speak with you."

"Send him in."

Janice walked in with a man about her height, but he was definitely larger in width. His uniform reflected he was a gunner. His eyes were swollen red, clearly he had been crying.

"What is it, Petty Officer?" Serenity had compassion in her voice.

"Petty Officer Borvis, Ma'am." He stopped a few feet from her. "Can I talk to you alone? It's a private matter."

"Certainly." Serenity turned to Carlson and nodded.

He knew what that meant; she was okay with seeing him alone. Carlson didn't like leaving emotional people alone with the Captain. So he was going to at least check him for weapons. Then he would stay close enough to the door to hear any confrontations. Emotions change quickly, sad can go to mad faster than Carlson could react.

"Petty Officer, we need to do a quick check for weapons, then we will step out." Carlson gave a nod to Janice that would indicate for her to take over.

She understood. "Turn around and put your hands on the wall." Janice pointed to an open wall near the door. She pulled out her chip reader and scanned it. The information came up on Carlson's screen too. It was processing. "Do you have anything on you that can poke, stick or otherwise hurt me?"

"No," Boris said dryly.

Carlson watched as Janice went through the pat down. She stopped a moment when she got to one of his legs. "What's this?"

In the same moment, Boris swung his elbow back, hitting Janice in the chest. Janice stumbled back. Carlson called for help on his radio and rushed in. Boris swung his right arm around, trying to strike Carlson.

Carlson stepped back to avoid the hit. Janice knocked him to the ground. While Janice grappled for his arms, Carlson put his knee on the back of Boris's neck. As Janice pulled his arms back, Carlson restrained him.

The door flew open. Carlson had his weapon halfway out of the holster when he saw it was two Security Forces patrolmen. Boris was screaming something. "...my sister is dead! It's her fault. I'm going to kill her!"

Janice reached down the same leg and pulled out a large knife. She looked it over. "Pretty big for typical ship duties."

Carlson radioed the Code Green. He read over his scanner. "Petty Officer Third Class Boris Santiago. Currently on emotional leave." He was likely awaiting evaluation once they would arrive for repairs the next day.

As Boris was taken from the room, Carlson went over to Serenity. She appeared scared, something Carlson had only seen once before. "Captain?"

She looked up at him. Her eyes met his. Carlson wanted to hug her, but he couldn't. "This is one guy who couldn't handle the emotional toll of a military conflict. It happens. No one is hurt."

* * *

Serenity had just watched Carlson and Kanter take out a man who appeared ready and able to kill her. She turned away to hide her fear. The day after hearing Mathews was released, someone tried to kill her again. That couldn't be coincidence.

She looked Carlson right in the eyes. *I need you Mike*, she thought. *I need someone I can trust.*

"This is one guy who couldn't handle the emotional toll of a military conflict. It happens. No one is hurt."

She nodded.

Carlson lowered his voice to a whisper. "Mathews is in prison. This has nothing to do with him."

She wanted to tell Carlson the truth right then. *Mathews is out, Mike. No one knows where he is, but he is free.*

"I know. Just so soon." She raised her voice a bit, looking past Mike at Janice. "That was certainly a surprise."

Janice rubbed her chest. "I'll say."

Chapter 7

It **didn't** take long to get the ship repaired. Clearly all hands were at work on the matter. The crews of the repair docks and the Australia had been working as fast as they could to get the ship repaired. The media was faster.

It took only six hours before the first media shuttles showed up. They stayed outside the restricted area, but Serenity knew they could see what they needed to. Within eight hours the Australia was all over the news.

The media played their cards well, as they always did. They danced just on the line of The Truth in News Act. No one speculated on the cause, but they just kept showing the footage. After that, family came forward reporting the Navy had told them their loved ones were killed two days ago while serving on the Australia.

After that came the emails asking questions. The Navy needed to explain why people had died and why the Australia was so badly damaged. In just a few minutes Serenity would watch her friend, and Navy Public Relations Officer, make an official statement.

After which, she would need to get to the conference room for a formal, confidential, meeting. It was to be held on secure channels; a face to face meeting would attract attention. Attention was the enemy right now. Why the meeting had to be after hours was beyond her understanding.

So she sat on her couch in a dress uniform watching the news, careful not to glance in Carlson's direction too often.

She needed to tell Carlson; he had a right to know. She cursed Admiral McCorvick for telling her about Mathews. If she didn't know, she wouldn't have to worry about telling Carlson. She wouldn't have to wonder when

Mathews was coming back.

It was made worse by the fact that she trusted Carlson, and she was keeping this secret from him. Well, she was keeping two secrets from him. She was attracted to Carlson, something she had hidden from even herself for some time.

But when she heard he spent all that time with her in sickbay she thought perhaps he was more than just her bodyguard. Perhaps what he said was true. Perhaps he just felt responsible.

It was a silly thing to be thinking about right now. Her ship was attacked, she was attacked again, and here she was wondering if Carlson liked her. Was this why McCorvick hated young Commanding Officers?

She was thinking too much.

A picture of a Podium with the Earth Navy Seal showed up on the screen. The news announcer said something about the conference starting.

Tracy Kelly walked out to the podium, her rank and title showed on the screen. She was just a few months older than Serenity. She, too, had been in command for a brief moment, but she took McCorvick's deal. It seemed to pay off for her. She was the commanding officer of the Navy Public Affairs office. That was something to be proud of.

But the Navy was about space. Or at least it was to Serenity. The thought of doing any type of desk work scared her. If it was forced on her, she would likely get out. Fortunately, no one could do that. Yet.

"Two days ago, an unknown craft attacked the Earth Navy Warship E.S.S. Australia. Captain Christina Serenity, of the Australia, ordered the hostile ship to stand down. The vessel refused to comply with those orders, and the Australia had no choice but to take defensive action.

"However, the shuttle was prepared for the defenses of a warship and rammed the landing bays of the Australia. The warship was boarded by an unknown group in civilian clothing, but clearly well trained.

"The Security Forces teams on the Australia were able to hold off the boarding party and regain control of the ship. Regrettably, Navy and Security Forces did suffer minimal human losses. The Navy finds this unacceptable and has launched a full investigation. However, it is too early to make any conclusions."

With that, the media unleashed their onslaught of questions. Most of which Tracy replied with the usual, "I can't comment on that." Or, "We just don't know at this time."

One reporter called out, "We've heard that the Martians had warships in the area. Is that true?"

Tracy had a look of confusion. Serenity knew that wasn't supposed to be public knowledge. Serenity expected the "no comment" line.

"That is true. We've contacted the Martian Government to seek their cooperation in our investigation."

* * *

Serenity felt stupid sitting in the empty conference room by herself. Kanter and Carlson were there, but they didn't say much. But this room was the only place, besides the bridge, with the transmission encodings strong enough to comply with the security clearance level needed for this meeting.

The large screen displayed five "Waiting for Party to connect" screens. Serenity was surprised to be the first to connect, but she wasn't about to be late to a meeting of this caliber.

Admiral McCorvick connected next. "Ah Captain, you are early as well."

"Yes, Sir."

"Are you all right? I got the report about this Petty Officer."

"I'm fine, Sir. The protection team handled it before there was any real danger to anyone." *Though it still scared the shit out of me.*

"Good." McCorvick was silent for several moments. "Serenity, the Army and Air Force insist on being in on this meeting. They don't get to be part of much anymore, so please pretend to enjoy what they have to say."

Serenity let out a small laugh, enough to humor the Admiral. "I will do my best, Sir."

As if on cue, Generals Mathew Lee and Heather Kent of the Army and Air Force, respectively, came on the screen. Shortly after a man in a suit came on the screen followed by General Valentine of Security Forces.

"Good we are all here," McCorvick said "Mr. Papavich, you know the Generals, but allow me to introduce Captain Serenity of the Australia."

Papavich nodded to the screen. "Captain, your crew performed well in the face of this attack."

"Thank you, Sir," Serenity said.

"Terrorism is bad enough, but when it appears to be condoned by the Martians it makes me sick," Papavich said.

"That's a bold conclusion, Diplomat," McCorvick's voice was dry. "They were there, yes. They fired on the Australia, yes. But can we hold them responsible for all of this? What do the Martians have to say for themselves?"

"Almost nothing. They claim they were fired on by the Australia while responding to the Captain's distress call. After that they tell me nothing more. There is something they are hiding."

"That I might agree with," General Kent spoke. "The records of our ship clearly show something different."

"The boarding party was well trained," General Valentine said. "A few of the men who fought them off swear the tactics are very similar to a Martian Marine Corps operation. Again, nothing we can verify but something smells funny here."

"What do we know of these Martian warships?" General Lee asked.

"M.S.S. Frontier is one. The other is the M.S.S. Phobos. Nothing strange about the Frontier. But all records show the Phobos was dismantled years ago. Never seen or heard from since then, until now."

"So do we know if the Australia was the target?" Serenity didn't mean to speak that questions allowed, but no one seemed to mind.

"I think you may have stumbled onto something you weren't meant to find," McCorvick said.

"I disagree," Major Valentine said. "It was awfully well planned out for a 'Crap, they found us' type of situation. Let's not forget they had Command Codes for the Australia's systems. Unless you have a lot of compromised command codes, I would speculate that it was the target."

"They were supposed to be on near-Earth duty. It was a last minute change that brought them to Border Patrol," McCorvick said.

"Perhaps that was why they seemed to be a little unprepared. Perhaps they planned to attack us on Peace Day," Kent said.

"That makes more sense than I care to admit," Lee said.

Serenity had to agree. If you wanted to make an attack on an Earth warship, one with a huge statement, that was the day to do it. It was certainly a scary thought.

"God, I hope you are wrong, General," Papavich said. "Has anyone tried to claim responsibility for this?"

"No." McCorvick was quieter than Serenity had ever seen him. Even his tone softened. "I don't like the idea of terrorists, and I certainly don't like the idea of a terrorist attack on our ship during Peace Day. Do you know how many civilians would have been on that ship?"

"I don't like it either, but it's a strong possibility," Lee said.

"I would cancel the Civilian visits for tomorrow's events," Valentine said.

"Every time we get a bit of information you want to cancel," McCorvick shook his head. "I am not canceling these events. The media outcry alone will be hell to manage."

"That's just my official suggestion, Admiral. You can do as you see fit. You usually do." Valentine made to attempt to hide his sarcasm.

"Okay, enough," Papavich said without much force. "We can guess all we want but your guesses won't get answers from the Martians. And we need answers. We all have the Prime Minister down our necks about this. There is a possibility of war in this, however small, and it's time for answers."

"Then perhaps the Prime Minister should have been less liberal when it came to slicing our budgets," Lee said with an equal amount of anger and jest in his tone.

The other Generals let out a laugh; McCorvick was the only one not to.

"Something like this was bound to happen. When you divide the human race into separate governments, it is only a matter of time before they disagree. The Unification Wars were to join the human race and we just hand the Martians their own government."

"If we'd refused, there would have been war. The Unification Wars were about bringing peace," Kent said.

"Now is not the time for political discussions," Papavich said. "That choice was made a long time ago. Let's focus on the issue at hand today."

"The Diplomat is right. I believe the investigation needs to start with this mystery ship. This supposedly dismantled Phobos." Valentine looked to Serenity. "I don't envy your mission."

"Two things are clear here, Captain. First, this attack was an act of terrorism. Second, Mars is hiding something," McCorvick said. "I want you to find out what they are hiding."

Chapter 8

Janice woke up sick to her stomach. At first she dismissed it as nerves; she never liked shuttle rides. She was slated to visit the planet. The Captain had put the crew on a cycling leave. But, slowly the problem worsened and she headed for sickbay.

This had to be the brightest area of the ship, the colors were all light. A few pictures that were supposed to inspire healing flashed up on the unused monitors. It wasn't working. Her stomach still complained.

The Doctor walked up to the table. The dark skin of his shaved head reflected the bright lights of the room. He was reading his tablet. He looked up and put on a comforting smile.

"I'm Doctor Farven. Here for stomach problems—" He checked the tablet, "Officer Kanter?"

"Yeah, at first I thought it was nerves but it's been getting worse."

"Alright, let's see what we have here." The Doctor began the typical examination. After several moments he spoke. "You're Carlson's new partner, right?"

"Yes. He seems well known around here." Janice waited for the Doctor to check her throat. "I know he has been here a while, but on a ship this big?"

"Well I should know him. He was here for weeks, barely left to go to the bathroom. I had to make them bring him food so he'd eat." Doctor Farven entered something into his tablet. "He really took it hard, especially when we thought she might not make it."

She thought about a clever way to get more information from the

Doctor, without letting him know she was searching for information. "I didn't know he took it so hard."

"We all did, Janice. Captain Serenity is well respected and liked on this ship." The Doctor waved over the nurse. "Sandra will give you a nasal spray to help with the nausea. It seems to be a case of food poisoning. You should be fine in a couple of days. If it gets worse, come back."

"Thanks Doctor, you've been helpful," Janice smiled, until her stomach protested her positive mood.

Had this been why Carlson was so secretive about his partner? He did take leave just before she arrived, his file showed that. Carlson did say his old partner was a traitor. The pieces were there, but they seemed impossibly out of place.

* * *

Carlson stood on the deck gazing out at the beauty of the Niagara Falls. He knew what mandated leave meant; they would be taking an extended tour away from Earth. This was his favorite place to visit. It was easy to think here.

He had been too cold with Janice. She didn't deserve his bitterness from Mathews. She was taking the job seriously enough and that was what really mattered. Mathews was never as serious about it as Carlson was. Perhaps Janice was a better fit for him anyway.

Carlson felt a tap on his shoulder. When he turned around he was shocked to find the Captain standing there. "Captain?"

"Not today. I am on leave. Christina is fine." She smiled at him.

"You should have a team here, even on temporary leave."

"Mike, the Doctor cleared me to go without one. I needed a break. Besides, you are here." Serenity paused, but spoke again before Carlson could protest. "I thought I might find you here. I've heard you mention it before."

"It's a beautiful place and a good place to come and think." Carlson turned back to the falls as Serenity moved next to him. Carlson spoke a bit quieter. "There has been a lot to think about."

"And there really hasn't been much time to think." Serenity's hand took hold of the rail next to Carlson's. "Care to talk about it?"

"I've been a bit closed off from my new partner, Janice. I picked her because I figured she wouldn't be too serious about the job, she would leave quickly and I wouldn't get too attached. But, she is taking things seriously and..."

Serenity waited a moment before finishing his thought. "You don't want to get close to another partner."

"Roger was my best friend. There wasn't anything he didn't know about me. I thought the same was true for him, but it seems there was one thing he was hiding. Worst of all he hurt someone..." *Hurt someone I care about.* "He hurt you, betraying his oath, his planet, and our friendship."

"I understand. The things he did to me cannot be undone. The emotional pain is sometimes worse than the physical." Serenity caught Carlson's glance. He hadn't known there was any physical pain. "Yes, I still get pain in my hip and sometimes my arm. I told them it went away. I didn't want to lose my command over a lengthy rehabilitation. Please don't say anything."

Carlson could say something, and technically he was duty bound to say something. His job was to protect the Captain, but to also protect her crew from a Captain who might not be fit to command. It was his job.

And by not saying anything was he any better than Mathews? Was he not betraying his duty by keeping quiet? Carlson stared into Serenity's eyes, there was a bit of plea in them. *She trusts you enough to tell you the truth.*

"Of course not." Carlson swallowed the lump in his throat. He couldn't do it if he wanted to. She smiled and turned back to the view. Carlson watched the sunlight dance off her blonde hair. He wanted to kiss her then. The view, her beauty, and the release of a heavy burden made it feel right. But they could never be. He had found an impossible love.

"I always wonder why he did it," Serenity finally spoke. The moment of romance had passed. "That keeps me up some nights. How did he get away without giving an answer? He didn't even get the damned needle." A tear streamed down her face. She slumped onto the rail in emotion. "He did the unthinkable to me, and they let him live."

Carlson did the natural thing and put his arm on her back. She turned quickly and embraced him tightly, burying her face in his chest. Carlson froze, his arms unmoving before finally hugging her back. He could feel her sobs, the wet warmth of her tears soaked his shirt.

"I wish I could explain." He didn't know what else to say as he looked down at the top of her head. "At least we know he can't get out."

She pushed her way back from him. Carlson released quickly but she still knocked his arms away. Carlson thought she was angry, but as she stared up at him with her red, swollen eyes Carlson saw something different. The same look from when they arrested Boris.

"What?" Carlson said as she turned away. "You can tell me. What is it?"

Serenity walked away. Carlson thought about letting her go, but only for a second, before he walked after her. He didn't want to chase her, so he kept pace behind her. Was he saying something wrong? Had their embrace caused her some concern? No, Carlson knew it was more than that. She finally turned around as they reached the parking lot for the gift shop.

"Damn it, Mike." It wasn't anger in her voice, but a bit of relief. "I know something. Something I shouldn't know, but the damn Admiral thought he was doing me a damned favor. I wish I didn't know. It's even above my clearance."

"Oh, I see." Carlson didn't really understand but if it was above her clearance he didn't need to know more.

"You should know, you need to know to do your job. But more so, you need to know because of what we're going through." Serenity took a deep breath. "Mathews escaped."

Carlson struggled for a breath. It felt like someone had punched him in the chest. He struggled for the words. They came out soft and weak. "That's impossible. No one escapes New Alcatraz."

"He did. They are trying to cover it up, or at least stall for time. You needed to know." Serenity paused a moment. "I could lose my command for telling you—hell I could go to New Alcatraz myself..."

"I won't say anything." Carlson swallowed hard. How could he say anything? She was clearly telling him as a favor. The mood was dark. He needed to lighten her spirits. "I suppose I owe you two secrets now."

Serenity gave him that smile he needed. She gave him another hug and walked away. This time Carlson didn't follow her.

* * *

Janice waited for Carlson as he got off the shuttle. Her stomach was still aching, but she would never rest without answers. Carlson looked worn out as he walked toward her. She almost regretted meeting him here.

"Hey Janice, I can't really do much now. I'm beat."

She turned to walk with him. "Yeah, well I need to talk to you. It really can't wait anymore."

"Okay." Carlson stopped and slumped down on a bench by the door. "Sit down, let's talk then."

Janice did. She was worried about it, and it did a number on her already touchy stomach. She took a few breaths and spoke slowly as not to anger him again. "I want to know what Mathews did. The hints are not enough. But clearly the reason you treat me the way you do has to do with him. I found out you spent a lot of time in sickbay with the Captain. I got a feeling it has to do with him."

"You are right. Roger Mathews is a traitor. But, before that he was my closest friend." Carlson faced Janice. Not a hint of anger was in his face. He had gone cold. "Mathews and I were working the late night shift, just as we do now. Mathews needed more coffee, and hell, I could've used a cup. So I went out to go get some. I knew it was against the rules, but hell, it wasn't the first time we had covered for each other."

Carlson took a deep breath. Janice saw a quiver in his lip. She put her hand on his shoulder. She could feel him relax.

"Anyway, on my way there I realized I forgot my Payroll Card. When I got back to her quarters, the doors had been locked. I hadn't locked it and my security codes didn't work.

"I radioed backup. Then had the door forced open by Control. As soon as I got it open, laser fire came flying out at me. More officers arrived. At the first pause in fire, we charged in. One officer was shot and killed. I found myself pointing my L-pistol at Mathews."

Janice's arm fell off his shoulder. She didn't know what to think. A Security Forces Officer had killed another.

Carlson nodded at her as if he knew what she was thinking. "I found the Captain in her room with an electro-knife stuck into her left hip. She was beaten, and had a stab wound in her arm. She had a sheet tied around her throat, unconscious but alive. She barely made it. She still doesn't remember much of what happened; just that he started demanding information. But..."

Carlson broke down. His head hung low in his hands. The sobs choked back by a vain effort to control his emotions. Janice didn't ask why it had happened; it was clear Carlson didn't know.

Janice regretted knowing now.

Chapter 9

Serenity rubbed her face as if she could somehow wash the tiredness away. She was slated to meet the Fuji here in an hour. The Admiral had told her they should have some preliminary information to help her start investigating the Phobos. That seemed the best place to start.

Truthfully, it was the only place to start, but it was a long shot at best. It wasn't very likely that the Martians were going to simply let an Earth warship enter their space to do some poking around, especially not in the current political climate.

The console at her seat buzzed. A message from Naval Command. A couple of field promotion tests had come in. One was of utmost importance to her. She stood up. "Lieutenant Commander, come with me."

Zimmerman stood, gave his familiar smile to Carlson and Kanter, then followed the Captain to her office. Serenity stood by the door, ushering Zimmerman in. She turned to Carlson giving him a nod to wait outside the door. He understood.

"Zimmerman, I have some good news." Serenity paused. "I just got a list of some promotions from some of the last minute testing. Can you make sure to notify the correct people as soon as practical?"

"Of course, Ma'am."

"Also, make sure you fix your uniform." Serenity watched as Zimmerman scanned over his attire. A slow grin crept to her face. She chuckled, and he looked up. "Commander Zimmerman now, congratulations."

Serenity put out her hand and shook his. She always liked telling people they were promoted. It made her happy to see her crew succeed.

"Have they given me a permanent assignment? I mean, I had hoped that since we didn't have a Commander—"

"Naval Command has assigned you here, permanent assignment," Serenity said. "Now, Commander, I have something you need to handle at once."

"Of course."

"We need to assign the new primary bridge crew." Serenity had lost some of her primary crew members to promotions and transfers while they were in dock. "We will keep Lieutenant Sanchez on weapons, she has a way with the gunners. Assign Lieutenant Morgan to Engineering. Of course we still have Major Kingsworth for Security Forces. Not that I would have had a say anyway."

"What about Navigations and Comms? Anyone promote, or come in on the transfers?"

"No. I am thinking Ensign Willard would perform well." Serenity went behind her desk. "She did really well when she was thrown into the last combat situation, our only one."

"I don't know, Ma'am. She seems so... inexperienced. She didn't even pass the Lieutenant test."

"She is young, but she is smart. Some people don't test well." Serenity sat down. "I say we give her a chance. Keep an eye on her and we can reevaluate if needed. But I am guessing it won't be necessary."

"I suppose only time will tell."

"Good. Get them all on the bridge in 30 minutes. I want them in place and ready before the Fuji gets here."

* * *

The Fuji was thirty minutes late. So far, they were not answering any of their frequencies. It bothered Serenity that they weren't answering at all. No one went radio dark unless there was trouble.

"Ready Stations," Serenity said to no one in particular. The klaxon sounded and the lights on the bridge dimmed. The yellow alarm lights came on.

"Captain, I have the Fuji on radar. Moving at full speed to our current location," Willard called out. "They are still not responding."

"Maybe they can still hear us. Request they slow to half speed. Move us to a defensive position," Serenity said. "Ship scans?"

"Looks like they are badly damaged. I am detecting multiple hull breaches and it appears the weapons systems are damaged. Life support seems normal, but I am having trouble getting good readings," Morgan said.

"Willard, what's their course in response to ours?"

"No change, Ma'am. They are on an intercept course, but not a collision course."

"They could be chased," Zimmerman said.

Serenity nodded. "General Quarters, Battle Stations."

The bridge alarm lights went red. Serenity didn't know what to think of this situation. She surely couldn't fire on an Earth Vessel. She could fire a warning shot, but then what?

The Fuji was a destroyer, it should have been able to handle its own. A com loop might work, if they were close enough.

"Morgan, can you get a loop so we can talk to them?"

"I can in a few minutes. They should be getting close enough."

"Captain, a ship is arriving. No ship ID yet, they are too far out," Willard said.

"Try the Fuji now," Morgan said.

The speakers cracked for a moment, the quality was never good on a loop. "Thank God you are here. They attacked us out of nowhere, not even a warning. Fast ships too, they are right on top of us."

"Slow to half speed," Serenity said. "We can move to defend you."

"We can—" The transmission ended.

"I don't know what happened," Morgan said. "It was cut off."

"The perusing ship ID just came in. It's the Fuji."

"There can't be two Fuji's, Ensign," Zimmerman said.

"That's what it says, Sir," Willard said.

"Move us away, half speed."

"The Fuji is hailing us," Willard said. "The chasing one."

"E.S.S. Australia, this is E.S.S Fuji. That approaching ship is hostile. You have my command codes encoded, verify and reply."

"I'm checking now," Zimmerman said.

"Open a transmission." Serenity waited for a nod. "This is Captain Serenity, stand down and go to all stop while we verify."

"They are slowing," Willard said.

"The codes verify. Recent additions," Zimmerman said.

"Contact the other Fuji." Serenity waited.

"They won't respond," Willard said.

"Fire a warning shot." Serenity paused for the sound of the Cannons. There were two loud blasts.

"They are turning off their current course," Willard said. "Moving towards neutral space."

"Did they ever get in visual range?"

"No, Ma'am. The Fuji, the real one, is all stop."

"Move us into visual range, open the channel." Serenity stood up and paced the floor. " This is Captain Serenity, the codes have been verified."

A picture came on screen. The balding man, with more grey in his hair than black, appeared on the screen. "Captain Walker, here. I'm glad we got here in time."

"Go to ready stations," Serenity said, the other ship had left radar range. She turned back to the screen. "What is going on here?"

"We are not entirely sure. We stumbled on that ship while on our way here. We were surprised to find it was showing our signatures. As we moved into visual range, they took off. When they lost us, we headed here, only to find them again." Captain Walker shrugged. "I'm afraid I got more information on that ship than I did on the Phobos."

"Not helpful at all. Did you get anything?"

"Dismantled two years ago. That is all we can find. I can't even get history reports on the old Phobos. The contacts I could find wouldn't talk about the ship," Walker said. "The best I can give you is a last known location from two days ago that a merchant gave me. It's a remote location in Neutral Space."

"It's going to be like finding a needle in a haystack, but thanks for what you have. We'll be underway." Serenity closed the transmission. "Ensign Willard, set a pursuit course after that unidentified ship."

"Captain, the last known location is the other way. Out past Jupiter," Zimmerman said. "Should we check that out?"

"We may. But there is a reason that ship came here."

Chapter 10

Carlson sat at the small table next to the Captain's bedroom door. He hadn't said much to Janice in the couple of weeks since he told her what Mathews had done. He felt bad about that. Only just prior to telling her, he had resolved to be a better partner.

But if he hadn't said much, Janice hadn't said but a few words. She seemed to act awkward around him, but that could have been just as much his own imagination as it was true. The night shifts were certainly getting longer.

Carlson reached into his shirt pocket and pulled out a deck of cards. "You play poker?"

"I have," Janice said, not even turning to face him.

"Let's play a game, it will pass the time." Carlson started shuffling the cards.

Janice finally turned around. "I don't think I want to play."

Carlson set the deck down. "Listen, I know I've been a bit of a jerk, but you've proven me wrong on a lot of things. It wasn't fair for me to put a label on you just because of some test scores. And it certainly wasn't fair for me to treat you rudely because of my last partner. But, if we are going to continue down this path, this is going to be a long 10 months for both of us."

"Your label was right. I just skated through PS school so I could get a quick assignment and transfer back to patrol for that promotion." Janice leaned forward on the table. "But you lit the fire under my ass when you called me on it, and I figured I had better do the best I can for the year we were stuck together. But, this baggage of a best friend/partner who turned traitor, that's a big pill to swallow."

"I may have chosen you for the wrong reasons, but I am glad I did. You did well with Boris, and you made sure to get yourself up to speed. That says a lot about you." Carlson fidgeted with the cards. "I can't do anything about Mathews. It happened. If you think it's a tough pill to swallow, imagine how it is for me, or even the Captain.

"I really don't have any friends on this ship. I'd at least like a partner I get along with. If you leave when your tour is up, that's up to you. But let's take our bad situation and work with it."

Janice nodded. She took the cards and started some fancy shuffle. "Tell you what, how about some rounds of Black Jack instead?"

* * *

Serenity laid in bed, unable to sleep. They'd been tailing the engine traces on that unidentified ship for a couple of weeks. It was like chasing a ghost's tail, but she was certain it would turn out to be a good lead.

What gave her the most trouble was the distance they were putting between themselves and the nearest Earth ship. If they did stumble into a hostile situation, it would be two weeks until a single one arrived. That was a thought that worried Serenity.

Her only combat experience resulted in her ship being boarded, her crewmen dead, and costly repairs. The farther into neutral space they got, the more nervous she got.

There were some advantages. She was starting to go into areas, even the Navy Research vessels hadn't been. They were jumping all over themselves to get her scans and to ask for samples and detours. Her mission didn't allow for detours, but she was happy to please a scientist or two with a sample. It gave the crew something to focus on.

And if they continued this trail, who knows what they might discover. The Navy rarely explored this far out of the solar system. She secretly hoped the trail would lead them to one of the other nearer solar systems. She would love to find a world that the Earth Government could colonize.

When Mars was granted independence, the Earth government became very concerned with the idea of colonizing any more planets. Serenity always speculated that that had to do with a concern of more divided governments forming.

There was still plenty of space around the solar system to discover. It was why Serenity signed up. But many who joined the Navy did so with the dream of finding new worlds, and she was no exception.

She heard the shuffle of a deck of cards, a sound that startled her. She hadn't heard Carlson play cards since Mathews was arrested. Perhaps Janice and Carlson were getting along now.

She could hear them talking, mostly Carlson. Why did it bother her that they were talking? Serenity knew why, but she was being foolish.

She thought back to Niagara Falls, Carlson standing there holding her as she cried. She hoped for a moment he might even kiss her. God, she wished he had. It would have meant he was reassigned, and that was a more devastating thought to her. But the kiss would have been magical.

It could have been their little secret. No one had to have know. But Carlson would have known and he would have said something. It was his job.

It was also his job to report her injury, or even her releasing classified information, but he didn't say a word. It was like he never gave it a second thought. She was foolish to tell him those things, and she was foolish to think there was something there between them.

Janice was a pretty woman. Perhaps they would find happiness together. Serenity cringed at the thought. She could always request Janice reassigned. No one would say a word about it. All Serenity had to say was she didn't trust her.

That was cruel to ruin Janice's career over her own petty jealousy. She couldn't do that, and she wouldn't. Carlson deserved a friend on this ship, and Janice seemed to be a good fit for him.

She was foolish to even be kept awake by this. *I'm a foolish, foolish girl.*

* * *

A whole night talking about little things with Carlson had been the fastest shift Janice had worked since she got to the ship. They covered everything from his childhood to the death of his parents. She'd talked about her family, her upbringing in Midwestern North America. They even swapped a few patrol stories.

She asked if he would join her for breakfast, and he agreed. As they made their way to the mess hall, Carlson had finished up a story about a bar fight on the ship.

"I never knew there was that kind of action on a ship." Janice followed Mike down the buffet line.

"Shit, this ship is as big as some cities. The recreation areas and quarters get the most stuff. But, it's to be expected." Carlson took a scoop of eggs. "The smaller ships might be a bit more boring. You could serve your whole career on the Australia and not know everyone."

Janice followed him to a table and sat down. "Just something you don't think about."

"So why were you so opposed to this year in space?" Carlson said between bites. "Too far from the family, a boyfriend you're missing?"

"Ha! A boyfriend." Janice over exaggerated the laugh.

"A girl with your looks, and you're acting like a boyfriend is a ridiculous assumption."

Janice felt a bit of heat on her cheeks. *Great, I'm blushing.* "Well, thanks. But no. No boyfriend. I didn't make much time for that. And I notice a lot of guys have a problem with dating someone with a bit of authority."

"You mean someone who could kick their ass," Carlson chuckled.

Janice let out a weak laugh. "Pretty much. And the guys in Security Forces tend to not be my thing. You know, don't shit where you eat and all."

"Yeah, that can get messy." Carlson looked down at his plate. Had he dated someone on the ship in Security Forces?

"What about you? Is there a girlfriend for you? Or was that your way of hitting on me?" Janice wished she hadn't said that last sentence the moment it slipped out.

Carlson let out a laugh. Which was a relief. Not that she would mind a date with Carlson. He was a good-looking guy, but aside from today he hadn't been too welcoming of her.

"I haven't dated in a while now."

"Why not? Because of Mathews?" Janice got the feeling there was something a bit complicated about her simple question. Perhaps it was his demeanor that gave her that idea. He seemed to stiffen in his seat. That could have been the mention of Mathews though.

"No. Way before him. I sort of have this crush on this girl. And every time I try to date someone else, I think about her." Carlson took the last sip of his Orange Juice. "We can't be together for reasons out of our control. To be honest, she probably couldn't care less about me. She doesn't even know how I feel."

"Seems silly to devote your love to someone who might not even love you back." This was a different side of Carlson. Janice would have never guessed he was the type to have a lost love back on Earth. "I'm not trying to criticize, but you should at least tell her what you think of her. Tell her what she means to you. If she doesn't share your feeling, you can probably move on. If she does, who knows, there might be a way to work things out."

"You might be right about that, Janice." Carlson stared out a window, a thought on his mind. "That has to be the best advice I've gotten on the subject, and you don't even know the whole story."

"Perhaps you can fill me in."

"Another time. I need some sleep." Carlson smiled at Janice.

She was confident she had helped out. Maybe she even made a friend. "Well, I suppose we have ten more months of graveyard to talk about it."

Chapter 11

Carlson walked onto the bridge with Janice. The Captain was seated in her command chair, Zimmerman to her right. That was uncommon for this hour. Carlson approached the other Protective Services officers.

"Hey Mike," the one said turning to acknowledge him. "They lost the trace on that ship we've been tailing for weeks. She's been here for two hours trying to find it again."

Carlson just nodded. It wasn't his place to comment on what the Captain was doing. But finding the faint signature of an engine after it was lost was like trying to get a scent once the rain had washed it away. You might catch a trace, but odds are it was lost.

Serenity looked over her shoulder and at Mike. She stood up and turned to Zimmerman. "I'm going to take a break, keep this heading and see what we can find."

She walked into her office, Carlson and Janice followed her in. She went straight to her couch and lay down. She didn't say anything for some time. When she did speak, her voice startled Carlson.

"Four and a half weeks chasing this lead and we've lost it like that. So damn strong, then suddenly it goes weak and we lose it." Serenity looked at Carlson. He had assumed she was just talking to the room, not him.

"I don't know enough about the engines of our ship, let alone this mystery one, Ma'am," Carlson shrugged. "What does Lieutenant Morgan think?"

"I haven't bothered him with it yet. Odds are, it means the ship slowed down here for some reason. The signatures on these engines are very close to our own, so you know what that means?"

"No, not really." This time Janice spoke.

"Probably a Martian warship," Serenity said. "Their designs are almost exactly like ours; they are a bit faster. In fact, they had about a forty-five minute jump on us; so in the four weeks, assuming they were at maximum speed like us..." Serenity was doing the math in her head. "They were probably here about twenty hours or so ago."

"So why would they have stopped here, and for long enough for the trail to go cold?" Janice asked.

Serenity jumped up. "They stopped! That has to be it. I don't know why I didn't think of it. Damn it Kanter, I could kiss you!"

Serenity ran over to her desk and hit a button. "Commander, scan for signs of debris. Maybe trash, debris, something. I have a feeling they stopped nearby."

* * *

Mathews stared at the picture of the man with that damned apple in his face. He was getting sick of this person contacting him. "You realize you could be jeopardizing both our goals by contacting me all the time. Someone will notice soon."

"I understand you have the Australia running around a month outside of Earth space," the disguised voice said.

"And what of it?" Mathews said.

"What are you doing about it?" the voice said. "She is out there alone. Now would be the best time. Do you have someone on board to take care of her?"

"I'll decide when the best time is. I have some enemies out there that will take care of this without implicating anyone."

"You already have a price on your head."

"No one knows I have left. The Earth Military isn't so stupid as to let my escape go public. They have gained the trust of the citizens that New Alcatraz is safe, and they think they have the most cost-effective, and most criminal-deterrent judicial system there ever was," Mathews laughed. "They announce I escaped and people will ask why I didn't get the needle. My crimes warranted life in prison; I should have been killed. Then they will want to know how I could escape. They will keep it under wraps as long as they can. You and I are the only ones who know about me."

"What about the people I hired to get you out?"

"Dead men don't talk," Mathews said. "What is it you contacted me for anyway?"

"I am not confident you can handle this. I want a little assurance," the voice said.

"Get me more contacts inside. I'll tell them what to do, through you."

"What makes you think I have any influence in the Earth Navy?"

"I know more than you think I know," Mathews said. "Now let me take care of my own business. I'll contact you."

* * *

Serenity ran out to the bridge. "How many?"

"Now four ships coming into radar range. They are moving fast. Unknown style, no known identity beacons."

"How the hell did the Martians get four ships out here?" Serenity panicked a bit. It was a trap the whole time. She had worried about that. No time for that now. "General Quarters. Scramble all three fighter wings. How long until we can get better scans?"

"At the speed they are moving on us, a matter of minutes."

Serenity analyzed the radar. They were fast ships, maybe destroyers. The Australia might be able to outgun two destroyers, maybe three if the fighters could help. Four would be hard.

"Captain..." Morgan hesitated. "Those aren't Martian Ships. There is nothing like them in the Martian or Earth databases."

"A secret Martian design?"

"If it is, they are using metal and construction methods way beyond anything I know," Morgan said. "I don't think it's human made."

"Let's not jump the gun here," Zimmerman said. He turned to the Captain. "We could be looking pretty hostile right now."

"At those speeds and their maneuvers, so do they. We are clearly being intercepted," Serenity said.

"They've slowed down. They appear to be coming to a stop about nine hundred meters out. If these readings are right, they have weapons ready," Willard said.

"Take a defensive posture. Target the closest ship and await orders," Serenity said. "Keep the fighters aft."

"Transmission coming in," Willard said. "Putting it on screen."

A dark brown humanoid creature appeared on the monitor. They had similar facial features, but its head flowed more cleanly into its shoulders, no real visible neck.

It wore what was clearly a uniform, decorated in ways that lead Serenity to believe it was clearly an officer of importance.

"Unidentified Vessel, I am Marshall Korvikan of the Royal Navy. You are trespassing in Zercowan space. Stand down and prepare to be boarded." His English was almost perfect. How was that even possible?

"I am Captain Christina Serenity of the Earth Space Ship Australia. I assure you we have no hostile intention. Our actions were simply a reaction to the state of your arrival."

"We've been tricked once too many by your people. We are not fools." Korvikan broke from his straightforward gaze, taking in what he could see of the ship on his own screens. Then he went back to his forward gaze. "If you will not stand down, we will destroy your ship."

"I assure you, we are no threat. We will leave if you want, but I cannot allow you to board my ship."

"Enough tricks," Korvikan shouted and the transmission ended.

"Captain, they're firing at us," Willard shouted.

Serenity waited for the hit. They missed. "Either they are terrible shots, or that was a warning."

"Should we turn and run?" Zimmerman asked.

"That will do nothing for us. They can outrun us, and something tells me they won't let us run. Try hailing them again." Serenity waited a moment. Korvikan came back on screen. "You speak of tricks from my people, yet I can assure you the Earth Government has no knowledge of Zercowan space."

"We dealt with humans just yesterday, and it was not a welcomed event."

"I'm brought here because I am chasing a ship, one that may belong to a different government. We are both humans, but not the same government. We have different leaders, different military—"

"The ship was of the same design as yours. This is another stall tactic." The transmission ended.

This time, all four ships fired just over the bridge. Only these shots were a lot closer to hitting the ship. Serenity knew what this was.

"Saber rattling," Serenity said out loud. "Have the fighters do a fly by. Not too close, but close enough to show we can play too."

"I don't think that's—" Zimmerman started to say.

Serenity raised a hand to silence him. "What do we know of those weapons?"

"They are energy based, similar to ours. They appear to be fired from an energy rail of some kind, perhaps centrally controlled," Morgan shrugged. "Best guess anyway."

"That could be an advantage for us." The ship's individual cannons would allow them to fire from multiple angles; they may have blind spots. Serenity sat down. The fighters were already returning from the fly by.

How could she play this right? That damned unknown ship had got her into this mess, perhaps intentionally. She wished she knew something about what they had done. "Zimmerman, did we ever find any debris?"

"Unknown debris, a lot of it was detected not far from here. We hadn't checked it out yet," Zimmerman said. "You think they destroyed that ship we've been chasing?"

"I think a Zercowan ship may have been destroyed," Serenity said. If that was true, this was going to take a silver tongue to get out of.

"They are contacting us again," Willard said.

"Make them wait a minute," Serenity said. She figured they had been all too friendly and that hadn't worked.

The Marshall came on screen. Again he glanced around before he went to the straightforward stare. He saw something different. The damned uniforms.

"I notice you look around our ship. Is there something you notice?" Serenity said.

"It could be more tricks," Korvikan said.

"Imagine the cost to outfit another crew with a different uniform, a different color for this ship even?" Serenity really hoped it was a Martian ship. If it looked like the Australia it was likely Martian, painted red. Hopefully it was the Phobos. "We just met you today, the other ship yesterday. A lot of work to deceive a friend we haven't met yet."

"Humans pretended to be our friends, exchanged gifts with us. When we felt it was safe to let them pass, they destroyed one of our ships, killing two thousand of our military. So we know a little about the lengths humans will go in order to trick a friend."

"That was the Martian's or, at the very least, a ship masquerading as theirs. That's the very reason I am chasing that ship, they attacked us just over a month ago." Serenity paused. "I can send you records of Earth and our two different cultures to verify my story."

"Doctored records."

"Marshall, I really understand your skepticism here. But what possible hostile intent can I have? I am alone. No other ship has arrived in the time we have talked." Serenity paused. She spoke to Sanchez, "Lieutenant, recall the fighters and power down the cannons."

Sanchez stared at the Captain with a look that asked, *Really?* Serenity just nodded.

She stood with her arms outstretched before the screen. "There, Marshall. Destroy us if you must. We sit here defenseless to show our goodwill. I can offer no more. As I said before, I can leave if you wish. But it seems to me that we at least have a common enemy, and perhaps we could even become friends."

"Fine. I will admit there is enough doubt in my mind," The Marshall said dryly. "Stay still. I won't fire on a defenseless ship, so it is best you remain that way."

* * *

Serenity would have been excited to talk to the Prime Minister, but given the four fully-armed ships watching her, her focus was on something else entirely. The rest of Naval Command was ecstatic over the discovery of other life. None of them seemed the least bit concerned, they were ready to destroy her ship.

The Prime Minister's seal showed up on the screen on her desk. She popped her neck and tried to relax. Taking a breath as the Prime Minister came on screen,

"Captain Serenity, I assume," he said. His voice was deep, but soothing. It calmed and reassured her.

"Yes, Sir."

"I have the Admiral here with me. He has relayed a lot of information my way. But it sounds to me like these Zercowans were pretty set on attacking your ship. You seem to have charmed them out of it."

"Well, I have at least delayed them, Sir," Serenity said.

"Nonetheless, good work." Serenity let a bit of pride escape to her face. She hid it again quickly. The Prime Minister only smiled back. "I hope we have a successful first contact. I have the Admiral sending another Warship your way. Of course, it will be almost a month before you see them. But, they have a diplomat on board. They will be able to pick up where you left off.

"Assuming you keep on good terms with these Zercowans, I want you to stay on the trail of the Phobos. I don't like this ship running around dragging Earth's name around.

"I believe you already prevented a terrorist attack on Peace Day. The Martian President won't give me many answers, but I think he may be just as puzzled by the actions of this Phobos as we are. Perhaps we can shed some more light on this matter. You understand the stakes, don't you?"

"Keep an alien race happy with Earth, prevent one ship from dragging us into a war, and try to do it fast," Serenity said. "I will do my best, Sir."

Chapter 12

"**F**rankly, I am getting tired of hearing from you," Mathews said. "And change that privacy image. I can't even enjoy a damned apple anymore."

"Someone is a bit touchy," the voice said. "Perhaps you already know why I have contacted you."

"No, I don't. I was pretty sure I was supposed to contact you next." Mathews really had no idea what the issue was this time. He was halfway back to Martian space, hoping to be nowhere near the Zercowans when they destroyed the Australia. "I am just tired of you bothering me."

"Then why don't you take care of the problem? Then I don't have to deal with you anymore," the voice said.

"By now she should be dead," Mathews said.

"You really should read the news. She is far from dead," the voice said. "She's a Goddamned hero now."

"What are you talking about?" Mathews pulled up the local news.

"She is being hailed as a hero. They say she prevented a terrorist attack planned on the Everest for Peace Day," the voice said.

"She was always the target of that attack."

"The Prime Minister stated otherwise in his address regarding the first contact with the Zercowans." The voice sounded annoyed. "So now she is a savior and an explorer. Her name and her ship are on every news channel here."

Hero Captain Discovers Aliens. Mathews just read the first headline. That could have been his name on that headline. "How does that change anything? Dead is dead."

"I thought I made it clear the last time that she was the target, not the whole damned ship. You don't think I know why you lured her way out there? Now she has the Prime Minister's attention."

"Then get someone else!" Mathews slammed down his fist on the desk. "I told you I would handle this how I wanted to handle this."

"You are trying to start a war!" the voice yelled back. "How does that benefit you?"

"My goals are none of your business," Mathews said calmly.

"After what I've done for you."

"There is nothing you can do about that now." Mathews's voice was flat. He had enough.

"I'll handle this myself. You will find your account very empty right now. I turned the information over to Security Forces, they've seized it all," the voice said. "I won't be contacting you again."

The transmission ended. Mathews pulled up his bank records. Then threw the tablet across the office. All of it was gone; all he had was what was in the Martian banks.

And how long would it be before the Martians turned him in? If his contact told them of his money, he likely mentioned his living arrangement on Mars. Of course, his contact didn't know he was in the Martian military, though he probably assumed as much. It was still likely, even in this rocky political situation, the Martians would turn him in if they went public with his escape.

Mathews took a breath. He could reveal his contact. He had a good idea who it was. No, they wouldn't go public with his escape yet. He had some time. The real question was his next move. His desk transmitter buzzed. "Yes."

"Captain, we have an Earth Warship passing through our area. Not far from us, but they don't appear to notice us."

"I see," Mathews grinned. "Move us to intercept, and go to General Quarters."

* * *

Two weeks spent at a standstill with four alien ships pointing weapons at the Australia was making the crew stir crazy. Fights were up all over the ship and patrol was swamped. So that meant more work for everyone.

Carlson had pulled rank on the matter, so he was put on the Captain for extended shifts and no time off. Janice hadn't complained once, even though he was sure she would have chosen to help patrol.

The Captain spent her shifts chatting with the Marshall and relations were certainly improving. The delay had been lengthy for one main reason:

Trust. Leaders of the Zercowan government wanted to ensure there was no trickery. They had lost a ship, and there was a need to have answers.

They were clearly more technologically advanced. If things panned out, like they seemed they would, this was likely to be a positive discovery for Earth.

Carlson let a yawn escape. Janice nudged him and handed him a cup of coffee. "Drink it quick. The Captain has plans to make some rounds in a few minutes."

Carlson took a couple of sips. He widened his eyes at the taste. "This tastes like pure grounds."

"It'll wake you up."

Carlson handed her back the cup. "It tastes like shit. You finish it."

She laughed. Carlson shook his head. Another set of rounds meant walking this whole ship while the Captain heard about the various problems. But Serenity had been clear that she would make these rounds because the crew needed to see her. And see that she was in high spirits.

"Should we go in and see what she needs?" Janice asked.

Carlson nodded. He knocked on the door twice, and then opened it slowly.

"Come in. We'll start rounds soon." Serenity was seated at her desk.

She stretched her arms up, her breasts pushing tightly on her uniform shirt. Carlson decided to focus his attention elsewhere before he was caught gawking.

"I am just reading these Security Forces reports. My whole crew is going to wind up in the brig soon," Serenity said.

"They're restless, Ma'am," Janice said, but she was watching Carlson.

Carlson made eye contact with Janice. She put on a wry smile, glanced down at her own chest, then back up at him. *Fuck.* She had seen him. Carlson just shook his head as if he was annoyed with Janice.

"Well, progress is good with the Zercowans," Serenity said. "Slow, but good. I can't blame them for being restless. Something about them bothers me, too. For one, these translators they use. I don't understand how they could learn a language as complex as English in a matter of twenty hours."

"They did say the Martians shared some gifts," Janice said. "Perhaps a computer file was shared with them."

"I can't help but feel like we're being deceived," Serenity thought for a moment. "Anyway, we are two weeks behind the Phobos now, if we can even pick up the trail. Though I think the Zercowans have an idea on where we can start searching. I am worried the Africa will get here before they make up their minds. That may escalate things."

The transmitter buzzed. Serenity pressed the button.

"Captain, three of the ships have left. I have Marshall Korvikan transmitting."

"Put it through." Serenity waited for the Marshall to come on her screen. "Marshall, I always enjoy our chats. We seem to learn a lot."

"I would agree, Captain. I have some good news. Our government has determined that your people were not responsible for the attack on our ship. They will allow you monitored access to our space."

"That is great news. Earth has sent a Diplomat. I don't expect they will arrive for another couple of weeks," Serenity said. "I am supposed to try and find the Phobos."

"Our mutual, shall we say... acquaintance. I can be of help there, too. I have managed to talk them into giving you the last known location of the Phobos. That's all I can give you, but it is something. It's also old information."

"Still, it is information," Serenity said. "I thank you. And I hope we meet again, on better terms."

"Me, too." Korvikan paused, "I've sent the information. You may be on your way."

Chapter 13

Janice woke up early. She spent two weeks saying that once she had a day off, she would sleep all day—and she wound up awake at the usual time. So the first thing she did was go for a jog around the ship. It was far better than using the treadmill in the gym, and she liked the chance to move. After that, she showered and changed.

The videos were boring. Either the Earth news broadcasts going on and on about the Zercowans, or it was some cheesy movie. Janice didn't have time for either. So she went out for a walk.

She decided she would make her way around, and then head to Carlson's quarters. She was really starting to enjoy his company. They actually had a lot in common. They enjoyed the same sports, had the same jaded views, a bit of a sarcastic sense of humor, and they enjoyed the same foods.

He was a good friend, and she didn't have any on the Australia. She didn't really have any friends at all. Most of her friends had abandoned her when she went into the Service. They were not exactly fond of the law. So perhaps it was best that she didn't associate with them.

Her last partner was likeable. But, she was also promotable and moved up to Corporal. That was when she found out she had better get specialty training if she wanted to promote.

So far, she wasn't sure she even wanted to go back to patrol. Patrol was more fun, more action, but she had a friend here now.

She knocked on Carlson's door. "Mike, it's Janice."

"Come in," Carlson called out. She opened the door. He was coming out of the bedroom with no shirt on. "Oh, good, it's open. I'll be right back."

Janice watched him walk away. For a lanky guy, there was some clear definition to his muscles. He looked good. Janice felt a flush come over her. That was her partner and friend.

"Would you put a shirt on, no one needs to see that." *You always were a charmer.*

"Ha! I thought you might like it, since you haven't seen a man in a while," Carlson teased.

The typical low blow banter she had expected. She took a breath, feeling somehow oddly relieved. "You wanna get something to eat? A drink? Something?"

Carlson walked out, his black undershirt on. "I don't know. I'm sick of being out around the ship. I was just planning on hanging here. You can sit if you want. My place is your place."

Janice sat on the standard couch. It was oddly comfortable for being military issue. Carlson handed her a soda and sat down in the chair near her. He cracked open his drink and took a sip. "So much for sleeping all day anyway, eh?"

"Yea, no shit." Janice leaned back.

* * *

Serenity settled into her command chair. The last known location of the Phobos had come up dry. There was nothing to go on in this area, and odds were they fled back in the direction of Mars. She planned to check the area more and tomorrow report to the Admiral.

"Captain, emergency transmission coming in," Willard stated. "It's the Africa."

"Put it on."

The speakers popped. "This is the E.S.S. Africa to any who can hear us. We are under attack and in need of assistance. We have been disabled and cannot move. Please respond."

"Respond," Serenity jumped up. Willard gave her the signal. "E.S.S. Africa, respond. This is the Australia."

The Captain of the Africa came on screen. His ship rattling and the bridge was dark, only lit by the red hue of the alarm lights. "Captain Serenity, thank God! The Martians came out of nowhere and took out our engines. We're giving them a hell of a fight, but I can't maneuver much. We need help."

"Send me the coordinates." Serenity waited for Willard to plug them in.

"At top speed, we are still four days away," Willard said.

"Set the course," Serenity ordered. She turned back to the screen. "Who is attacking you?"

"It's the M.S.S. Phobos. They demanded our surrender to the Martian Government after attacking our engines." The Captain paused, the ship shook again.

"I'm four days away, Captain," Serenity said. "Hold them off as long as you can."

The transmission ended. Serenity rubbed her face. They would be dead in four days. There was no way they could hold off a Martian warship that long. "Notify Naval Command, and try to raise a Zercowan ship. And get the Commander up here, now."

"Yes, Ma'am," Willard said.

Serenity felt hopeless. She had to wait four days now. Why now? Had the Phobos been hanging around here this whole time? If so, why didn't they attack the Australia? It had been a week since the Zercowans left the Australia to their mission. If he wanted to attack them then, there would have been no aide to arrive for weeks. Or, had they passed the Africa on their way back to Mars and decided to attack?

"Where is the Commander?" Serenity called out.

"On his way, Ma'am. It's only been a few minutes," Willard said. "I do have the Zercowan ship, The Derik's Eye, responding to our transmission."

Perfect, Marshall Korvikan. "Put them on."

"Captain, we have received the Africa's emergency signal," Korvikan said. "Our nearest ship is six days away. And there is little I can do anyway, they are outside our space."

"Fuck," Serenity said. "I'm sorry Marshall, excuse me. It is a bad situation."

* * *

"So I get to his place, and he has pictures of his wife up everywhere," Janice said. "Then—get this—he says, 'Oh, she is good with this.' Needless to say, I just walked out. Wound up walking all the way back to my place."

"Wow." Carlson sat back down and handed Janice another soda. "Just left the pictures out everywhere."

"You couldn't turn anywhere in the house without seeing one. And, he didn't even make anything up. Can you believe it?"

Janice had been regaling Carlson with one of her more horrendous dating experiences. They'd been trading personal stories for the better part of an hour, and Carlson enjoyed it.

"So, you ever get a chance to speak to this girl of yours, Mike?" Janice gave him a push on his knee. "You know, take up my advice?"

"I wish it were that simple." Carlson really didn't want to go down this path. He was smart enough to know that if he danced around it long enough he would spill.

"It's only as hard as you make it." Janice sat back and took another drink. "You gonna tell me, or do I have to go see the Doctor again?"

"Ha, even the Doctor doesn't know that." Carlson had heard it was the Doctor's bedside manner that revealed enough information for Janice to press Carlson about Mathews. "Only one other person does, and he's..." He's not in prison anymore. He swallowed hard and made himself say it. "...in prison."

"Oh, so the traitor gets to know, but not me," Janice laughed. "At least tell me about her."

Carlson had backed himself into a verbal corner now. He trusted Janice, but he had also trusted Mathews. Although Mathews hasn't said anything.

"Mike?" Janice leaned in again, before flopping back again. "Nah, if you don't want to tell me you don't have to."

"Really? Somehow I don't believe you're done hounding me on this." *Carlson you idiot, just shut up.*

"Yeah, it must be the Captain. I saw you checking her out." Janice laughed hard. Clearly she was just making a joke.

But, Carlson couldn't help the feeling of being caught. He let out a short nervous laugh. "You think you're funny, don't you?"

"Sometimes. Can you—" Janice looked Mike dead in the eyes. "Oh, my God. I'm right, aren't I?"

Carlson swallowed hard. That was that, she knew. Even if he didn't say a word, she knew. The moment of truth was here. He could continue to lie, and if she didn't report him their trust would be damaged because she would know he lied. Or, he could come clean and tell her, she reports it, and he gets reassigned.

Janice was his friend. He couldn't lie to her right now. And, if she did report him, they were at least a month outside of Earth Space. Maybe he could use the month to see what the Captain thought of him.

"Mike?" Janice prodded.

"This stays between us as friends, Janice. Off the record." Carlson stared at her hard. "Because jokes like yours can get me reassigned."

"Mike, we're friends. I'm not stupid enough to run my mouth." Janice put her hand on his knee.

"Fine, you are right." Carlson let a huge breath out. "I've liked the Captain for a while now. And, well, as I told you a while ago, she doesn't know and probably doesn't even think of me beyond my duties. There are regulations prohibiting us from even talking about this."

It seemed like it took ages for Janice to acknowledge him. Finally, she sat back. "Leave it to you to make love complicated."

"I guess so." That wasn't the reassuring response he had hoped Janice would give him.

"Though you guys would be a good couple, I think. Maybe you're right to wait it out for her." Janice looked over at him. "Relax, Mike. I'm not going to fuck this up for you. Like I said, I'm not going to run my mouth."

"Thanks," Carlson sunk into the chair. It felt good to say something about it.

"Stupid thing anyway," Janice took a drink. "Trying to regulate love."

Chapter 14

Serenity had planned for the possibility this was a trap. They were not going to come in full blast. They even came around from another angle, just in case. There had been no response from the Africa since the first transmission. Serenity expected there to be no Africa when she arrived.

"Slowing speeds. We will be arriving in long range radar here in, three. Two. One," Willard said. The crew was ready.

"What do you see, Ensign?" Zimmerman said.

"Nothing, yet. No ships in range," Willard said.

"Keep moving us in, attack speed," Serenity said. "And keep an eye on the area we would have been expected to arrive at."

Serenity couldn't sit. She paced back and forth, surely driving Willard and Sanchez crazy. They should be getting something soon. Even if it was just debris.

Willard's display lit up. Willard looked over her shoulder to the Captain. "Lifeboats, eight of them in the debris field. They have the Africa's beacon."

"Shit." Serenity had expected this, but really had hoped they would make it in time. She pinched the top of her nose between her eyes to hide the wince of pain in her hip. "Deploy the fighters and launch the rescue shuttles."

"Aye, Captain," Sanchez said.

Zimmerman came to the Captain's side. "There was nothing we could have done to get to her in time."

"Those survivors are likely to be hungry, and in need of medical aide,"

Serenity said. "Go down to the flight deck and orchestrate their arrival. I want them greeted with a hot meal and the Doctor as soon as they step off our shuttles."

"Yes, Ma'am," Zimmerman said. He turned to walk away.

"Commander..." Serenity waited for him to turn around. "Thank you."

He smiled at her and nodded before walking away. Serenity went straight to her office. She connected with the Admiral, who knew they'd be arriving now.

"You don't appear to have good news," The Admiral said.

"The Africa is lost, Sir. There are lifeboats, but we don't know their condition yet."

"Any sign of the attackers?" Serenity shook her head. McCorvick continued. "Do we know for sure it was the Phobos?"

"Not until we get the computer box from the debris. But, that is what Captain Sinclair said, Sir," Serenity said.

"The Prime Minister has been in contact with Mars. Their President won't deny the Phobos is a Martian ship, but he won't confirm it, either." The Admiral looked down, as if reflecting. "I'd expect a war after this, Captain. That ship is flying Martian markings, and the Martians won't say otherwise. Now it has destroyed an Earth Warship. All it is going to take is for the Prime Minister to get the proof he needs. That proof is on that computer box. Do you understand?"

Serenity didn't get what he was implying. "Do you need us to return home?"

"No, find that box. Use it to figure out where the Phobos went. Find that ship and get us some answers," The Admiral said. "There has to be more to this than even the Martians know."

* * *

"How many?" Serenity surveyed all the survivors of the Africa lined up for food or medical attention on the flight deck.

"There were forty on the boats, five were dead when we pulled them in. Thirty-five total," Zimmerman said. "Three of them are in bad shape. Doctor's working on them first."

"Forty men in those life boats?" Serenity knew they were designed to hold two, maybe three maximum. "Crammed together for that long, three days."

"They were very appreciative of the food, that's for sure," Zimmerman said. "They haven't been checked in yet. I figured they could eat first. We'll check them in before they get off the flight deck."

"Who's the highest ranking officer?" Serenity asked.

"I really don't know, Ma'am," Zimmerman said. "Would you like me to find out?"

"I'll go down there and look around." Serenity glanced back at Carlson. He looked worn down. They had been at General Quarters for some time. She turned back to Zimmerman. "We need to get them integrated into the crew, and move on quickly."

Serenity went down the lift to the flight deck. She looked around to see if anyone stood out. There was a group of five crewmen standing around joking, but the highest rank there was a Petty Officer. A man stood by himself, watching over all of the survivors. Serenity was surprised to see he was a Lieutenant Commander.

She hadn't expected a commanding officer to have made it off the ship. As she approached him, he glanced at her. He started straightening his uniform. Perhaps he was a new Lieutenant Commander.

"Relax, I'm not holding uniform inspections today," Serenity joked. The Commander stiffened up to attention. "At ease, I said relax."

"Sorry, Si—Ma'am," he said.

"I'm Captain Serenity."

"Lieutenant Commander Banks, Ma'am."

"And fresh out of Command School too. Or so I assume." She put out her hand and he shook it.

"Captain Sinclair was trying to get me to tone it down," Banks stared at the floor. "Rough past few days, I suppose discipline is what pulled us through."

"It had to be." Serenity took a few moments to let him reflect. "I must say, I'm surprised to see anyone of the command staff made it off."

"The Captain insisted I go. He said I could be helpful at tracking down the people who did this. I almost refused, but as I said, discipline is what sees us through."

Serenity nodded. "You will be helpful with integrating your crew with mine."

"You already won them over with the food. You didn't have to do that."

"The hell I didn't. I just wish I could have gotten here faster." Serenity felt the pain in her hip again. "Let's sit down and talk about this attack. I am betting you can get me information faster than that computer box."

* * *

Carlson was tired. They had been at General Quarters for too long. Worst of all, Serenity hadn't taken so much as a break the whole time. That meant Carlson and Janice had been on their feet. Now she was down here on the flight deck mingling with the survivors.

Carlson knew it was his own sleepiness that was giving him a bitter outlook. Truthfully, it was nice for her to come see these people. Three days in a jam-packed lifeboat was a situation he hoped he never had to live through. Of course, it was better than blowing up with the ship. Carlson wasn't sure by how much.

Now the Captain and this rookie Lieutenant Commander were exchanging playful banter. He was obviously flirting with the Captain. And Carlson was jealous.

He saw a twitch in the Captain's left leg, just barely there. In fact, he may not have noticed if he wasn't watching her butt move.

"Let's sit down and talk about this attack. I am betting you can get me information faster than that computer box," Serenity said.

Serenity and Banks made their way to a set of storage containers and sat down. Carlson looked at Janice and rolled his eyes. He had enough and just wanted to sit down himself. Janice gave him a nod of agreement. Carlson stood a couple of feet to the Captain's left. Janice stayed to the right of her.

Carlson would have preferred to stand behind the Captain, but these containers were too close to the wall. He would have felt pinned down, standing behind them.

Banks was going on about the attack on the Africa. Carlson could listen in, but frankly, he didn't care. He scanned the group of people.

They had all formed little groups. Clearly, these pods had come from different areas of the ship. Some of these guys didn't know each other at all until today. That wasn't surprising with the crew size of a warship. The groups had begun to intermingle. Before long these thirty or so survivors would be a close group.

Carlson stretched, let out a yawn, he had hoped to hold in, and stared down at his aching feet.

"GUN!" Janice yelled.

Carlson looked up and started running. A laser blast hit the wall just high left of the Captain's head. Carlson grabbed her collar and pulled her behind the container. A second blast hit the wall where her head had just been.

Carlson's vision blurred and he could see spots. He must have hit his head on the deck. Another shot fired. He struggled to get his L-pistol from the holster while lying down. Janice was yelling into her radio. He couldn't hear what she said over the noises. He checked the Captain. He was still lying halfway over her.

"You okay?"

She nodded at him. Carlson looked over the container. Janice fired two more shots and then leapt over the boxes a few feet from Carlson. Two more bolts hit right under Carlson. He fired once, then ducked.

"Five of them," Janice called to him. "I hit two of them."

Carlson scanned the area. The nearest exit was right through the line of fire. Janice took several more shots before the bolts flew past her. She ducked down.

The Security Forces teams had now moved into a good position and were engaging the suspects well. He looked at Janice. Then down to the Captain.

"We got to move, Ma'am," He said pulling her to her hands and knees. "Go when I say so."

He waited for a sign from Janice. She nodded, popped up, and fired at the suspects.

"Move now." Carlson pushed Serenity along as they ran to the containers Janice hid behind. There was another set just ahead.

Janice ducked behind cover, dropping her battery pack. Carlson popped up and fired three more shots. The suspects had slipped behind some shuttles.

Janice sprung back up. "Go!"

Carlson pushed Serenity along again. They got to the next set of containers, then slid in. Two bolts hit near them. Carlson couldn't tell where.

"We've got to get to that door," Carlson told the Captain. It was a good distance to move and there was no cover. "Can you make it? I need a full sprint."

"Yes."

Carlson saw something out of the corner of his eye. He swung around and caught Banks in the arm. The L-pistol Banks had fell to the floor. Carlson's other hand struck Banks in the chest. Carlson was then able to fling him to the ground.

Janice was by his side getting the restraints on him. Two other Security Forces Officers came running over. "Leave him, Janice. We've got to get out of here."

They ran for the exit, slid through and slammed it shut. Carlson took a breath while Janice covered the doorway, just in case.

"I think they are all down," Janice said, listening to the radio. "Yeah, five down, one in custody."

"Let's get the Captain to her quarters." Carlson started to jog down the halls.

* * *

While submitting his report, the adrenaline had burned off and rage replaced it. Five people plus Banks, an Earth Navy Lieutenant Commander, had attacked the Captain. He was the only survivor and he wasn't saying a thing.

Two other Security Forces Officers were injured—one was life threatening. Carlson was lucky with just a goose egg on his head. Janice walked with him down the halls of the Security Forces section of the ship.

Carlson stopped at the brig and stared down at the row of cells. Anger grew in him. The Captain had trusted Banks—extended a courtesy to him by feeding his men. She had been upset for four days while she tried to get there to save these men. And this Lieutenant Commander betrayed her, the Navy, and his government. He wanted to kill Christina. Just like Mathews.

"Open the brig," Carlson said to the man at the control desk. The anger leaked from his voice. The brig officer gave Carlson a puzzled look. "Now!"

The clear door to the row of cells opened. Carlson stormed down the aisle. He saw Banks sitting on the cot.

"Six!" Carlson yelled down the hall.

The door didn't even open all the way before Carlson had Banks against the wall by his collar.

"You son-of-a-bitch!" Carlson slammed Banks against the wall a few times, shaking him hard. "I swear I will kill you. You betrayed us, you betrayed her."

Janice pulled Carlson off of Banks. "God damn it, Mike. What are you doing? Back off!"

Banks dusted off his uniform. He let out a faint chuckle. "There is something going on here bigger than you know. Serenity will die, and you won't be able to stop it. There's a big price on her pretty little head."

Carlson lunged at Banks again. Janice and another officer held him back just well enough that he missed getting a hold of Banks again. "I swear if anyone hurts Christina, I will hunt them down. Every last one of you!"

They dragged Carlson out and the cell door closed. Janice pushed Carlson against the wall. She stared dead in his eyes, "Knock it off, Mike."

Carlson turned away. Janice grabbed him by the face and turned his head back to face her. "Mike. Listen to me. He isn't Mathews, Mike. He isn't Mathews."

The fight fell right out of Carlson. He shook his head. Not because he didn't agree with her, but because she was right. He gently pushed her back, dusted off his uniform, and walked out of the brig.

Chapter 15

Christina walked into the conference room. General Valentine was on the main screen. Major Kingsworth sat at one side of the table, Carlson was on the other side. She turned to the on-duty protection crew and told them to wait outside.

She hadn't seen Carlson in a couple days. The Major was adamant that he take some time off. Serenity had to agree. After the incident in the brig it was important he take a breather. She had thought that would be the end of it, until this meeting was called.

"What is going on now, Major?" She glanced over at Carlson. "I thought this was behind us."

"It was, until the Admiral thought otherwise," General Valentine said.

"I'm sorry, Sir. I assumed Major Kingsworth called for the disciplinary hearing," Serenity said.

"No, this is all your branch's doing," Valentine said. "The least he could do is get here on time."

Why had the Admiral taken such an interest in this case? She assumed it had more to do with Carlson than the case. Perhaps he worried because this happened from Mathews's old partner. But, Carlson really hadn't done much. He used far less force than the interrogators would have, and he got a confession.

The fact did remain that Carlson was not an approved interrogator and hadn't been authorized to use force on a prisoner. This was easily a Security Forces matter. Certainly not a matter requiring an Admiral and a General.

The screen split in two, and Admiral McCorvick joined the secure transmission. "Sorry I am late, General. Major, Captain. I hope we can be brief."

"I suppose that is up to you, McCorvick," Valentine said. "Since you expressed a need to know what is going on in a matter that doesn't concern you."

"Doesn't concern me? That prisoner was a Naval Officer. The rough handling of my Officers is my concern," the Admiral said.

"Fine. What are you concerned about?" Valentine asked.

"I believe I asked for a formal inquiry," the Admiral replied.

The General shook his head and looked down at something, probably the official inquiry documents. He began reading them aloud. Serenity tuned it out. It was the usual bureaucratic things like time and place and article numbers.

She glanced at Carlson. When they made eye contact, he hung his head low, focusing on the floor. He refused to look at her. That bothered her, and she was even more distracted.

"So what do you want to accomplish with all this, Admiral?" Valentine said when he finished.

"I think Carlson needs to be demoted to Officer Second Class and removed from Protective Services." The Admiral looked at Serenity as if seeking her approval. She turned away and watched the General's half of the screen.

"Major, Captain. As the ranking officers on the ship, do you object?" the General asked.

"I do," Serenity blurted out. She swallowed hard as if somehow her throat was to blame for her outburst. The Admiral gave her a puzzled look. Was he suddenly trying to protect Serenity?

"I object," Major Kingsworth stated.

"So much for brief," the General said. "Well, Admiral, make your case."

"Carlson entered a prisoner's cell, a Navy Officer, and treated the prisoner roughly. He had no authorization or training to handle approved force. He repeatedly slammed that prisoner against the wall," the Admiral said. "He is responsible for the Captain's safety, yet he lost complete control of himself. How do we know this could not happen in the line of duty? Carlson is not responsible enough for his current assignment."

"Not responsible! He has saved my life three times now, four if you count locking out the bridge during the terrorist attack." Serenity instantly regretted the outburst. It sounded just like she was a teenager explaining to her dad why Carlson was a good man. "I'm sorry. I just get the feeling this is some attempt to lump him together with the actions of his old partner."

"They were not just partners, but friends, Captain," the Admiral said. "Mathews did prove one thing: Occasionally bad eggs get through even the strictest enlistment standards of Security Forces. We have to recognize the early warning signs. That is what this is about."

"The fact remains, just prior to this incident the Corporal dived on the Captain to save her life," the Major said. "In fact, if you want to talk about bad eggs..."

"We're not here to point fingers, Major," the General stated.

"You are right. Carlson was disciplined in a level that fit his actions. While he wasn't authorized to use approved force to get answers, he did manage to get a sort of confession. One of the key pieces of evidence used to convict the prisoner yesterday." The Major read a tablet in front of him, "Carlson doesn't deserve this spectacle. It has been handled fairly and the matter was closed until the Admiral got involved."

"Ignoring these warning signs will cause him to behave in a manner that may cause safety issues for Naval personnel," the Admiral said.

"I am at my safest when Officer Kanter and Mi—" Serenity paused, did she almost say Mike? "When Officer Kanter and Corporal Carlson are working. That has been proven by their track record."

The Admiral gave Serenity a curious look. He glanced at Carlson, who was watching Serenity. The Admiral looked back to Serenity. "Captain, are you romantically involved with Carlson?"

"What?!" Serenity said. Her shock was real, but for a different reason. "What does that have to do with this case?"

Carlson stopped looking at Serenity. Shock was on the Major's face.

General Valentine shook his head, disgust on his face. "Are you trying to make this some sort of scene, Admiral?"

"Carlson used the Captain's first name in his fit of rage. A moment when he might forget to use formal courtesy to hide his relationship." The Admiral glared at Carlson.

Serenity panicked a moment. This was not how she wanted Carlson to find out her true feelings. If the issue was pressed, would she be able to lie so blatantly to two of the highest ranking Military officials on Earth. To top things off, her hip was really starting to hurt.

"Admiral, with all due respect, are you that adamant to remove Carlson from his post that you would throw out these wild accusations? The Commander and Major both use my first name. It's a very weak basis for this," Serenity said. "With how many times I have used regulations to get my way—even with you—you must know I would stick to them?"

"I suppose you are right, Captain. It was a fleeting thought and I probably should have thought it out more before saying something." The Admiral held his chin up. "I apologize, General. This wasn't the place."

"Can we get on with this?" the General said. He waited for any objections. "Well, I am sorry, Admiral. I just don't see any reason to reverse the Major's disciplinary decision here."

"I'm sorry to hear that," the Admiral replied.

The Admiral's side of the screen went black. The General shrugged. "Well, I guess we are done here."

Serenity stood up, fighting her sore hip. She brushed past Carlson and straight out of the room.

Chapter 16

The Africa's computer box pointed them this direction. It wasn't much to go on, they could have changed course a bunch of times in the week it took to cross Zercowan space. But something told Serenity the Phobos would take the quickest way through.

Time was running out too. Naval Command had made it clear the Prime Minister had heard all he needed to about this attack and the Phobos. It would take about a week to get the Earth Council convened, so any day the Prime Minister would be addressing them.

"Captain, I've detected a small Martian ship. A transport similar to the one that rammed us," Morgan said. "All signs show it has been derelict for some time."

"Are we still in Zercowan space?"

"No, we just left," Willard said.

"Contact them anyway, just as a courtesy." Serenity paused, "And put us to Ready Stations."

"No sign of other craft," Willard said as the klaxon sounded.

"I have a feeling about this, and I don't like it," Serenity said.

What was the purpose of this craft sitting out here in the open, clearly abandoned? Either the Martians had been here before, or that craft belonged to the Phobos. She was betting on the Phobos. She was also betting the Phobos would be back.

"We're attempting to bring it aboard now," Morgan said.

"Alpha group is out there," Sanchez said.

"What do you think of this, Commander?" Serenity said.

"I think we may have a big lead here. But you are right to be on edge."

Serenity took a deep breath. "The thought of the Phobos always—"

"Captain, three unknown ships arriving fast!" Willard called out. "The Phobos is here too, but they are stopping."

"Battle stations, hail those ships."

"I can't, they've blocked our transmissions. I can't contact anyone," Willard said.

"It looks like they have weapons ready," Morgan said.

"They have released what appears to be fighter craft of their own, drones maybe. No life signs," Willard said.

"Move into position to protect the shuttle. Scramble the rest of the fighters. Target those ships and fire!" Serenity shouted.

As soon as the Australia's cannons fired, the ship jolted from a barrage of return fire. Serenity braced herself against the jolts of the ship. It was a lot of hits.

"Keep us moving, Willard. They are hitting us way too much," Serenity called out. "Make sure we get that shuttle."

"They are working on it, but we need to stay still long enough for them to get it in," Sanchez said.

"Damn it. Willard, keep us steady," Serenity said. She felt the barrage of fire hitting the ship. "Damage reports?"

"Hull damage on decks fifteen, six, and two," Morgan reported. "Holds are in place. But we need to move."

"Sanchez," Serenity said.

"They are aboard."

"Three new craft, Captain," Willard said. "They are just like the one we took in. Moving in fast. Collision course."

"Lock down the bridge," Carlson said.

"I'm trying," Kingsworth said. "I am getting no response."

"Can we outrun them?" Serenity said. The laser cannons were hitting the shuttles with little effect.

"They are too close," Willard said. "All hands brace for impact!"

The collision knocked everyone off their feet. Carlson helped the Captain up. Janice tossed him a laser rifle.

"Captain, we've been boarded in three separate locations," Kingsworth said.

The bridge doors blew open. The creatures had a blue tint to their skin, almost translucent. Serenity ducked as a blue ball of energy shot over her head. Carlson fired back.

Serenity ducked again as the console in front of Carlson exploded. These creatures were taller, but their form was odd, though they stood erect like humans.

Carlson, Kanter and the Major were doing their best to hold them off as they filed in the bridge doors. The ship still rattled with shots coming in from the enemy vessels.

Serenity heard a scream, it was Willard. She was holding her left arm at the elbow, the remainder appeared melted away like a candle. Serenity rushed over to her and pulled her away. Another ball hit near her head, but she kept moving.

The Major slumped over a console, his neck melted in the same manner, his head slid down to one side. Serenity swallowed hard to avoid vomiting. She looked over Willard, no blood was coming out. As bad as she was in pain, she wouldn't bleed to death.

The shooting stopped. Carlson leapt over the Security Forces station. He shoved the Major aside. Janice kept her rifle trained on the dead creatures.

"I got us locked down, but farther away. We may not be as safe as that implies," Carlson said.

Janice ran over to the Captain. "She's good."

Serenity stood up. "Carlson, can you get me reports from the rest of the ship?"

"They have tried to get to the engine room and the flight deck," Carlson replied. "It appears the fighting is growing sporadic."

"Captain, the Zercowans are arriving. They've stopped at their border," Zimmerman said; he was sitting at Willard's station.

"The ship has heavy damage in several areas. Those shuttles didn't stay lodged in our hull, so we are having trouble keeping containment. Large areas of the ship are cut off," Morgan said. "Structurally, we are fine, the ship is operable."

"The enemy ships are withdrawing," Zimmerman said.

"Disengage them, make for Zercowan Space," Serenity said. "Carlson?"

"Fighting has stopped."

"Look!" Janice pointed to the bodies of creatures. They seemed to melt away, like ice.

"Captain," Zimmerman said, distracting Serenity from the odd sight. "Marshall Korvikan."

"Put it on," Serenity waited. "We could have used your help, Marshall."

"I'm sorry, Captain. We can't engage anyone outside of our space. It's the law," Korvikan stated.

Serenity took a moment to keep her aggravation from showing. "Can you at least track the Phobos? We are in bad shape here."

"That I can do, Captain."

"Captain, they have fully withdrawn, we will be over the border soon," Zimmerman said.

Serenity surveyed her bridge. Willard was in tears, barely aware of her surroundings. Serenity couldn't imagine.

"Damn it, Carlson. Release the lock down and let the medical crew in."

Carlson nodded. "They are on the way up."

Chapter 17

Serenity stood on the flight deck. The craft they had brought in took up a lot of space on the deck. Crews were working all over it. But that wasn't why she was here.

A small Zercowan craft sat to the right. Security Forces crews were checking in the Marshall. She didn't want to have company on the ship in the condition it was in, but she also didn't want to travel five weeks back to Earth for repairs. So as aggravated as she was, she smiled.

The Marshall walked up, alone. The rest of his staff stayed at the shuttle. He handed them all small devices and gestured to his ear. Carlson put it on.

The Marshall said something to Carlson in his own language. Carlson nodded and said to the Captain. "They're translators."

Serenity put hers in her ear. "That's it?"

"Yes," Korvikan said. "There are a lot of dialects of our language, a device like this is necessary for our people to work together. The fact it figured out English so fast, well, that was a pleasant surprise."

"Well, that's something else," Serenity said. There was no delay or anything. Serenity would have sworn English came from Korvikan's mouth. Even if the Zercowans did receive English language files from the Phobos, Serenity was skeptical it would work so well. But now wasn't the time to challenge the Zercowans. She needed their help.

"Thank you for having me aboard."

"I only wish we were in better shape," Serenity said.

Korvikan looked to Carlson and Kanter. "Fellow Officers?"

"No, I'm sorry," Serenity said. "Earth Captains, among many others, are protected by a Protection Team. They are part of Security Forces, a separate branch."

They started walking. "Branches? Like a tree?"

Serenity let out a laugh. "I guess so. The Earth military is divided into four branches. On this ship you will see Navy and Security Forces. Navy handles space defense. Security Forces is the law enforcement of Earth."

"We only have one branch... or I guess it would be a trunk," Korvikan said. "Police is a different issue all together."

"I'll give you a tour of the ship if you'd like," Serenity said "Then we can head up to the bridge and start the docking process with your repair facility."

"A good idea."

* * *

Janice was bored with the Marshall and the Captain's discussion of all things Earth Navy. For one, most of it was common knowledge. Well, she supposed it wasn't for Korvikan. He seemed nice enough, and he had a good sense of humor.

Janice noticed a Navy crewman walking down the halls toward the Captain and the Marshall. His insignia showed he was an engineer, but he had a holstered L-pistol. He paid his respects as he walked past. Janice was still bothered. Engineers rarely carried weapons; of course the ship had recently had a hostile encounter. Kanter looked over her shoulder. The engineer was drawing the L-pistol.

"Gun!" Kanter yelled while tackling Korvikan.

A shot fired. Carlson drew his L-pistol and used his left hand to shove the Captain against the wall. He fired twice hitting the crewman both times in the chest. The third shot hit him in the head. The crewman collapsed to the ground.

Janice saw blood on the ground. *Shit!* She was too slow, the Marshall was hit. Then a stinging crept into her leg. She looked at it and saw a hole in her pants. She touched it and pulled her hand away. Red coated her palms.

"Janice, talk to me." Carlson wasn't facing her. He was checking for more threats.

"I'm hit in the leg. Looks like the Captain and the Marshall are fine."

Carlson radioed control. He kept watching the hall one way. Janice, still lying down, had her L-pistol pointed the other way. She felt a bit dizzy. The pool of blood around her was growing.

Serenity went over to her side. "You are losing too much blood, Janice."

"Where are the medics?" Korvikan asked.

Serenity tore off the leg of Janice's pants. She tied off a bandage as best she could. "They have to wait for it to be safe."

A voice came over the radio. "We're coming around the corner. Watch for friendly fire."

Janice saw two Security Forces officers come around the corner, weapons out. She lowered her weapon, unable to hold it up anymore.

The other officer checked the suspect, kicking away his weapon. "He's dead."

"Get those medics in here, and they better fucking run!" Carlson yelled at them. He holstered his weapon and came to Janice's side. "Hang in there."

The sides of her vision began to darken. She couldn't even feel her leg anymore. She felt disconnected from the rest of her body. "Carlson, I don't feel so good."

Carlson's mouth moved, but Janice didn't hear anything. The black overtook her eyes.

Chapter 18

Serenity watched Carlson sitting in sick bay. He hadn't moved. Was he like this when she had been here? Did he refuse to eat, like he was now? Had it been this hard on him?

"At least he talks," Doctor Farven said. "He wouldn't say a word for four days when you were here."

"She'll be fine?" Serenity asked.

"Remarkably, yes. She should pull through; thanks to that blood you donated. She may be weak for a while, but she should heal up fine," Farven said. "Our blood supplies are low. We were not prepared to take so many casualties so far from home."

"The ship is almost repaired. After that, we will have to start taking blood donations from the crew," Serenity said. "I'll reward them somehow."

Korvikan stepped into sickbay. He glanced around a moment, then found Serenity. He walked over to her. "Sorry to interrupt, Captain."

"It's fine."

"We're about done with repairs. I am going to be on my way soon."

Serenity took a breath. Two days with the Marshall around had been hard. All the extra security had been harder. The Marshall refused to be scared away by the attack. She had to admire his courage.

"I have to apologize again. I just don't understand it."

"Don't apologize to me. I take no offense," Korvikan said. He looked to Janice. "I won't be able to thank her I'm afraid."

Serenity looked at the Marshall. She saw genuine concern in his expressions. But she couldn't help but wonder how much was a show. The hidden information about these attackers and the odd ability of this translator to understand English so well, had her convinced there was a lot the Zercowans were not sharing. They were the closest they had to friends this far away so she chose her words carefully.

"Tell me. We are still cracking that Martian shuttle. Who attacked us?" Serenity said.

Korvikan shifted his stance. "Captain, I... I am not supposed to say."

"You realize this hidden information cost my crew dearly. We didn't know we had enemies out this far, other than one lone warship." Serenity gestured around the room. "See what silence among friends has caused."

"I can't." Korvikan walked to the bedside of Willard. "Ensign? Did I understand the rank correctly?"

"Yes, Sir."

"Not many survive the hit of one of those weapons. They are horrible devices. The pain alone kills most that the shot itself spares."

"It still hurts," Willard said quietly.

"Doctor. Do your people have prosthetic limbs?"

"They do, but they are nothing compared to the real thing. Not good enough for Ensign Willard to return to the bridge."

Korvikan returned his stare to Ensign Willard. "The bridge, what post?"

"Navigations and Comms," Willard replied.

"We have very good robotic limbs. I'll share it with you, Ensign. They are remarkable. You will forget it is fake. It will certainly get you back on the bridge where you belong." Korvikan turned to the Captain. "You're Captain needs you there."

"Well... Why..." Willard couldn't speak.

"You're welcome." Korvikan walked to the Captain. "I can't share everything, but I am doing my best to make this right. Please understand."

Serenity knew exactly what was going on. He had his orders about these translucent enemies. Serenity nodded. Not a nod of satisfaction, but of understanding.

"I'll tell you something: There is a lot you will discover in those computers about them." Korvikan turned to walk out. He stopped and turned back. "I would really hope you might allow your crew some time on our planet. This one is beautiful and they could use the break."

"Thank you," Serenity said. "For everything."

She watched the Marshall leave. She wasn't sure how much he was hiding and how much his government was hiding. But she had little choice but to accept whatever assistance they provided.

Serenity looked back over at Carlson. He hadn't moved in some time. His face buried in his hands, he just stared down at the floor. Serenity walked over, he barely glanced up at her.

"How you holding up, Mike?" She put her hand on his shoulder.

"I'm better now that the Doctor says she will be okay." Carlson stood and stretched. "I think I will stay with her until she wakes up."

"I understand. What do you think the motivation for attacking the Marshall would be?" *What is my problem? A chance to comfort and be with Mike, and I bring up business.* "I mean, if you're up to talking about it."

"I filed my reports, of course I didn't speculate." Carlson paused a moment. "Let me pose a question. How do you think the Admiral would have reacted had the Marshall died on your ship?"

"We'd be sent home, for sure. The delicate relationship we have with the Zercowans would be shattered," Serenity said.

"Someone doesn't want Earth getting involved with the Zercowans, or more importantly, someone doesn't want you near the Phobos." Carlson sat back down. "The million dollar question is, who?"

* * *

Serenity woke up to her desk buzzing. She didn't remember falling asleep. She was reviewing repair reports. She hit the button on her desk.

"Admiral for you."

"Okay," Serenity said.

"Please tell me you have good news," The Admiral said, almost before his picture was on screen.

"Engineers have determined the craft are used for mining some type of unknown mineral. The hull is very thick. It is exactly like the one that attacked us. The computer shows this mineral is likely what is in their weapons. It seems these aliens are called the Borvians. The Zercowans and the Borvians have been at war for some time. Perhaps as long as time itself."

The Admiral shook his head. "And they told us nothing of them. I understand their good nature, but we could have avoided needing their charity if they had just said something."

"Perhaps they would have mentioned it to the diplomat we lost on the Africa," Serenity said.

"Well, we do know that the Phobos was responsible for the attack on your ship."

"That is a fair assessment," Serenity said. "But it still doesn't prove if the Martians know what this ship is up to. I think we should go after the Phobos, now that we know where they are."

"Damn it, Serenity!" The Admiral slammed his fist down on the desk, tilting the camera sending his transmission slightly. "Do you know what kind of pressure I am under to prepare for a war? I have only five warships here now, only two are really combat ready. The Aircraft Carriers are still being staffed. I am trying to mobilize a fleet that has never had to fight. Now, my only warship Captain with combat experience is five weeks from Earth and wants to go deeper into space. Hostile Space at that."

Sure, now she was the experienced Captain. "We don't have all the facts, Admiral. We can't go to war on half the information."

"The Prime Minister decides that, not me."

"Admiral. We are already out here, what is a few more days?" Serenity asked.

"Fine. But you are on your own. I hope those Zercowans are as helpful as you seem to think they are."

Chapter 19

Carlson sat at the bar. It was empty. A lot of the crew took up Serenity's offer: Donate blood to sick bay and get shore leave on the Zercowan planet. Carlson donated blood, but he stayed on the ship.

Janice woke up and was progressing well with the Doctor. So he gave her some space and tried to resume his own life. Besides, Willard and Janice got to talking and there was little room for him in the conversation. That's how it often is with girl talk. So, he sat here with his face in a glass.

"You gonna just drink all night?"

Carlson spun around at the familiar voice. He jumped up and hugged Janice. "Holy shit you're walking again."

Janice took a seat next to Carlson, who then sat down. "You didn't go down to the surface?"

"Nah, maybe another time," Carlson said. "What am I gonna do, run around there alone?"

Janice gave him a smile. They sat there quiet for some time. Carlson saw a Navy guy looking over at Janice. He'd turn away every time Carlson saw him. "You know that guy?"

"Know him? No. We were in sickbay together for a while," Janice said. "Why?"

"He's been checking you out. He turns away whenever I catch him. You should go talk to him. He's not going to come over here."

Janice looked over at the guy again. "Nah, I'm not gonna leave you alone here."

"Me? I think I will be okay. Go." Janice didn't move. "Okay, I will then."

Carlson walked over to the guy.

The guy put his glass down and his hand up. "I'm not looking for trouble."

"Neither am I." Carlson shook his head. "My friend over there thinks you're good looking. Go talk to her."

"Friend?"

"Yes, now just go." Carlson sat down at another table.

The guy approached Janice at the bar and they started talking. The bartender came over and wiped down the table. "You're a fool, Mike."

"How's that?"

"You're going to let a girl like that get away. I've seen the way she stares at you."

"It's not like that. Janice and I are friends." Mike shrugged, "I got someone else that's on my mind."

"Since you've been comin' here you've let women slip away, one by one, always with this 'someone on my mind' crap." The bartender shook his head. "It's really none of my business."

"You're right. It's none of your business," Carlson said.

The bartender walked away. Carlson watched Janice and the guy laugh. They got up and walked out of the bar. Janice glanced back and gave Carlson a brief grin. He nodded ahead, letting her know he was fine and she should go.

The bartender walked back up and handed Carlson a drink. "This one is on the house. You need the counseling."

"You always pry and I always get a free drink," Carlson laughed.

He went back to reflecting in the pool of auburn liquid. There was a lot for him to think about. He heard the bar door open and turned to see. Serenity stood there looking around.

She was beautiful with the bright light from the halls illuminating her. Carlson saw her stop scanning the room when she found him. She walked over, her protection crew waited at the door. Carlson stood up.

"Captain, what a surprise."

Serenity gestured the nearest table. "Please, we're off duty, Mike."

"Is this a good idea?" Carlson had meant to say that to himself, but it came out. "I mean, with the Admiral already asking questions."

"I'd say we're friends, Mike. I can have a drink with a friend," Serenity said bluntly.

"Well, I am glad for the company." *Glad for your company.* "I just set Janice up with some guy and I was thinking I'd be sitting around alone."

"Well then it works out that I am here," Serenity said.

Had she come here looking for Carlson? "Listen, about that whole inquiry thing, I'm sorry I acted like I did."

"That was just the Admiral doing what he thought was right. It wasn't right for him to assume you'd be like Mathews just because he was your partner."

"You don't think I could ever do what he did, do you?"

"Of course not, Mike," Serenity hesitated.

Carlson knew why she hesitated. She didn't really know Mike couldn't be like that. She didn't really know Mike that well. He finished the drink in his hand and slouched back in his chair. The alcohol relaxed him a bit. "I bet you're thinking you can't really be sure about that."

"You'd be wrong," Serenity said with a very matter-of-fact tone. "Not even close."

"So, what are you thinking?"

"Have you ever wondered what an alternate reality for yourself might be? If just a few things were different," Serenity said.

"Not sure what you mean."

"Like, if I was not a Captain would it be so awkward that we are sitting here talking? Would we be able to talk freely?"

Awkward was the understatement of the century, he would love to be able to talk to her freely. By now Serenity had finished a drink and they both sat quietly as the bartender brought them another.

He thought about what Janice said to him. *It's only as hard as you make it.* They were five weeks from Earth, he couldn't be reassigned right away, except maybe to patrol. Was now really the time to confess... in a bar?

"You know, I still owe you two secrets," Carlson said.

"I suppose you do," Serenity said. "I hope they're good ones too."

Carlson took a huge gulp of his drink. He'd thought about how he'd say it many times. Something romantic. "I think you're cute."

Fuck. That was his opening line. The Captain just stared at him. Carlson closed his eyes. This was going to end badly. "I mean, you're funny, nice, compassionate, and one of the most attractive women I've met. I've felt this way for a long time, and I just never said anything."

"Mike, I..." Serenity stopped.

"I know, I know." Carlson shook his head. He'd messed this up bad. He said it to her in a bar; what was he thinking? Carlson rubbed his face.

"No, it's not that. Words have to be chosen carefully here," Serenity said.

This is where the reassignment would be brought up. Carlson's heart sank. First, she would let him down gently, then she would run out of the room and contact the Admiral at once.

"There was a reason I was so dodgy with the Admiral's questions. A reason even why I found you at the Falls. I..." Serenity paused again. Here it comes. "There are certain confessions we can't make right now. Not if we want to continue to be... friends."

There was just enough of a pause for Carlson to understand. She felt the same way, at least enough to want to get to know him better. Carlson nodded his head. "You're right... friends."

Serenity leaned in close to whisper. "I want to know you better, Mike. I really do. But you know what publicly dating you would mean."

Carlson just nodded.

"Mike, it's our secret. We'll hang out more, or something. But we just can't have a relationship. Or we don't see each other for a long time. Or maybe ever again."

She was right. Carlson knew she was. Or, she could be letting him down gently. Carlson wasn't sure which was happening right now. "I know. It's the reason I've never said anything."

Serenity's face lit up. "You're the only guy I have wanted to get to know better in many years. Please understand, I am only being this way because it has to be this way."

For some reason, Carlson didn't feel any better having told Serenity.

Chapter 20

Security Forces Captain Howard was acting in the Major's role until they filled the position, which could be some time away. The reports on the attempted murder of the Marshall were his first order of business.

Carlson had turned in his report the evening of the incident. There were some other investigations going on, and they finally turned up a lead on the suspect's friend. There was a knock on the door, and then a Navy crewman entered.

"Ah, Carey Barnes. Thanks for coming to see me so early."

"I'm going to just assume this is about my friend." Barnes had the tone of a snot-nosed kid.

"In fact, it is. We wonder why he might want to kill the Marshall of a Zercowan ship."

"I don't... Wait, I thought he shot a Security Forces officer." Barnes' posture shifted suddenly.

"He did. Did he say anything?"

"I already told the investigators, but no, he said very little to me. We were scheduled to play darts, he was late. A little while later we were being sheltered in place while Security Forces handled some situation. I later found out he had shot a Security Forces officer."

"What do you think of Security Forces killing your friend?"

"They may have been a little excessive. I mean, shooting him in the head is a bit much. That's just my thoughts though."

"By 'they' do you mean Security Forces or the Captain's protection detail?" Howard pressed a button on his desk. Two other officers came in.

Barnes looked back. "Wait, what is this about?"

"We found a note in your belongings that has a Security Forces Officer's name on it. Janice Kanter."

"Yeah, I met her in a bar last night. We were in sick bay together for a time." Barnes stopped.

"We found a list of instructions from your friend. They were telling you certain information you needed from a member of Protective Services on this ship." Howard pulled up a list on his tablet. "Command Codes, Captain's routines, hardest areas to protect the Captain. Any of these sound familiar, Barnes?"

"This is outrageous. I don't know what you are talking about." The two officers restrained Barnes, he didn't resist much. "He must have planned for something I didn't know about."

"When you came in for questioning, we left a torture kit out for you. Do you remember that? Well, it doesn't matter. It was tracked to your office. We recovered it at your gunnery station," Howard stated. "So, why?"

"I'm not talking."

"Fine." Howard couldn't help but grin. "You're under arrest for conspiracy to commit murder against an Earth ally, conspiracy to gather naval secrets, treason, attempted murder of a Security Forces officer, and theft of government property." Howard spoke to the officer, "Take him to the brig until I can draw up the Force papers. I have a spare kit we just found."

* * *

Janice was supposed to be happy today. She got the Medal of Valor today for her acts to protect the Marshall. Instead, she spent her time giving statements to investigators about her date last night.

Apparently a few dates and then torture were in the plans. She liked this guy too. He was nice, sweet, and didn't seem to care one bit that she was Security Forces. Apparently, he already knew that.

She thought about canceling with Mike. She really didn't want to hang out and celebrate this medal. She could always do it later. Mike would understand.

But, here she was about to walk in to the mess hall. She opened the door, and saw a large group of people. Great, Carlson had planned a party. She wished even more she had canceled. But, she put on a smile.

Carlson came rushing forward. She couldn't help but hug him. "I know I should have told you, but Janice, I wanted to have a little surprise get together for you. You don't get the Medal of Valor every day."

"I really wish you hadn't," Janice said.

"Don't let that punk ruin this." Carlson looked her in the eyes, "Janice, go have fun."

"Okay, Mike. Okay." Janice pushed him aside. She saw Ensign Willard. She looked nice dressed in her uniform. Her hand wasn't even noticeable, because it appeared real. It acted real. She didn't even have to learn how to use it. Janice decided she would start her round with Willard. A woman would understand man troubles far better.

* * *

Carlson found Janice sitting alone eating some cake. She had done well with the crowd, she deserved some time to herself. He walked over to her.

"Good cake?"

"As good as you can find on a Navy ship," Janice said. "I know I was kind of a bitch about the party, but thank you."

"You're entitled. I understand twisted love life problems all too well." Carlson sat down.

"He was so nice and charming too." Janice pushed the cake away. "I have not found a man to suit me yet. You know, I want more to life than just this job."

Carlson hadn't thought about it much, but all he had was this job. A life outside of work, or even outside of the ship, had never occurred to him. "I guess that is one advantage to working on Earth."

"I guess." Janice sat up and looked past Carlson.

Carlson turned around to see Serenity walking up to the table. The rest of the party was winding down. Most everyone had left or was leaving. Serenity gave Carlson a smile.

Carlson leaned in. "While you were out last night, I told the Captain about how I felt. In a sort of alcohol-induced way. I'll fill you in later, but she wants to be... *friends*. Understand?"

"Sort of, I guess," Janice said.

"Then we are on the same page." Carlson turned just in time to greet the Captain. "Captain."

"Please, none of that now. No formalities," Serenity said. "Can I join you?"

"Sure, Mike and I were just talking about—"

"About how good the cake was." Carlson held up Janice's plate.

Serenity laughed. "That I doubt."

"Well the cake was mentioned," Carlson laughed. He felt comfortable just sitting there with Janice and Christina. "Janice just wants to get me in trouble."

"I would never," Janice put on a fake show of shock.

That was all it took. The Captain chimed in with a quick shot and they began talking. Hours passed as they sat there talking about nothing in particular. For a moment, Carlson forgot they were on a Warship weeks from Earth and trying to prevent a war. There was no Phobos to chase, no lives being lost, and no one out to kill the Captain. There was just three friends sitting at a table, enjoying a few drinks, and telling a few bad jokes. It felt good.

Chapter 21

Korvikan had managed to get Serenity an audience with the Zercowan Derik, the leader of their people. Serenity thought she might talk to military leaders, or maybe a diplomat, but not the leader of the whole race. Her stomach twisted and turned with the thought of it as the shuttle approached the planet.

Carlson and Kanter protested her leaving the ship to go to the planet. Serenity could understand their concern, but how do you refuse the hospitality of a world leader? She even had to argue with them about bringing rifles. Ultimately it was their choice, and she was glad they finally conceded to her wishes.

It was a beautiful planet. The water ways were a light shade of violet. Even the greens and blues of the land looked almost painted on. Serenity thought it was much brighter than Earth.

The entry into the atmosphere was easy, and before long they were on approach to a large, jade-colored building. The Derik's palace. Serenity was mesmerized by the sight. She almost forgot why she was here.

She had to get help from the Derik. Earth wouldn't be sending any other ships to help her chase the Phobos. A ship that was likely mining weapons materials in, or very near to, Borvian space. Korvikan had told her this would be a nearly impossible task. The Zercowans were so imbedded in their defensive ways that asking for them to go on the offensive would be difficult.

Carlson was first to step off the shuttle. Serenity kept sneaking peeks out at the palace. It was a beautiful building, with massive archways and beautiful architectural details that flowed nicely with the landscape in the background.

Finally she took a step out. Korvikan was standing there to meet them. "Captain, I am glad to have you here."

They exchanged handshakes. Another man, in fancy dress, approached them slowly. Korvikan moved to the side, and bowed towards the man. "May I introduce Derik Platterik, the blessed leader of the Zercowans."

"It is truly a pleasure to meet you, Derik," Serenity bowed in the same manner as Korvikan.

"The honor is mine. Though I had expected my first meeting with humans to be with a diplomat."

"I hope we have not disappointed you." Serenity was using the regimented tone of formality.

"Not at all. I would rather meet you given the situation you want to discuss." The Derik gestured to his palace, "Let us go inside."

They walked in silence through the large passages, the ceiling was at least twenty-five-feet tall. Murals decorated it with images that appeared to be both religious and historical. The windows overlooked an ocean, Serenity could see the water hitting some rocks along the beach.

"I really must make some time to spend on one of your planets," Serenity said, still gazing out the windows.

"You didn't visit Darsin while you were there for repairs?" The Derik sounded disappointed.

"There were a lot of things for me to accomplish in a very short time."

"Make time for yourself, Captain," the Derik said. "It is the most important thing in life."

"Good advice." Serenity glanced at Carlson for a moment.

The Derik looked at him as well, "I am glad to see they are back to work. Korvikan and I are close. I owe a debt to Earth for training such a fine military."

"They do their jobs very well. Thank you."

Korvikan rushed ahead to a door and opened it. As Serenity walked in to the conference room, with equally tall walls, she realized there should have been some echoes. She heard none.

The room was filled with Zercowans, presumably advisors. The Derik waved his hand and they all left quickly. Korvikan stayed. Serenity thought about having Carlson and Kanter leave, but decided not to.

"Sit, please." The Derik waited for Serenity to sit before seating himself. "I am sorry we did not warn you of the Borvians or their hostility. My military advisors insisted it was not a good idea. Korvikan objected repeatedly, but I chose to follow the advice of my advisors. It is my own fault that you suffered so many losses."

"I appreciate that. But there was a lot more to that attack than missing information." Serenity paused, "It might be helpful to know why you have been at war for so long."

"Long is an understatement, Captain. No one alive remembers a time when we were not fighting. It has just been part of our lives," the Derik let out a sigh. "We are a race of science and discovery. We use our technology and science for the benefit of everyone. The Borvians are not so scientific, but they want to be able to discover weapons and other unethical uses for technology.

"During the bloodiest parts of the war, the Borvians claimed some of our space and planets. Since then, the attacks dwindled down to almost nothing. There was never a declared peace, it just seemed to happen.

"Then the Phobos came, and attacked our ship. They came offering friendship. The majority of the fleet that met them left. One ship remained to escort them to our nearest planet. The Phobos destroyed that ship. Since that time, the Borvians have resumed their aggressive behavior." The Derik paused, "I'd be interested to know your history with Mars."

"Centuries ago, Earth was divided into many countries and space exploration was limited." Serenity wished her history was better. "The Unifications war was fought for reasons I'm afraid I am not too sure of. The result was a united Earth government. After peace was cemented, space exploration became a priority. Over time, we developed the ability to make other planets livable. The infancy version was our own moon. Later, we were able to terraform Mars.

"Politics comes into play, but the Martian colonists wanted to be considered a Colony. They wanted limited independence. However, the Colonists had different ideas and beliefs than the Earth Government. I would guess that was why so many of them chose to go to Mars in the first place.

"Over time, they wanted their full independence. At first Earth refused, but the threat of war was a real possibility. At this point, peace was all we knew. The threat of a war, no matter how small it may have been, was not something we wanted. So Earth granted that independence.

"We've been at peace with the Martian government for as long as anyone remembers. Even my grandparents can't remember anything but Martian and Earth governments coexisting. My ship was attacked by what we can only assume are terrorists. The Phobos was nearby. It destroyed an Earth Warship. And the Martians won't tell us anything about the ship." Serenity took a drink from a glass nearby. "Now all records would point to finding the Phobos in Borvian space. We are about to start a war with Mars, and I get the feeling the Phobos is playing both sides."

"Getting deep into Borvian space will be hard. There are not many gaps in their patrols. And your one ship will not be much of a match for the Borvians. They are a race ready for war always," the Derik said. "Of course, we can help provide defense for your ship, in our space, while your fleet forms."

"There will be no fleet. The Navy cannot send any ships because they are preparing for the war. When there has been peace for so long, you don't keep a large military. So what ships we have are preparing to defend their home," Serenity said. "It was my hope that the Zercowans would be able to commit some ships to help a friend."

"I can't," the Derik said. "We have had a policy of defense only. It is the way of our people. I can't possibly send any ships into what will be seen as an offensive attack. This is why Korvikan was forced to stay on the border while you were being attacked."

"When we arrived, that seemed a very aggressive stance you took with us," Serenity stated. "Perhaps that same aggression should be shown to the Borvians."

"The aggression we showed you was in defense of our space and our ships." The Derik stated.

Serenity stopped to collect her thoughts. Challenging the Zercowan's customs would not get her what she wanted.

"I have to figure out what the Phobos is up to. I am hoping for your support in a crisis situation for our people. If Zercowans were about to fight each other, wouldn't you do whatever possible?"

"Of course, Captain."

"So will we, so will I." Serenity paused. "My ship will be going into Borvian space to find the Phobos. We have to find out what we can expect from that ship, the Martians, and these Borvians. It could prevent this war."

Serenity let the words sink in for a moment. Then she continued. "You know what will happen if I go alone. You know we will likely die trying. You expressed regret for not helping us earlier and for the losses we suffered from it. Yet, you are willing to repeat that mistake again? We say on Earth, the best defense is a good offense."

Korvikan leaned in and whispered in the Derik's ear. The Derik stood up. "Excuse me for a moment."

Korvikan and the Derik left the room. Serenity wondered if she had angered the Derik. But, she would have been even more foolish to just accept "No" as the answer. She stood up to stretch and walked over and refilled her glass.

A loud argument could be heard in the halls outside. Serenity couldn't make out words, but she could tell it was passionate. She returned to her seat.

The Derik walked back in; Korvikan followed. The Derik didn't sit. "All right Captain, I have a very angry Military advisor who sees no logic in helping you. However, Korvikan feels we can't afford not to help."

Serenity stood up, she planned to leave as soon as the decision was made. Either to show anger for a lack of help or to not allow the Derik time to reconsider.

"I will commit only two ships, to follow your orders. But, I insist that Korvikan serve on your ship. I have two ships at stake here and I will not lose them because you misunderstood something about the Borvians." The Derik gave her a stern look.

"It will have to do. I thank you for this. It won't be forgotten." Serenity bowed. "Thank you again."

Chapter 22

Carlson went into the Security Forces section of the ship. He walked over to the Major's office—well, now it was Captain Howard's office. That took some adjustment for him to realize the Major was dead. He knocked on the door.

"Corporal, come in please," Howard stood. "Sit down."

Howard walked over and closed the door to the office behind Carlson. He went over to his desk and sat on top of it. "Patrol picked up a guy today. They thought he was just another drunk, angry with the long shifts and the ship's losses. He was wielding a pipe and screaming about something."

"Okay." None of this really had anything to do with Carlson.

"When the team returned to patrol, they found an emergency weapons locker had been busted into. A few L-rifles and a few L-pistols were stolen.

"Wouldn't you know our drunk crewman was actually very sober. He originally said he was playing drunk to get the time off. Needless to say, Patrol didn't buy it."

"I'm sorry, Sir. But how does this involve me?" Carlson asked. He was tired and still had to work that night.

"Okay, well. When the interrogator came in, he spilled it. Apparently saying his orders were to cause a distraction because an undercover Security Forces officer was going to take some weapons. That they were handling a mission for Naval Command to remove the Captain from command. He claims the Captain is rogue." Howard picked up a coffee cup. "It sounds to me like a solid lead on why people keep going after the Captain."

"What does Investigations think?"

"What Investigations?" Howard laughed. "With the losses we have suffered from the attacks, I can't even keep minimum patrol levels. I dissolved the Investigations division to cover patrol. The only reason there is still a Protective Services division on this ship is because I can't touch it."

"So, you want me to look into this possible secret organization?" Carlson asked. "Not part of my duties, Sir."

"Then no one does, Corporal. I can't spare anyone to do it."

"Fine." Carlson wasn't about to sacrifice the safety of Serenity over a staff shortage. "I guess I will start with this suspect."

"He's dead. Choked himself to death." Howard slid his tablet over to Carlson. "All I got is his file with some known friends of his."

Carlson read the tablet. There had to be fifty names on the list. "I don't have time to go over all of this. It could take months to cross check all these names."

"Welcome to Investigations, Corporal."

* * *

Serenity had been sure to make an extra hour before bed each night to play a game of cards with Mike and Janice. She enjoyed the time with Mike most, though she found she enjoyed Janice's company as well. There was something friendlier about hanging out with them than a lunch with Zimmerman or Korvikan. She supposed it was what friendship was supposed to be.

She had been spending a lot of time with the Commander and the Marshall. She was learning a lot about Borvian customs, Borvian naval warfare, and the best tactics to use. It was fascinating and boring combined into one mess of a situation.

She expected to arrive at the Zercowan border where she would meet with the two of their ships that would form their small, likely ineffectual, fleet. She wasn't looking forward to these next few weeks sneaking around in hostile space hunting for the needle in a haystack.

She folded the hand. "I got nothing."

"Me, either." Janice tossed down the cards.

Carlson laughed. "We need to play for money."

Serenity was actually starting to think this may be the best way to date someone. Secretly hang out with them and claim they were friends. She had learned a lot about who Mike really was. His parents were both dead. He had one sister who rarely spoke to him since his parents' accident. He didn't watch many sports or TV. He seemed to make friends easier with women than men. She smirked at that.

"What's so funny?" Carlson asked.

"I was just thinking…" Serenity said.

"You've got to share now," Janice said.

"You ought to try having to be forced into accepting 'just friends.' It seems to be working for Mike and me," Serenity said. She noticed Carlson look down. "What?"

"I mean, we have learned so much about each other, but I..." Carlson met her stare. "I mean, it's good we're friends."

Serenity thought Carlson understood what she meant by "just friends" when they talked. She just couldn't say they were dating. But were they even really dating? They were never alone, there was no romance. They were just friends.

The whole thing was bullshit. It was the way things had to be for now. "We'll just have to see how this plays out."

Chapter 23

Janice didn't bother going to sleep. She knew they'd be meeting the Zercowan ships today and then it would be drills. That meant ready stations, which meant she was back to the bridge. So she tagged along with Carlson to meet with Willard.

Willard had been on Janice's mind recently anyway. They hadn't talked much since they shared sick bay together. She was nice, and Janice was feeling a bit like a third wheel with the Captain and Carlson's friendship, whatever that mess was. She figured Willard would be a good person to hang out with should they need their alone time.

When they walked into the mess hall Janice noticed Willard right away. She took the lead in front of Carlson and walked up to Willard. "Francesca, it's good to see you."

"Janice." Willard stood up to greet them. "I didn't expect you."

"Just tagging along." Janice sat down after Willard.

"Thank you for meeting with us, Ensign." Carlson took a seat. "Did you find anything unusual in the transmissions to the ship?"

"Not, much." Willard pulled out a tablet. "There is all the typical incoming mail and data transmissions. It would be impossible to know where to start there. The amount of data coming in on a daily basis is hard to narrow down."

"Anything audio?"

"Well, I checked all the voice transmissions coming and going. If it was coming from Earth, or outside the ship, then that narrows things down a lot. But, it will take some time for me to break down the signal to see if anything was piggy backed in. Again, without knowing where to start it could be a long time." Willard read her tablet. "There isn't anything sticking out."

"I know you have other priorities, but if I give you a list of names, would that help?"

"It can't hurt," Willard said.

* * *

Willard was the last of the crew to come on to the bridge. Serenity checked her watch, she wasn't late. Serenity watched her take her station. The ability of that hand was amazing.

Korvikan took his seat in the Lieutenant Commander chair. Serenity sat. "Slow us down, Ensign."

"Yes, Captain."

Serenity turned to Korvikan. "We don't have time for the drills. The Prime Minister will address the Earth Council tomorrow. I need something soon." Serenity saw no ships on the radar. "Where are they?"

"I don't know."

"Captain, we are getting transmissions on Zercowan frequencies, they aren't coming in translated," Willard said.

A message played over the speakers. Korvikan looked at the Captain. "It's a distress call, a few minutes from here."

"Set the course, Battle Stations." Serenity took a breath. "As soon as we arrive, engage the enemy."

"Captain," Zimmerman leaned in, "we're required to transmit a warning first."

"We need to make an impression," Serenity said. "You can report it if you wish."

"No, Ma'am."

"Captain, we're arriving now," Willard said. "Six Borvian ships and two Zercowan ships. Now, five Borvian ships."

"Captain, those are normally patrol ships for the inside of Borvian space. I can't remember a time I've seen them outside it." Korvikan paused. "They shouldn't be much of a match for us."

The ship rattled once, and then another volley of cannon fire could be heard.

"Minor damages on that hit," Morgan said. "I have one small breach contained."

"The Borvians have lost two more ships." Willard paused. "They are hailing us."

"Earth vessel, this not concern planet Earth. Stand down, act of war if continued."

"Their translators are not as good, Captain."

"You are attacking an Earth ally. Surrender your vessels and prepare to be boarded." Serenity signaled to end the transmission. "Have a boarding team ready. If, by chance, they surrender I want to take their ship. There will be valuable information on it."

"Captain, they have one ship left. It's in bad shape," Sanchez said.

"They are transmitting," Willard said.

"Earth vessel, we stop fight. We will follow instructions. You board."

"Cease fire, Sanchez." Serenity paused. "Send the boarding instructions."

"Captain, the boarding shuttles are delayed. Alpha group had a malfunction. Charlie Group is scrambling now."

"Fine, make the Zercowans aware of our boarding operation." Serenity leaned into the Marshall. "What is the typical reaction from the Borvians when boarded?"

"They have always complied. They rarely are taken alive, they tend to transcend themselves. Essentially, it is suicide. Their bodies decompose quickly, or dissolve."

"The shuttles are away, Captain," Sanchez said.

"Captain! They've discharged some kind of projectile," Willard said.

The ship rattled for several moments. "Status?"

"The shuttles, they're gone. The fighters are gone too," Willard's voice shook. "No debris..."

"Destroy that ship." Serenity slammed a fist on her chair.

"I've never seen that weapon before," Korvikan said.

"How many people were on those shuttles?" Serenity said to Captain Howard. She already had an idea.

"Forty-five," Howard said.

"We don't have the numbers for this." Serenity knew it. This had to be a tactic to delay them. She wouldn't let them win. They were slowly chipping away at her numbers, while they easily could sacrifice three ships. "Let's get underway for the first waypoint."

She could feel anger swelling up inside her. It was all she could feel right now. More of her crew dead and it couldn't seem to be stopped. Not only were human lives being lost, but her mission was being endangered. If any more crew died, the ship would be in no position to take on the Phobos. It was a jaded way of looking at it, but it was the facts of war. She needed to calm down. She went straight to her office.

* * *

Carlson followed Serenity. It was clear she had been upset by the shuttles being destroyed. Carlson closed the door. Janice looked at him, she saw it too.

Serenity took a paperweight off the desk and threw it across her office. It smashed into the wall. "We'd be lucky to stop a damned ant trail in the God damned mess hall without someone dying!" She hit her desk.

Carlson thought about keeping his mouth shut, but felt like he needed to try to comfort her. "You're taking this too hard. It's not your fault. Not even the Marshall knew about that weapon."

"Oh, come on." Serenity never even looked at him. "What the fuck do you know about running a starship? You're a bodyguard."

Carlson took a breath to hold his temper. "Yes, Ma'am."

Carlson didn't like this at all. He could feel a rush of emotions coming up. He did his best to hold it in.

Janice marched over to the Captain. She took her by the arm and turned Serenity to face her. "Who the hell do you think you are?"

"You're out of line," Serenity stated.

"Am I?" Janice paused. "I can turn this fit of rage into an incompetence of command. Carlson may try to save your ass, but I won't. In the end nothing may happen, but I can make your life hell until the Doctor evaluates you. I won't hesitate to draft the forms.

"The lives we've lost are nothing compared to what we might lose in a false war. This crew sacrifices itself for you. They trust you and they'll do almost anything just because you said so. So grow up and act like the leader you have to be."

Serenity walked over to her desk. Her voice was calm now. "Don't talk to me like that again."

Carlson just took the scene in. He said nothing, didn't even move. Their relief crew came in. Carlson just walked out.

* * *

Serenity sat at her desk. Still taking in the words Janice had told her. She was the leader of these people, they did count on her. She watched Carlson walk out.

Oh God, Carlson. Serenity had done that to Carlson. The protection crew handed her the paperweight she'd thrown. A large painted rock with a laser inscription: "Thanks for visiting Niagara Falls".

* * *

Janice chased Carlson. "For God's sake Mike, slow down."

Mike spun around and faced her. For a second, Janice was scared. "I'm putting in for a transfer to patrol."

"You don't mean that, Mike."

"The fuck I don't." Mike's voice was softer now. He turned and started walking. "She doesn't need me, or want me, so I'm done."

"Mike, she is just mad." Janice walked after him. "She has been under so much stress for the last two months. She has done well to contain it."

"Son-of-a-bitch," Carlson said. "All those times I have saved her life."

"Mike, if you transfer out, she could die." Janice stopped him and waited for him to make eye contact. "There is a group on this ship trying to kill her. Can you really walk away from her now?"

Janice watched Carlson's eyes. Finally, he hung his head. "I'm just hurt. I'll get over it."

Chapter 24

They had taken a roundabout trip to the Borvian border. They didn't want to come in from the most obvious approach. They had spent a lot of time going over battle plans and tactics, and all the "what ifs" you could imagine. But, that wasn't what had Serenity up early. It was the man sitting outside her bedroom door.

There was no more point in denying it any longer. She was only doing it in hopes she wouldn't slip up and let it show. She loved Mike. The time they had spent together, she really knew him and she loved him. There was little she could do about it.

She could resign her command. The Admiral would love that and she would be able to have Carlson. She wasn't ready to be out of command. But this outburst had made her realize she could drive Carlson away. Sure, she can apologize for her anger, but how long would Mike wait for her?

She got out of bed and went outside the bedroom door. "Janice, can I have a minute with Mike?"

"Of course," Janice walked out of the room.

Carlson stood up. "Yes, Ma'am."

He has to be formal now? "Mike, I just wanted to tell you sorry for the rage I showed. This has been a really stressful time and I've been trying way too hard to hold it in." Serenity tried to look into Mike's eyes, but he just stared straight ahead. "Damn it, Mike. You are not just some bodyguard to me. I owe my life to you many times over. But—well, it's more than that..." *Here goes nothing.* "Mike, I love you."

Serenity finally got Mike to make eye contact with her. He just stared at her for a moment. "Christina, I... well. I love you too. I just didn't expect that."

"Mike, I just had to deny it. I didn't want anyone else to see it. But, I can't keep doing this charade with you. You had to know."

Carlson stared at her, and then pulled her in for a hug. Serenity felt comfortable there, her head rested on his chest. She didn't want to move, but she forced herself to pull back.

She looked up at him for a moment. Mike kissed her. She melted in his arms. She forgot where she was for a moment. She hadn't felt so at peace in a long time. Then it was over.

"Mike..." He smiled at her. Serenity smiled back. "I'll resign my command when we get back to Earth. Until then—"

"Wait, no." Carlson pulled away. "You can't do that. There is a good chance there will be war when we get home. The Earth needs you. We can keep this under wraps."

"Mike, you deserve more than that."

"You deserve this ship. And right now, this ship needs you. There will be a time and a place for us to go public. But, right now isn't it." Carlson paused. "There is something going on bigger than us. We love each other, we know it now. No one else needs to."

There was a knock at the door. Carlson shifted back to his post by the door. Serenity rushed away toward the couch. Janice peaked in. "Day shift is here."

* * *

Serenity sat on the bridge, a little more optimistic about their mission. Things just didn't seem all doom and gloom. They were arriving at the Borvian border now.

As soon as the ship stopped, she saw the radar screen filled with contacts. "How many?"

"There are twenty-five, all with weapons ready." Willard hit a few buttons. "The Phobos is on long range radar."

Serenity didn't feel so optimistic anymore. "Battle Stations."

Twenty-five Borvian vessels, of all different sizes and shapes, were sitting there waiting for the Australia to arrive. The countless meters of Borvian border and they knew she was coming here. She turned to Korvikan.

"I don't know, Captain. That's not a patrol fleet, that's for sure." Korvikan shrugged his shoulders. "Either we are really unlucky, or they knew we were coming."

"They knew we were coming. The question is, how?" Serenity said. "Willard, hold here. I don't want to drift into their space."

"Try hailing the Phobos," Zimmerman said. Serenity gave him a puzzled look. "What? Stranger things have happened."

"Okay, try it," Serenity said.

They didn't have any battle plan for this. If they couldn't somehow open up dialogue with this fleet, then they would have no choice but to retreat.

"A Borvian Vessel is responding."

"Earth vessel, you are forbidden from entering our space."

"This is Captain Serenity of the Australia. We're here to speak with the Phobos. We have no issues with you or your people."

No response. Just silence. Did they not understand her? Finally the speakers cracked with a reply. "The Phobos does not agree. Leave this area at once. Do not enter our space."

Willard ended the transmission.

"I'm open for suggestions…" Serenity surveyed her bridge staff.

"We won't be any match for them. We'll be destroyed in minutes," Korvikan said. "Fighting can't be an option here."

"I am not ready to throw away all these weeks of planning," Serenity paused. "Anything?"

"Even if we flank the Phobos, the fleet will tear us to shreds before we can do much damage to her. Let alone have a talk with their Captain," Zimmerman said. "We need to withdraw and regroup."

Serenity didn't want to admit they were right. If this failed, she knew what the next step would be. The Admiral was sure to send them home. This was her last chance at the Phobos. Her last chance to prevent a war. She just couldn't give the order to attack.

"Turn us around, Ensign. Set a course for the nearest Zercowan planet."

Chapter 25

"**It's time** to come home, Captain," the Admiral said. "I can't justify it any longer. Your crew levels are low, your supplies are low, and your hopes of getting anywhere are lower."

"I understand, Sir. But I just—"

"Serenity, I understand you want to succeed. But the mission had a low success rate from the beginning. Come home."

"But, Sir."

"No more. Christina, you've proven me wrong on many things. You've proven your worth." The Admiral paused. "You're a damned hero here."

"I sure don't feel like a hero."

"The good ones never do." The Admiral shook his head. "Head back for Earth. We'll see you in five weeks."

* * *

"I can't give you much on these transmissions. But they are definitely coinciding with the attacks on the Captain," Willard said. "The messages are being piggybacked through Naval Command messages. They are usually recordings. So it really could be anyone between here and Earth doing it."

"What about that list? Did anything come up with those names?" Carlson swiped through the screens of information Willard had sent to his tablet.

"Forty-three names on that list live in the area of the transmission relay services," Willard said. "That's about all I can get. It could take years to unscramble this piggyback without original files to compare to."

"Janice, start looking at those names. See if something coincides with the times of these transmissions." Carlson sighed, "Anything else?"

"I notice that every one of these transmissions has this image in the cache. Probably a privacy image." Willard turned her tablet to show Carlson.

A man in a suit and bowler hat with an apple over his face. Carlson recognized the image; it was very old artwork. Not much help to him. "Janice, see if any of those suspects like apples."

The three of them laughed.

Willard stood up. "I better go."

"Well, thanks for everything, Ensign," Carlson said.

"Still on for movie night tonight?" Janice asked.

"Yeah, I'll see you then."

Carlson watched Willard walk out of Janice's quarters. "I didn't know you and Ensign Willard hung out."

"Francesca is her name, Mike. As shocking as it is, I do have friends besides you."

"It is a surprise." Carlson pushed her shoulder.

"Will you shut up and check this out?" Janice turned her tablet to him. "This woman, a Junior Lieutenant Sarah Hunter, has been off-duty most times these transmissions come in. And on the last one, she was written up for leaving her post without authorization."

"Is she off now?" Carlson asked.

"Yes." Janice checked her tablet again. "Should we get a BET team in place?"

"Yeah, that would be best."

* * *

The Boarding and Entry Team was stacked up outside the door. Carlson and Janice waited to the rear. It wasn't their job to make entry. These guys were trained for it.

The Imager had confirmed four people were inside these quarters. Of course, once the door kicked in, they could go anywhere.

BET had rifles ready and kicked in the door. An instant later the sound of a stun grenade went off. The team flooded the room quickly. They were yelling orders.

Carlson was the last one in, his L-pistol drawn. One person went for an L-pistol on the table. A member of the team had their rifle in his face. "Don't even think about it."

Carlson knew from the Imager that someone would be in the bedroom. He went straight to that door. Janice followed him. He looked at the three suspects in the main room. None of them were Hunter.

"Security Forces! Come out with your hands in view," Janice called in.

Hunter was in there, she likely had a weapon or two. She definitely had the advantage. "Sarah, I know you're in there. There is no way out. You need to come out with your hands in view."

"Fuck you, grey shirt."

"Well, at least she is talking." Janice shrugged her shoulders.

"Sarah, there are two ways this can end. You can either come out on your own, or we are going to have to come in and get you."

"Come in, I dare you."

"She is on the back wall." A team member with the Imager said. "She is by the bed, with two items in her hand, probably L-rifles."

Carlson knew those quarters. The bed would block her lower view of the door. "Keep talking to her, Janice."

"Sarah, come on out while this is still something we can work out."

Carlson lay flat on his belly and began to crawl his way into the bedroom. The bed would hopefully block enough of the view that he could slip in without Hunter seeing.

"If you wind up killing one of us in all this you won't stand a chance. Right now we are talking about some small weapons charges," Janice said.

"Don't feed me some bullshit," Sarah said.

Mike got to the back wall. He could tell by the way Hunter's legs were positioned, she was facing the door, on her knees. She was probably leaning on the bed with the two rifles.

Carlson popped up and pointed his L-pistol at the side of her head. "Drop those weapons!"

As soon as Hunter let go of them, Carlson pulled them away from her. Janice rushed in, and restrained her. Carlson stood up. Hunter looked at the P.S. pin on Carlson's shirt.

"Protective Services, huh? Took you long enough to figure it out."

* * *

Carlson sat in an interview room. This room was for interviewing those that were not suspects. The door opened.

"Lieutenant Morgan, come in. I won't keep you long."

"I heard one of my Juniors was picked up."

"Yeah, what can you say about her?"

"Missing a lot of time since we got out here. I thought maybe it was being away from Earth. I didn't officially document anything until recently." Morgan pulled out a note pad. "But I wrote it down in case it became an issue."

Carlson read it over. At first glance the times seemed close. "Can I hold on to this?"

Morgan nodded. Carlson handed it to Janice. Janice thumbed through it. "Thanks, Lieutenant. You can go."

"She's the one." Carlson said when Morgan left. "Someone has been piping information to her."

"Yeah, but who? All the messages were wiped clean. Can't find one copy of anything." Janice tossed down the notepad. "It's a weak case at best. She isn't talking, either."

"What about the other three?"

"Two of them were new to this. They thought she was Security Forces. I guess she told them she was working undercover and that there was evidence the Captain needed to be stopped. They'll testify against her, but that's not gonna be enough to stick much on her, other than weapons charges and some impersonation charges."

"The third guy?"

"He's her boyfriend. He won't talk much, either," Janice said.

"Let's see if he will talk to us." Carlson stood up. "Come on."

They walked over to the brig. They found him sitting in his cell. Carlson waited for the cell door to open. "Glen Young?"

"Yeah, so?" He appeared no older than twenty and had every bit as much attitude.

"I told you he wasn't going to say nothing. You wanted to give him a second chance," Janice said. Carlson was pleased she knew exactly how he wanted to play this.

"I'd hoped you might want a chance to make this right." Carlson got down on one knee next to Young. "You see, Sarah is in there right now pinning this on you. Claims you just used her quarters. She is in tears in there saying you promised she wouldn't get caught."

"You're lying." Young didn't sound so sure.

"You don't get it. We got you on treason. You're getting the needle, man. As soon as we get home, you can stand in line with the others and get your medicine." Janice turned to Carlson. "Can we just go?"

"Leave him alone for a minute. This is a lot to take in. First, you have BET break in and haul everyone off. Then, to find out the woman you love is so easily using you to get away with murder."

"I don't believe you." Young rested his head in his hands.

"I know it's a lot to take in, but once I leave, the interrogators are gonna go with what she said. She's willing to talk, you weren't." Carlson paused. "Listen, I know she gave you the promise of love forever, and she probably told you that you both needed to keep quiet. But she is counting on the fact that you won't talk. It was part of her plan."

"I can't..." Young said.

"Come on, Corporal. Let's go." Janice walked away.

Carlson shook his head. He stood up and turned to walk away.

"WAIT!" Young shouted. "Sarah was getting these messages. I really didn't want to be a part of it. But, man she is a wild one in bed. I just couldn't help it. Then, I fell in love. Or maybe it was just lust. I'm not sure. Anyway, she'd get these messages from someone. Then she'd wipe them clean."

"So who sent them?" Carlson said.

"I don't know. There was just this stupid picture of a man with an apple head." Young took a breath. "I saved them."

"You said she wiped them clean," Carlson moved closer to him. "If you are messing with us to buy time, you won't find it works in your favor."

"No, she does wipe them. But, I guess part of me knew she might sell me out. She played them, we'd fuck, I'd copy them while she cleaned up. Some insurance in case she did this to me." Young slumped into the cot. "They are in a wall panel in my quarters. It's the panel with her initials scraped into the bottom right corner."

"You did the right thing, Young." Carlson walked out. The cell door closed behind him.

* * *

"Sarah said nothing. They are still trying, but she is quiet as can be. There hasn't been one approved force technique to make her talk." Janice lounged back in the chair.

Two patrol officers came in. One tossed a brown envelope on the table. "Right there where you told us."

Carlson opened it up. Tablet chips were inside. He pulled one out and plugged it in. A date and time came up. "This is just before the attack on the Marshall."

The image came up. That man in the suit with the apple over his face. What was the name of that painting anyway? Well, it didn't really matter.

"Sarah, I have another assignment." The voice was disguised too. I guess they shouldn't be so lucky. "I need to find a way to get the Australia home. We don't need to be out playing with these Zercowans. They are not beneficial to us..."

Carlson stopped it. "Well, this isn't going to lead us to the kingpin, that's for sure."

"Well, maybe not right away," Janice said. "Let's see if Willard knows how to unscramble this. At least, get a voice."

"That could take weeks." Carlson tossed the chip back in the bag envelope.

"We got weeks before we even get home," Janice said. "For now, we need to watch all of these. There may be a slip up somewhere."

Chapter 26

They were halfway home now. There was no convincing them they could turn back now. Serenity had hoped something would change and she could be sent back to prevent this from getting ugly.

Apparently, some cooler heads had prevailed and the Earth Government had stalled on declaring war. The Council wanted more evidence, and all the evidence was on the Australia. They had the prisoners, the Africa's computer box, and their own computer records.

Serenity already knew there was nothing to refute that the Phobos was a Martian ship. It was certainly a depressing trip home. She knew what was waiting for her. A reinforced crew and a presence on the border.

Both sides had been rattling the saber. Martian ships would cross into Earth Space, and claim they had a navigational error. Or Earth Ships would perform practice maneuvers right on the border. It was a game of cat and mouse and they were playing with people's lives. The real question was: Who's the mouse?

It was nice to get back to her quarters at a reasonable hour. She knew Carlson and Janice would be in soon. Then it would be a few more rounds of poker and a kiss from Carlson.

That was the extent of her relationship with him right now. It was enough, for now. She hoped to be able to come clean soon. Maybe now that she was a hero, Naval Command would be a bit more understanding. Maybe all Carlson had to do was move to ship patrol.

Serenity didn't like the idea of that. Carlson may have rounded up the traitors on her ship, but Mathews was still out there. She told Carlson that

Mathews had to be the man behind that apple. But Carlson wouldn't entertain any speculation at this point. He'd just say "Ensign Willard is working on it."

* * *

Janice watched as Willard took off her uniform shirt. The tight undershirt clung to every curve of her body. Willard's breasts were smaller than hers, but her stomach was just as flat. Willard was a bit thinner and less muscular than Janice. Her proportions were correct.

She was checking out Willard's body. She wasn't just admiring the beauty of another woman, she was ogling. Willard looked over at her. Janice decided turning away would make it more obvious.

Willard blushed. "What?"

"I was just thinking—I don't see you at the gym, but you stay so thin," Janice said. "I'm jealous."

"I go to the gym." Willard sat down. "I mean, two weeks before my mandatory PT testing. But I go."

Janice laughed. She admired Willard. Her blue eyes sparkled just a bit. She let out a nervous laugh.

"You don't talk too much about dating. You have a boyfriend back home?" Janice said. "You can't be having the same bad luck as me."

"I don't date men. At least not since college." Willard paused a moment. "It was a big issue for my family."

"Really? There are some places still that backward?" Janice paused. "Sorry, no offense."

Willard laughed. "The world may accept a person's right to love and marry who they want, but not all faiths do. My parents are very Catholic. It's one of the few churches left not to budge on the issue."

Was that why Janice was checking out Willard? Did she somehow know that Willard was attracted to her? "So it wasn't something you always knew?"

"No, I think I knew from the beginning. But it's not exactly something I think about. I suppose I could fall in love with a man, it just hasn't happened. I really don't know." Willard paused. "Really, I think it is just people's need to classify everyone that has led to labels. I'll love whoever I love."

Janice thought that over for a moment. She and Janice were friends. That was that. "So, there is just enough time for a movie before I have to be at work."

* * *

Carlson dealt the cards to Janice and Christina. "It sure is taking a while to get those transmissions unscrambled."

"It's a lot like taking apart a strand of yarn. Only once you get all those little strings apart. You then have to cut them all up and piece them back together in the right order," Serenity said. "If she gets even one of those done by the time we get home, I'll be impressed."

"It bothers me to know someone is still out there doing this," Carlson said. "Why would someone want to harm you?"

"I've been asking myself that since Mathews." Serenity turned to Janice. "You're awfully quiet."

"I've just been thinking about Willard." Janice tossed her cards on the table. "Did you know her whole family disowned her?"

"She always has been the quietest one on the bridge. I assumed it was because of her low rank," Serenity said. "I'm glad she found a friend in you, Janice."

"She's a good person. The only reason I don't invite her for our game is because, well, you know."

"Yeah, it's probably best," Carlson said. "But, she seems nice enough."

"No, we can't go sharing this with too many people," Serenity said. "Sooner or later it will leak out. Just the three of us need to know."

Chapter 27

Willard sat alone in her quarters. She really wanted to show the Captain she was good at her job. She had been spending all her off hours trying to crack this voice disguise. It had to be the best work she had seen.

There were only about three more days until they would return home. She had to get it done by then. Janice was depending on her for this. She finally had a friend on this ship and she wasn't about to make her mad.

Friendship hadn't been easy for Willard. She was generally a shy person, which is why it amused her that she ran the Communications for an Earth Warship. If Janice hadn't reached out to her at sickbay, Willard would have never said a thing.

She stopped and studied her left hand. She wiggled the fingers. She touched it. This was the most remarkable thing she had seen. There was no way for even herself to tell it was fake.

Then, suddenly, she saw it. The right sequence for the voice—it was right there. She frantically moved it around. She got several sentences, but that was it.

She played them. She scrambled for her transmitter. "Janice, you have to get here now!"

"I just went to bed, Francesca."

She played the sentences again.

"Is that from those chips?"

"Yes."

* * *

Willard, Carlson, and Janice had crowded around Serenity. They loaded the chip into the conference table. The apple faced man came on screen. Serenity knew they had big news, but this just looked and sounded the same. "The voice is still disguised."

"It's coming up."

The voice changed. Serenity nearly fell out of her chair. She couldn't believe she was hearing McCorvick's voice. "That can't be."

"It's him. I compared it with his actual transmissions," Willard said.

"I haven't told the General yet. I thought you'd want to know first," Carlson said.

"The Admiral has been trying to kill me." Serenity couldn't believe the words as they came from her mouth. She could feel herself struggle for a breath. "Why?"

"That, we don't know," Janice said.

"What happens next?" Serenity looked up, the image made her queasy. "Take it off the screen."

"He'll be arrested, I'm sure," Carlson said.

"Call the General," Serenity said. "If I go to max speed we can arrive at Earth by late tomorrow."

* * *

Admiral McCorvick sat at his desk. The Australia had just arrived home. He was working out personnel transfers to get her fully staffed. War was not far off. That had not been what he had hoped for.

There was a knock at his door. Then General Valentine came in. He did not want to listen to the General today; there were too many other things to deal with. "General, I trust you know I am busy."

"I am sure. But we took in a number of prisoners from the Australia today. I thought I'd see what you thought about that sudden level of violence on that ship."

"You could have messaged me that."

"I was in the area." Valentine sat in the chair in front of the Admiral's desk.

"What is it you need, General?" The Admiral knew there was about to be some request for a favor.

"I'm just hoping for some information." The General fished out a card from his pocket and began twirling it around in his hand. He gestured to a painting on the wall. "What are your thoughts on these attempts on the Captain's life?"

The Admiral was nervous now. That was a little too direct for his liking.

He reached for his desk drawer, but how would he explain a dead General in his office? "I'm concerned there must be a traitorous group on that ship. Perhaps a bit too strung out from the sudden thrust into combat missions."

"Hmm, I thought you might." Valentine sat up.

"I might what?"

The doors opened and four Security Forces officers came in. General Valentine stood.

"Lie to me, Admiral. You looked me in the face and told me wonderful lies. And you were so good at it. I'd have never known."

The officers pulled McCorvick from his chair. He didn't fight. There was no point. As they restrained him, Valentine read from the card he held. "You are hereby in the custody of Earth's Security Forces. You will be required to make a statement, but may wait for lockup to do so. If you refuse to answer any questions, court-approved force will be used to get accurate answers. This is considered your one and only warning before questioning."

"What is this all about, General?" Admiral McCorvick saw Captain Serenity walk in. Corporal Carlson and Officer Kanter were behind her. Why hadn't he managed to get them reassigned?

"I had to see it for myself," Serenity said. "I couldn't believe it. I just wanted a command, that was all. You would really kill me for being defiant of your attempts to remove me?"

"Damn you, Serenity!" McCorvick refused to give the overdramatic confession. "I'm not the only one you have to worry about, Captain. You've angered the wrong group of people."

"Admiral, you are charged with treason, murder, attempted murder, murder for hire..." The Admiral tuned out the list of charges. They'd have him put to death by the day after tomorrow.

* * *

It didn't matter how short a day in court was, Carlson didn't like it. He wasn't going to attend. He didn't have to. The evidence he had was written in his reports, that was all the judge needed. But he had to go. To make sure the Admiral was properly sentenced for his crimes. He'd already seen one person escape their rightful punishment.

The judge listed off the charges, as numerous as they were. Finally, when he finished, he said, "What is your plea?"

"Not guilty."

"I've read the prosecution's case. You and your lawyers have responded. I've seen evidence in the form of tapes recorded in your voice and sent to Sarah Hunter, a prisoner who was executed yesterday on a guilty verdict of treason. I've heard from the technicians who evaluated those recordings as one hundred percent authentic. Technicians found the privacy software you had on your computer, along with this "Son of Man" picture set as the privacy screen.

"Your statement still provides no real explanation for any of this. Let alone explain why you would be driven to kill such a heroic Captain. I just can't find any reason to acquit you. Therefore, it is my ruling that you are guilty of all charges. Since treason carries the death penalty, you are sentenced to die immediately."

The judge hit the gavel.

Carlson followed them as they put the Admiral in the execution room. The Admiral was put in a chair and strapped in. A button was pressed and the needle came out of the chair sticking the Admiral in the back. He didn't even move, until he stopped breathing. Then he slowly slumped down. The doctor took his pulse and a stretcher was brought in.

Carlson turned and walked away. He'd seen enough. When he got in the halls, General Valentine chased after him and Janice. Carlson shook the General's hand.

"Damn good work on this one, Mike. You too, Janice." The General shook her hand next. "Who knows how long it would've been to unearth this. The Prime Minister is raving about this. You've done well. I owe you a big favor on this one."

"Someday, I may need a favor from the General," Carlson smiled. "Just don't retire until I've used it."

Chapter 28

Serenity didn't like the looks of her new crew roster. The shuttles were unloading, but she didn't have time to get down there. Most of them were either fresh out of basic training, or fresh off a desk. She didn't like such an influx of inexperience.

She had orders to attend to, if the new Admiral ever contacted her. She didn't know who was replacing McCorvick but she felt bad for him. He would have a heck of a mess to clean up, that was for sure.

McCorvick was a topic she tried not to give much thought, but it was a lot like a gnat in the room. You tried to ignore that buzzing, but you always wound up trying to swat at it. And that was what she kept doing. Swatting at the thought of the man that had been giving her orders was also trying to kill her. She wondered how many orders she blindly followed that ultimately put her in the situation of being attacked.

She wasn't going to be so blind in following orders anymore. She would just have to do what she knew was right. She needed to trust her gut.

Her desk transmitter buzzed. "Yes?"

"I have Admiral Kelly on the line for you, Ma'am."

Kelly? Could it really be that Tracy was promoted to Admiral of the Navy? Must be someone else. Serenity didn't even know Tracy made Vice Admiral. "Put it through."

And there—on the screen—was her friend. Tracy Kelly was sitting in what used to be McCorvick's office. "Christina, how are you? It's been ages since we've talked."

"It has. I didn't even know you were in line for the top seat," Serenity said. "Congratulations."

"I wasn't. It's a political and public relations promotion. I know it. I just made Admiral, for crying out loud." Tracy shook her head. "McCorvick shattered the trust of a lot of people, including the public. Well, I've been the face of the Navy for so long. Naval Command feels that if they promote me they can regain some trust with the people, and maybe a few politicians too.

"Of course they haven't said that, but you don't promote this high without knowing the game. Once the Navy is done with me, I'll be pressured out. I'd love to be sitting back in your shoes. You did the right thing standing your ground."

Would they really use Tracy as a pawn? Serenity knew they likely would, it was part of the game. "Well, congrats again."

"Thanks. It's just one thing after another. We really need to get together and catch up."

"We should," Serenity said, but it was unlikely to happen soon. "I assume it's time to get to orders."

"The Phobos is a dead subject. We have a lot going on here right now. We have a diplomatic vessel out in Zercowan space. There are a lot of talks about an alliance. So, there is the possibility of more exploration out that way—but not now. The Martians have been spewing propaganda about these attacks being staged. That they are just a method for us to get back in control of their planet.

"The issue now is a research ship. The M.S.S. Logic has been exploiting gaps in the border coverage. They jump into Earth space and then they are gone before we can intercept it. I want to know what it is doing. I'll provide you with coordinates to the next patrol gap. Go there and see if you can intercept the Logic."

"Okay." Serenity waited for a moment. "This is going to be a delicate operation. You do realize this could be the sparking point for a war."

"There are a lot of sparks, Christina. I'm trying to prevent the fire." Tracy disconnected the transmission.

Serenity sent the coordinates to Ensign Willard, then hit the transmitter. "Ensign, I've sent you some coordinates. Once we're done taking on crew and supplies, proceed there."

* * *

It was Carlson's turn to meet the new Major. He didn't really care who the man was, but he requested to see both Janice and him. So here he was waiting for the man, who was late.

"He hasn't even been on the ship two days and we're already in trouble." Janice nudged Carlson.

"Probably some sort of 'this is how it is' type of talk," Carlson shrugged. "To make sure we know our place on the bridge."

Carlson hated this. He had done it once with Kingsworth. At the time, he was the new guy just coming on the bridge. Kingsworth was able to tell him all types of formalities and procedures he "had better follow." Carlson later realized he didn't have to follow half of them because he was Protective Services.

The Major came out. He was tall, blond hair cut close. He seemed a bit pudgy around the midsection. Carlson and Janice both stood.

"Sir."

"Ah, Corporal Carlson and Officer Kanter, sorry I am late. I am still trying to get the hang of this ship." He put out his hand. "I'm Major Nelson."

"Sir," Carlson said.

They walked into the office. Nelson gestured to some seats at his desk. Once they had both sat, Nelson took his seat behind his desk.

"So tell me, Corporal, it is my understanding that you work the bridge at General Quarters."

"I do, Sir." *Here it comes,* Carlson thought.

"I see." Nelson read some papers. "I also see here you've been recently disciplined for use of force."

"Yes, Sir." Carlson could not hide the aggravated tone.

"I suppose we can overlook that given that you exposed a Navy traitor."

"*We* did, Sir." Carlson gestured between Janice and himself. "I haven't done anything alone."

"Except stop Mathews," Nelson stated.

Carlson's blood still boiled at the mention of that name. He took a deep breath.

"Even then, I had help from other officers." Carlson's voice was harsh.

The Major turned to Janice. "Janice Kanter, by far one of the worst graduates from Protective Services training. I mean, given your abilities in every other training you've done."

"Is there a point to all this, Sir?" Janice asked.

Carlson wanted to tell Janice to just relax, but he didn't want the Major to think Carlson somehow controlled her. The Major didn't say anything right away. Carlson realized this just might be some kind of test. The brass always had some idea for a way to test how people act under pressure.

"I didn't think so, Sir," Janice said.

"You do realize that saying 'Sir' after every sentence doesn't give you the ability to say what you want to me," Nelson said. Janice attempted to speak, but Nelson continued talking. "I see that your school record is a point of annoyance for you. Given your proven abilities, I would say that is a good thing."

"I am starting to agree with Janice, and wonder why you called us in here." Carlson leaned forward to focus on the Major the whole time. "Is there something in our record that puzzles you?"

"No. I just like to meet all the senior people for each department. Typically it involved Lieutenants, and they are always so fidgety with a new boss." Nelson let a grin creep on his face. "Though it appears enlisted men are less impressed."

Carlson laughed. It wasn't a test, just a game. "I think I might like you."

"We'll see how you feel about that in time," Nelson said. "I'm no fool. I know when I have no say in what you guys do. But, I don't like you working on nights. You are the primary crew. You should be on when the Captain is awake."

Carlson's heart sank. He didn't want to be on days. This meant his nightly card game with the Captain, and the closest thing they had to dates, was over. He could protest it right now, try and fight it. But, the truth was, he had no say in the matter.

"I prefer the nights, Sir," Janice finally spoke. "It would be easier on us if we stayed there."

"Not for me it wouldn't," the Major said.

"Why don't you assign someone else as the primary then?" Carlson spoke. He glanced at Janice. "I don't think we mind giving that up."

"Why are nights so important to you two?" Nelson looked right at Carlson when he said it.

Had something come out in his voice or body language that had given him the impression it was really important to Carlson in particular? Carlson didn't really know how else to push it, other than to be a jerk. So that was the route he took.

"Why is it so important we be on days?"

Nelson put a smirk on. "You like your nights that much, huh?"

"We do," Carlson said.

"Well, tough shit, Corporal." Nelson's face went straight. He stared hard into Carlson's eyes. "I can be a jerk too."

Carlson thought about flying off the handle. But instead, he let out a sarcastic smile of his own. He likes mind games, let's play mind games.

"Actually, Sir. I hoped you might move us." Carlson relaxed in his seat. "I am glad I won't be around when you tell the Captain. If that is all, Sir?"

Nelson stood up. A little bit of puzzlement flashed on his face for just a moment before he hid it. "Of course."

Chapter 29

"**I don't** like this at all," Serenity said. For two days now Carlson had been assigned to day shift. It was a permanent change and she already missed their nightly talks at the card table. It was her chance to unwind and tell him about her day.

"Not our choice," Janice said.

"And there really is little I can do about it." Serenity knew that was the case. She could probably make a big deal about it. But that would only raise eyebrows. "It doesn't mean I have to like it."

They walked on to the bridge. Major Nelson stopped his work to acknowledge them. Serenity glared at him. She knew he must have had his reasons, and it was probably the simplest way to do things. Serenity wouldn't put Willard on nights as the primary Navigations officer.

"We've just detected the Logic on long range radar," Willard turned back.

"Ah, right on schedule." Serenity sat down. "General Quarters. Move us to block her escape route."

"I have the fighters deployed," Sanchez said.

The research vessel was small. There wasn't much to them, they were not designed to fight but to discover. They were typically outfitted with only one or two cannons for defense. Of course, they didn't usually trespass.

"Open a transmission." Serenity got her cue. "M.S.S. Logic, this is Captain Serenity of the E.S.S. Australia. You are trespassing in Earth space. I have orders to take your ship. Stand down and we will send over our boarding parties. Your cooperation will make this easier."

"They have not responded. Their engines are still powered," Willard said.

"The fighters have them surrounded," Sanchez said.

"Have the fighters take out the engines," Serenity ordered. "Repeat my last transmission."

"The fighters are engaging," Sanchez reported.

"They are responding," Willard said.

Serenity stood. A man with grey hair and an aged face wearing a Martian Naval uniform came on screen. "Captain Serenity, you must be trying to start a war."

"One might say the same of you, Captain..." Serenity said.

"Captain Fisher."

"I'm just following orders, as I am sure you are," Serenity said. "But, you keep sneaking your way into Earth space. And then you slip away. We'd like to know why."

"We are clearly no match for a Warship. But I can assure you my government will not take this lightly."

"I was never one for politics." Serenity turned to Willard. "Send the boarding instructions."

Serenity sat. She had expected a bit more fight from them. They had given up awfully quick. There was a slight twinge of pain in her hip. Then she thought of something.

"Willard, send a request of aid to any available ships in the area."

Zimmerman turned to Serenity, "What am I missing?"

"I wonder who is trapping who," Serenity said softly enough only they could hear. "We won't be alone for long."

"Captain, I am detecting the M.S.S. Phobos just inside Earth space aft of us," Willard called out.

"So they came home too." Serenity found that interesting, but it was for another time.

"The boarding party is meeting zero resistance on board," Nelson said.

"The North America and the destroyer Shasta have arrived and are requesting instructions," Willard said.

"Explain our situation."

"The Logic is under our control," Nelson said. "We can send over the techs."

Serenity nodded to Morgan.

Willard turned back to face the Captain. "Urgent orders from Naval Command, we are not to engage the Phobos unless engaged."

"What?!" Serenity exclaimed. "Have they lost their minds?"

"That's what it says."

Serenity thought for a moment. She wasn't going to follow orders blindly anymore, that was what she had said. She looked to Zimmerman.

"There has to be a reason, Ma'am," Zimmerman said. "The fact that the Phobos is home could suggest something else is going on."

"The technicians are on their way to download the Logic's computers," Morgan said.

"The Phobos has fled," Willard said. "Direction of travel is Mars."

Serenity hesitated and the Phobos got away. "Damn it."

* * *

Mathews watched the Australia. She was right there, Captain Serenity. This was his chance to end this. "Move us to engage them."

"Captain, I have the Martian President on transmitter. It's urgent."

Mathews was sick of dealing with him, but the Martian President was the only thing separating him from his fate at the hands of the Earth Government. Without his friendship, the Martian Federal Police would likely turn him in. And, even if he could escape them, he wouldn't have a ship to get to Borvian space.

Which was another problem. The President wanted him back here, in Martian Space. That was only delaying things for him. He stood up.

"Put it to my office." Mathews stopped at the door of his office. "Hold position here. If they come after us, get me."

Mathews closed the door. He sat down at his desk and mentally prepared for the butt kissing he needed to do. He pressed the transmitter.

"Mr. President, how are you?"

"How am I? How am I!" The President paused for only a moment. "Besides the fact that you keep instigating Earth, I'm just peachy."

"I have not instigated anyone, Mr. President," Mathews said in a controlled tone. "I told you, the Africa attacked us. I had no choice but to defend this ship. It is Earth that is instigating this."

"And why are you provoking them now?"

"Now?" How did he know exactly where he was? Had his Navigations officer said something?

"Right now. You are in Earth Space interfering with their operation."

"Oh, well, I saw the Logic was under attack. I was going to aid them." Mathews knew that wasn't very convincing.

"I am aware of what is going on over there. There is a reason none of the three other ships in the area are responding to assist."

"Oh?" Mathews hoped he might get an answer.

"Just because you report only to me, doesn't mean you get to know everything I know." The Martian President took a sip of coffee. "Now get your ass over here, you have five hours to arrive. If you are not here by then, I will declare your ship rogue. I can't stall the Prime Minister of Earth any longer."

Going back to Mars meant they could pull his computer and see what the ship had actually been up to. This would also show his lies. He didn't yet know how he could access that computer. His command codes were not high enough.

"Yes, Mr. President." He couldn't go rogue. Most of the crew wouldn't follow him that blindly yet. "You mentioned war, Sir."

"It is a real possibility if I don't explain away some of your actions. I don't want to fully claim your ship just yet. This could ruin our mutually beneficial plans."

"Our Borvian friends would be helpful. And if I—"

"Just get here. The clock is ticking."

Chapter 30

More supplies and more crew were coming on board. Serenity knew that meant they were either preparing for war or another lengthy mission. Of course, no one on the station would say. Maybe they didn't know, more likely they were just keeping their mouths shut.

She'd turned over the computer information from the Logic to the geeks at Naval Command. Last she heard, there was no explanation for their behavior. Either there was hidden information, or the Martian's were playing some game.

Both sides were still playing games, but the indicators were there. The pot was heating up, and soon it would boil over. Serenity had given up on trying to hold it off. She was one Captain, and if the Prime Minister wanted war, she wasn't able to stop it.

The other thing that put Serenity on edge was that she hadn't had a chance to talk to Carlson since he was switched to days. This was even worse now, and she was growing tired of hiding it. But, what could she do? She couldn't bear to tell him that it wouldn't work out. She didn't want this to fall apart.

It was too early to think about that. Besides, she had a lot of other things to worry about. Maybe that was why they didn't want Captains dating on their ship.

Her transmitter buzzed. "Yes?"

"Captain, a visitor arrived for you on the last shuttle," Zimmerman said. "I sent her to the conference rooms, but she insisted on meeting you on the bridge. She left some time ago, but this was the first moment I could spare."

"Who?"

Before Zimmerman could answer she heard someone on the bridge call out. "Admiral on the Bridge."

"Damn it, Zimmerman, a damn Admiral is here and you didn't warn me!"

"Not just an Admiral, *the* Admiral," Zimmerman sighed. "She said you wouldn't mind."

Admiral Kelly was on her ship! She jumped up and ran to the door of her office. She straightened her uniform and opened it. There stood Admiral Kelly, her fist raised to knock. Serenity snapped to attention and saluted.

Kelly returned the Salute. "Captain, mind if I come in?"

Serenity moved out of the way. "No, not at all, Ma'am."

She couldn't figure out why the Admiral was on her ship. In most cases, unannounced visits from Admirals were never good. Kelly instructed her protection team to wait outside.

Kelly closed the door. "Okay, no more formalities. I'm here as a friend. We'll just say it was a surprise inspection."

"Tracy, you could have called."

"Then it wouldn't be a surprise, Christina." She put her arms out and Serenity hugged her.

"So, how is everyone? The kids?" Serenity asked, sitting on the couch.

The Admiral pulled out a picture. "It's Kevin with the twins, Scott on the right and Sam on the left."

Serenity took the picture. Tracy with her husband, both smiling. The two boys on either side. If Serenity remembered correctly, they were three now. There was happiness in that picture. A different kind of happiness than she had now. A career could only bring so much happiness for anyone.

"How is your husband?" Serenity handed the picture back.

"He is good. He is still teaching at the elementary school. He likes the promotion. I am home even more than I was as the Spokesperson, and a lot more than I was on a ship." Kelly tucked the picture away. "What about you? You ever going to settle down yourself?"

"I don't know. I don't foresee it happening anytime soon. With the Navy in need of Commanding Officers and, well, you know this is what I wanted from the Navy." Serenity paused. *Or this is what I thought I wanted.* "You were the one that was gunning for the youngest Admiral. I just wanted to be a Captain, someday. Somehow I got it this young."

"Somehow?" Tracy laughed. "You're the smartest damn person the Navy has seen. You could be doing this job if you want."

"I'll pass." Serenity waved her hand, dismissing the idea.

"I just have never heard of anyone in your life. I just want to see you happy," Tracy said. "You've always had all the guys hanging off of you, I just thought the one would have popped up by now."

"Okay, Tracy." Serenity was done with this topic. "Let's get something to eat, huh?"

"Great." Tracy stood up. "Before we go, I may as well give you your new orders. You want them now or before I go?"

"Now and get it over with," Serenity said.

"The Derik has been talking with our diplomats about alliances and other mutually beneficial partnerships." Tracy paused. "They wish to see the Phobos hunted down. Bottom line is, that ship has caused regular attacks by their enemy the Borvians. They haven't seen the ship in several weeks, we know that's because it is here now. But, the Derik believes this is a common denominator to our problems.

"The Prime Minister agrees with sending you, even though we are in a hostile situation here. But if things escalate to war, then I suspect the Borvians will join. That means we need more help. The Zercowans may have a defensive fleet, but they still have far larger a Navy than us."

"So it's back on the Phobos. You know the ship Naval Command wouldn't let me attack," Serenity shook her head. "Now I've got to find it again."

"The Martian President had asked that if we found the Phobos we allow them to handle it. We had assumed this might mean that Mars was not entirely sure what the ship was up to. In any case, that was why the Logic was so easily captured." Kelly rubbed her head. "The ship went to Mars, and we don't know what happened from there."

"Fine, we'll get underway tomorrow." Serenity stood up. "Let's just go eat."

Chapter 31

Carlson woke up to someone knocking on the doors of his quarters. He had hoped it was Christina. That was who he had dreamt about. He tried not to sound groggy when he called out.

"Hello?"

"Corporal Carlson? This is Sergeant Biehl, from night patrol."

Carlson knew him. Carlson climbed out of bed and walked out to the door. He opened it and gave Biehl a dirty look.

"You know, I work days now so I sleep at night," Carlson let out a small laugh that sounded more like a grunt.

"Yeah, this seems like something you might want to know about. It has to do with the current night PS crew."

Carlson was awake now. "Okay, I'm listening."

"One of my officers, Holts is his name, noticed a Protective Services Officer walking down the halls. The man's uniform was torn and had small stains on the front. He contacted me because he just didn't think something was right.

"So I came down there and met with him. Officer Holts pointed him out to me and told me he saw him coming from a janitor's closet on Deck Ten. He was sure he came out of the closet, but couldn't prove it. Anyway, I caught up to him. He said his name was Daniels, new to the ship."

"Yeah, Daniels and his partner Gibson both arrived from Justice Station yesterday," Carlson said.

"Well, he said he was on duty and that he was just in a fight with someone who had threatened the Captain. He said he was going to get a new uniform from his quarters."

"That seems odd," Carlson said. "Did you check into it?"

"I contacted Australia control, they said he was scheduled on duty, but they didn't know of any conflicts. That was when I came here to see you," Biehl said. "I figured if you were worried about it, then we should all be."

"Call my partner, see if she will come here."

Carlson went to his room. He closed the door and started getting dressed while using his tablet to contact Christina.

"What?" The groggy voice answered.

"It's me," Carlson whispered.

"Mike? Do you know what time it is?"

"Daniels and Gibson, the new guys, did they come in?"

"No, Mike. The swing shift crew said they would be working a double shift. The new guys were sick."

"Thanks. I will explain more later." Carlson lowered his voice. "I love you, bye."

Carlson, now in uniform, holstered his L-pistol and walked out. "Better contact the Major, Biehl. Something is definitely wrong. I recommend they lock down Deck Ten near that closet."

"Okay." Biehl paused. "Should we stop Daniels?"

"Yeah. Run a locator on them?" Carlson heard another knock on the door. It was Janice, half asleep and pissed off.

"This had better be good."

"It is. I'll explain on our way to Deck Ten."

* * *

Carlson examined the closet door for some time. Janice didn't know what he was studying it for. Carlson glanced back at Sergeant Biehl and Officer Holts.

"This is it, huh?"

"Yes," Holts replied. "I can't know for sure if he was in there, but I swear I saw the door close behind him."

"Did you scan Daniels' chip?"

"No, he is one of ours."

"I don't think he was." Carlson opened the closet. There was nothing there but mops and brooms. "Help me empty this out."

They began moving buckets and brooms. Janice moved out the last bucket. A wall panel fell off. Janice screamed. There were two eyes peering up at her from inside the wall, just below the floor.

Carlson didn't know Gibson or Daniels, so he didn't know if this was one of them or not. He wore a Security Forces uniform, as best Carlson could tell.

His mouth moved, Carlson jumped back. "Fuck, he is alive! Get a medical crew in here. They may have to cut him out from Deck 9."

"Help." His voice was weak.

"What's your name?" Janice wouldn't be able to do a chip scan.

"Gibson."

"Who did this?"

"I don't know." Janice had to lay down on the floor to hear Gibson. "I tried to fight him, but I couldn't. He took my chip."

"He cut out your ID chip?" Janice couldn't believe the pain Gibson must be in.

"Yes."

"Save your strength. Medical teams will be here soon."

As Janice stood up, Carlson whispered in Janice's ear. "We found Daniels. He's dead on the floor of his quarters."

* * *

"I hope you are right about this, Mike." Nelson walked with Carlson down the halls. "The whole ship is locked down at this hour."

The halls were lined with staff, all awaiting a chip scan to verify their identity. "Sir, one of our own had his chip cut out. He is damn likely to bleed to death. There is something going on."

"I know. I am going to get hell from the Captain for this."

Carlson saw a man in a Security Forces uniform heading out to the shuttle bays. The problem was, he didn't carry himself like an officer. Or at least, Carlson thought something was wrong with it.

"Officer," the Major called out.

The officer turned around. "Major."

"Are you working?" Nelson asked as they walked up to him.

"No, just trying to help. Apparently the shuttle bay had some kind of night training so there is more staff than they expected."

Carlson read the man's shirt. It said he was Gibson. Carlson's first reaction was to draw his weapon, but he held off. Nelson gave him a glance. Carlson knew the Major understood and was handing it off to him.

"Gibson, you're the new Protective Services officer," Carlson smiled at him. "I thought you were working right now with the Captain?"

The Gibson imposter glanced down at Carlson's shirt. His eyes widened a bit. Then he nodded. "I should be, but Daniels felt really ill. He couldn't make it in. Can you imagine missing your first day? That's why I had to come down here and help. Pull my own weight and all that."

This guy was a good liar, even when forced to improvise. That made Carlson more nervous. He knew the shuttle bay was short staffed, that was why they were on their way down. He seemed to be able to adapt quickly.

"Did you already get your scan done?"

"Nope." The imposter turned around.

The Major walked over to scan his chip. The scanner beeped, reading a chip. Carlson saw it read with all Gibson's information. The Major read it.

That was the moment the imposter struck. A hard elbow, knocking into the Major. Carlson tried to go after him right away, but the Major blocked him.

The imposter ran for the nearest shuttle. Carlson and the Major drew their weapons and ran after him. Laser fire hit the top of the wall, just over Carlson's head. Carlson ducked behind some drums that he hoped were not fuel. Gibson, or whoever he really was, took cover behind a shuttle.

"I don't know who you are, but you are not Gibson," Carlson called out. "We have Gibson in sickbay. So whatever you planned to do is over now. You're making this harder on yourself."

"I don't plan to be captured, Mr. Carlson," the man yelled back. "Not even by you."

Carlson signaled to the Major that he would try and get closer. He made a run for one of the shuttles. Laser fire streaked by. Nelson fired back at the Gibson imposter. Carlson dove on the slick floors and slid behind the shuttle. He could see the unknown man run behind another shuttle.

"I'd like to avoid any more bloodshed," Carlson called out. "I'd just like some answers."

"You know, you really have become a thorn in our side, Mr. Carlson," the man said. "What better way to get close to the Captain than to be her protection."

"That didn't work the first time." Carlson was able to make a run for a nearby transport. He knelt behind it, his L-pistol pointed at one of two shuttles the suspect could be behind. The Major ran over next to him.

"Yeah, well, we've been underestimating you." The imposter walked out. The L-pistol was now pointed at his own head. "Even now, against the odds, you are here to stop us again."

Carlson threw up his left hand. "Wait—"

The imposter pulled the trigger. The blast of the laser bolt blew through his head.

Chapter 32

It had taken Serenity a week just to get a lead on the Phobos. She stopped every shuttle, transport, and cruise ship passing in the outer solar system. She was most interested in those that came from Mars. Hoping one of them might have seen the Phobos there.

Secretly, Serenity hoped they wouldn't see it there, because if the ship was in orbit of Mars, there was little she could do to intercept it. She doubted the Martians would just let her in.

Finally, an Earth Luxury Cruise ship had some details to help her. They were reluctant at first, but when Serenity threatened a boarding party, they had plenty to talk about. People pay a lot of money for that cruise, they don't want to see Security Forces BET running through, heavily armed.

They had seen the Phobos traveling in a direction that indicated they were likely heading for Borvian space again. That seemed to be the most logical choice. They saw the ship two weeks ago, so they were likely halfway there.

Serenity set a course for Zercowan space. They should see she was on this. Plus, a stop there would allow her a chance to take on supplies and let the crew get a day to relax. She'd pick up the search from there.

Kanter and Carlson were standing by the door. Her office was the closest thing they got to privacy so any work she could do there, she did. She was glad to have Carlson working with her. She felt safer.

Safer was a relative term now. It seemed that taking down the Admiral hadn't ended the threats to her life. She wasn't too surprised by that, but she had hoped it would end with him.

The only known motivation for the Admiral was her age, and that seemed weak at best. But he did mention a group of people. She looked over at Carlson.

"Who do you think might want me dead?" Serenity was surprised by her own casual tone.

"If we knew, we might have a better chance of figuring this all out," Carlson said.

Serenity hated that he avoided the questions, surely he had some idea. It was his nature—pretend he wouldn't speculate, and then do so anyway. "Come on, Mike."

"Fine. It could be your command codes, it could be your age, it could be you've disrupted someone's plans. It could even be that attack you foiled on Peace Day. It could be all those drug runners you foiled."

"The last one sounds most plausible, but I don't see them performing acts of terror," Serenity said. "Besides, there hasn't been a terrorist group with any real power in centuries."

Carlson laughed. "The thing about terrorists is, there is no face or uniform to identify them. They could be anywhere. They work secretly for as long as needed and when the time is right, they surface from seemingly nowhere. There is no reason some of the more powerful drug cartels couldn't see you as a threat. And as long as I've been on this ship, drugs have a presence in the military."

Serenity didn't really care much for the humor Carlson found in the topic. Perhaps it was a bit cynical for her taste. But he was right, she did stop a lot of illegal runners when she was working near-Earth patrols. A lot more than the other Captains.

"Perhaps we are dealing with one delusional man." She, of course, was referring to Mathews.

"Someone has to be giving these people resources," Janice said. "Mathews can't be doing this from prison. Perhaps the Martians?"

Serenity nodded. Serenity and Carlson knew he was out, but the fact remained the same. Someone would have to be aiding him, someone with money, influence, and supplies.

"That is the public and the politicians' initial reaction. Terrorists are hard to label, so they see all the Martian involvement. We will likely go to war with a country that is being played as bad as we are. Neither Mars nor Earth have any idea who is really manipulating who." Serenity stood up.

"Two governments shouldn't end decades of peace over a misunderstanding." Janice shook her head.

"If only it were that simple." Serenity walked to her door. "Let's make some rounds."

Chapter 33

Serenity sat on the bridge. All the preparations were in order for their arrival at Zercowa, the Zercowan home planet. Serenity had actually considered taking some time off the ship to see the planet. The small glimpse she got when they visited the Derik's Palace had been tempting her to see all their planet had to offer. After four weeks of travel, the crew was ready too.

When they arrived, she was to make contact with the Peacemaker. Then, within several hours, they would be able to start trips to the surface. Serenity had worked out the numbers with their government. They didn't want to get too overwhelmed with humans. Rules were thoroughly explained. No one needed an interplanetary incident. There would be a lot of dignitaries around.

The ship slowed down. "Take us into a high orbit with the Peacemaker."

"Captain, I don't detect the Peacemaker. In fact, I don't detect any ships." Willard keyed her console. "Just the planet."

"Morgan, check the radar," Serenity said. "This is their home planet, there are ships all over. Willard, all stop. I don't need to run into anything."

"There is some type of radar jamming occurring," Morgan said. "It's coming from a small probe. It seems to be a limited field. If we move forward, we may get out of it."

"Move us forward, slowly," Serenity said. "Try reaching the Peacemaker." Serenity didn't like flying blind. "General Quarters, too."

"Peacemaker is responding, but the transmission is weak."

Static filled the transmission. "Australia... attack... Phobos... badly..."

"Captain, I'm getting radar," Willard paused. "The Phobos is not up close. There are two Zercowan ships, badly damaged. The Peacemaker has minimal damage and one Borvian vessel has no damage. There are a lot of fighters out too."

"Move us in. Scramble the Fighters." Serenity stood up. "Our first job is to protect the Peacemaker. If we can, we will chase down the Phobos. Open a channel to the Borvians and the Phobos."

Serenity took a breath. She certainly hadn't expected to run into the Phobos so early. This was too weak of an attack to be any attempt at the Planet itself. Willard nodded to her.

"This is Captain Serenity of the E.S.S. Australia. You are trespassing in Zercowan Space, attacking an Earth Diplomatic Vessel, and attacking an Earth ally. Stand down your vessels."

"The Borvians are moving to flee. Should we attack?" Willard asked.

"No, move to engage the Phobos," Serenity said.

"Captain, the Phobos is responding." Willard sounded shocked.

Serenity was a bit shocked too. The ship that never said a word, was finally going to have a voice. The image of a woman, with dark black hair pulled back to a pony tail, in the familiar red Martian Naval uniform, came on the screen.

"Captain Serenity, I am Commander Rikta of the M.S.S. Phobos. You are interfering with a Martian military operation. We have no quarrel with Earth."

"Commander, that seems to be the point of debate. Since you've destroyed one Earth Warship and you seem to always be around when Earth is attacked," Serenity said. "Is your Captain sick?"

The transmission ended. Serenity looked to Willard.

"They cut it from their end, Captain," Willard said. "Zercowan Royal Navy has asked that we provide planetary defense due to the damaged nature of their ships, but the Phobos is turning to flee."

Shit! Serenity cursed to herself. She was here to get the Phobos. She could easily outrun them, but she couldn't leave the Zercowans alone.

"Stand down." Serenity let the disappointment show in her voice. "Contact Naval Command, relay the events."

Serenity paced the deck of the bridge. There was likely to be a response from Naval Command on this.

"Captain, Admiral Kelly for you," Willard said.

The Admiral came on screen. "A Martian Vessel attacked an Earth Diplomatic vessel. I guess we will add this to the list."

Serenity nodded.

"Well, Captain. I have some news of my own. Remember our little deal with the Martians about the Logic? Well, the Logic turned up nothing and the Martians have yet to say what is going on. So, an ultimatum has been issued by the Prime Minister. He wants them to either claim the ship, or deny it, within seventy two hours."

"Sounds like war," Serenity said. "Should we be heading home?"

"No. You are already out there and, clearly, so is the Phobos."

"Captain, we have hostiles arriving," Willard interrupted.

"Excuse me, Admiral." The transmission ended. Serenity saw fifty contacts on the radar. "That doesn't look good, Ensign."

"Three Martian warships and thirty Martian fighters," Willard replied. "Just arriving now. The Phobos is one of them."

"Are the fighters still out?" Serenity said.

"Yes, Captain," Sanchez called.

Three warships this far from home was not a good thing. The Martians appear to be planning their own preemptive strike on the Zercowans, perhaps to keep them out of the war. That meant Serenity had to do her best to show Earth was their friend. There would be no retreat this time.

"Captain, twenty Borvian vessels arriving. The Martian warships are moving in. The Borvians are following them. It's a wide formation," Willard said. "Two more Zercowan ships arrived, two more are about two hours away. Naval command is monitoring our communications and bridge."

Serenity shook her head. The last thing she wanted was to be watched. "Hail the Martian ships."

"Captain, the Derik is transmitting. Audio only."

"Captain Serenity, this is the largest offensive I have seen in years. We can't let Zercowa fall."

"It's not good odds, Sir. But I will do my best to hold them off until more of your ships can arrive." Serenity took a breath, "I will not leave."

The transmission ended. Willard turned back. "The M.S.S. Independence is responding."

"E.S.S. Australia, we have no hostility to Earth. These Zercowans attacked a Martian Vessel."

"First, I won't stand down. Second, the Phobos attacked an Earth Diplomatic Vessel. The Zercowans provided aid." Serenity paused. "Third, does this mean the Martian Government is claiming responsibility for the Phobos?"

"I'm not authorized to answer that. We have our orders. If you don't withdraw, Mars will not be responsible for what may happen."

"They ended the transmission, Captain," Willard said. "I have the Admiral."

"Captain, this is a bad situation," the Admiral said.

Serenity bit her tongue to show her annoyance with the obvious statement. "I know, we are here." So much for that. "It will be a while before anyone else comes to help. Two Zercowan ships, two damaged

Zercowan ships and my fifteen fighters are not going to hold off much. Obviously, they don't know what the Phobos is really up to."

"Captain, it's not our job to figure out their internal affairs. You need to stand down and withdraw."

"There is no way we can do that." Serenity had given her word. She wasn't going to follow orders blindly.

"Excuse me, *Captain*. I'm not giving you a choice."

"Admiral, Captain, if I may?" Carlson asked.

Carlson never spoke on the bridge, and certainly not during a transmission. Serenity spun around in her chair, staring at him coldly. Carlson leaned in.

"We have not been here long enough for them to be responding to aid the Phobos. How did those ships get here on such short notice?" He stood back up.

Zimmerman spoke. "So, either they have been waiting for us to arrive and they are using this morning's attack as an excuse. Or, the Phobos reported it was attacked weeks ago."

"I think the latter is more likely, but the timelines are all real fishy here," Serenity said. "The bigger picture is this: If I turn my back on my word now, Earth will just have one more enemy. Or at the least, no friends."

"You won't come out of this alive, Christina." There was no authority in Kelly's voice.

"I know, but it is the right thing to do," Serenity said.

"Fine, do your best. We'll be listening in. May God have mercy."

"Hail the Independence." She turned to speak to Zimmerman. "This is it, here goes nothing. "

"Captain Serenity, I thought we were done talking." The speakers replied, no visual again.

"I wanted to know how your government was able to get two warships out this far in a matter of hours, minutes really."

"You're joking."

"No, I am not. I don't make jokes. Just ask my Commander." It is interesting how quickly military discipline goes out the window when you're faced with death.

"Captain, this doesn't have to do with Earth. How we got here is not relevant."

"It is. You see, the Phobos just attacked the Zercowans here not long ago. We arrived to stop it, but only by dumb luck. Somehow you've got a whole fleet—one that is well coordinated and requires assistance from the Borvians—ready at a moment's notice."

There was a long pause. Serenity thought for sure the Independence had disconnected.

"I don't have to answer the questions of Earth Captains. You have only ten minutes left."

Willard spoke. "The Borvian ships are withdrawing."

Someone doesn't care to stay when the truth is exposed, Serenity thought. Perhaps the Borvians didn't care much for being used.

"Independence, I suggest you forget about counting down. We are not leaving. You've provided no clear explanation for your actions." Serenity paused. "Oh, and don't expect much help from the Phobos. We've yet to see them join in a fight."

The transmission ended. Serenity sat down.

"Orders?" Sanchez asked.

"If we are attacked, we will handle the warships. Let our fighters take on their fighters. We'll watch how the Zercowans react." Serenity saw the Martian warships moving in on her position. "No one engages unless they fire on us first."

She thought this could well be a ploy to get her to fire first. Thirty Martian fighters flew over the bridge dome. The Warships were within meters of the Zercowan ships, and holding. The Phobos still sat out at the edge of radar.

"Captain, intercepted transmission. I only got part of it."

"...ove to engage." That was the Independence.

Commander Rikta's voice came on. "Independence, we take orders from the President."

"We won't be able to hold an attack alone. Your Borvian friends are cowards."

"You can handle this. My Captain will not move in."

"Your damned Captain won't even speak for himself. I will not lose my rank because of you."

The transmission cut off. "I lost it, Captain."

Serenity watched the radar as the two warships started to withdraw. She had done it. She had talked her way out of certain death.

The ship shook violently and didn't stop.

"Captain, we've been engaged," Sanchez said. "We are returning fire."

"Ensign, move us away. They are unloading on us," Serenity called out. She could feel every hit tearing into the right side of the ship.

There was a brief pause in the shaking. Then it started again.

"We are starting to get hull breaches. They are focusing on us," Morgan said.

"Keep us moving away, Willard. Get us rolling to expose to other areas that haven't been hit," Serenity ordered

"We are making quick work of the fighters," Sanchez said.

"Captain—" Willard's console sparked and exploded in a flash of fire. Serenity flinched as Janice pulled Willard away from the burning station. Morgan rushed in to extinguish the flames. Flames grew, but the automatic extinguishers kicked in and began pouring water on the bridge.

"Morgan, get navigations up on your console," Serenity wiped the water off her forehead.

"We lost engines. The power relays have overloaded, blowing out most of the navigation systems. The backups are coming online, but they won't be much good with no engines," Morgan said. "We're in a slow roll."

"Commander, take the controls, see what you can do for us," Serenity said.

"Captain, we've lost almost all our cannons on the right side," Sanchez said. "When we roll around to that side again, we're fucked."

Several more large jolts hit the ship. The large view screen at the front cracked. "Sanchez, watch out!"

Sanchez dived out of the way. The glass fell and shattered over her console. Carlson ran over and helped her clear off the heavier pieces.

"Multiple hull breaches, fires on several decks. I would say about forty percent of this ship is unusable," Morgan reported. "Shit! We lost the pressure in the flight deck. These containments aren't holding anymore."

"What about them? For fuck's sake, we've got to have done something to them!" Serenity yelled, the constant pounding of water on her face made it hard to think.

"Marginal to moderate damage on both warships. There appear to be no fighters left. We are starting to get increased support from the Zercowan ships," Zimmerman said. "We've got to do something."

Serenity saw sparks from the Major's console. The water was seeping into the cracks in the watertight casing.

"Major, get away!"

Another huge jolt rocked the ship. The Security Forces station sparked and flamed up.

"Can we get something for engines, Morgan?" Serenity turned to face him.

"I can try."

"Don't try! Just do it if you want to live through this!" Serenity yelled.

Flames had now begun to consume the back part of the bridge. The fire control systems were not able to hold on any longer. Suddenly the shaking stopped.

"Report."

"The Martians are disengaging." Zimmerman coughed from the smoke. "Six Zercowan ships are arriving."

"We need to get out of here!" Kanter yelled at the Captain. The only exit was consumed in flames. "Everyone into the Captain's office."

Serenity waited for everyone to get into the office before she did. Zimmerman was last.

"I got a message to the Zercowans to protect us."

Serenity ran in and Carlson sealed the door. Serenity heard the sound of the airtight seals taking hold. Now they were all trapped in her office to die. Serenity was just glad they had managed to fend off the attack.

"Can you get the air off the bridge from here?" Zimmerman asked Morgan.

"I can use the Captain's console." Morgan ran over to her desk.

After a few moments, there was an odd creaking sound. Then several moments later, it happened again. It had to be the sound of the bridge losing air and then regaining pressure.

"We should be safe."

Carlson opened the door slowly. Serenity walked past him onto her bridge. The fire system had shut off. There was nothing but burn marks, damaged consoles, and metal carnage.

Serenity knew one thing for sure: The first battle of the Earth Martian War was just fought.

Earth lost.

Chapter 34

Carlson marveled at the beauty of the planet. He found himself wandering around the downtown shops and parks of this Zercowan city. It was nothing like the downtowns he knew from Earth. There were no skyscrapers or towering condominiums despite the population of the city. There wasn't a building taller than four stories in sight.

He walked down a path, into a park. The path was arched with trees, creating a tunnel. He thought the park would be densely populated with trees—that was all he could see as he approached it—but when he exited the tunnel a large open field was present. The trees circled the park, the city that surrounded it could barely be seen.

Carlson sat on a bench by the lake. The water was violet. Small fish—that seemed more like birds—swam in the water. He watched the Zercowans playing games in the grass, having picnics, and walking along the paths. None of them gave Carlson a second look.

He sat there waiting for Janice—but, secretly, he hoped Serenity would show up like she had on Earth. Carlson had grown to understand that, for now, all he could expect was sporadic moments with her. But in that little bit of time he had learned a lot about Christina, and he knew she was worth waiting for.

* * *

The ship was in docks, once again, and it drove Serenity crazy. Lieutenant Morgan had already made it clear that if they had been in Earth

Space the Australia would have been scrapped. Fortunately for them all, they were not.

Zercowan and human engineers were working all over the ship; they had already managed to restore communications and open up large areas of the ship that had been closed before. As a reward for the crew's hard work, she gave them shore leave, letting them take cycles on the planet. Morale was low, and she hoped this would provide a boost.

The Admiral came up on Serenity's screen. "Admiral, you'll have to excuse me for taking your call in my quarters. I still don't have a working bridge."

"I'm just glad you are okay. I understand the Australia is in pretty bad shape."

"She is, but they are working hard to get her back in service. I imagine it is going to be some time before we can get underway." Serenity shook her head. "We didn't do so well out there."

"I'm not sure there was much more that could have been done." Admiral Kelly read over her tablet. "Let me get you up to speed.

"We had a diplomatic meeting with the Martian government. They are playing word games, but you can rest assured that the Phobos is a Martian-controlled ship. There was a large meeting with the top military minds on Earth. They seem to agree that the Phobos is a source of confidence for the Martian President.

"We are sending the Churchill out to assist you and the Zercowans with the Phobos. The hope is to crush their President's hopes by taking out the Phobos. I know the Churchill is a destroyer, and it would be nice to get another warship, but that won't happen."

"I understand," Serenity said. "The Churchill should arrive about the same time we are repaired. If we can get repaired that fast."

"Let's hope so."

* * *

Janice spotted Mike sitting on a bench by the lake. She called him over. "Come on, Mike. I don't want to sit here. Let's go walk around the shops."

Carlson let out a sigh and rolled his eyes. "Shopping, really?"

"I didn't say I would buy anything." Janice slapped him on the shoulder. "It'll be fun."

They walked out of the tunnel of trees and returned to the downtown. Janice peered in a few windows, but she didn't seem to care much for Zercowan style. She stopped when she noticed Carlson wasn't next to her anymore. When she turned around, he was staring in the window of a shop.

"I thought you didn't like shopping." Janice walked back to him.

"Check this out." Carlson was pointing to a ring in a jewelry store display case.

A woman inside the store waved them in. Janice opened the shop door. Carlson followed her inside.

"I saw that ring," Carlson said.

The woman had already pulled it out of the case and handed it to Carlson. Janice admired it over his shoulder.

It was a shiny black metal ring. Imbedded in the black metal was a silver line that waved around it. Just before the top, the silver line broke out from the black and wrapped around a clear gem. First glance led Janice to think it was a diamond; but as Carlson moved it, she saw the light reflected off of it much differently, changing the color of the gem at different angles.

"That is a beautiful ring," Janice stated. "You should get it for Christina."

"I think it's a bit early for engagement rings, Janice." Carlson handed the ring back to the clerk. "It's very nice."

"It's made of Holrenite, a precious metal on one of our planets." The sales lady pointed to the silver line. "This is silver, from Earth. We took it in trade from one of your people on that Diplomatic ship. This gem is called Riomander's Eye. It's named after a monster in one of our ancient tales.

"We just made it yesterday. There isn't another one like it, and there won't be. We are out of silver."

"We're just barely getting to know each other." Carlson told the sales lady. "It is very nice."

"Love knows no timetable," the sales lady said.

"It's a bit more complicated than that." Carlson turned to Janice. "You ready?"

"I'll meet you outside. I want to look at these necklaces."

Carlson walked out. Janice could see the disappointment in his face. She knew it likely had little to do with the ring; but if things ever worked out for them, Carlson deserved something nice. She waited for a moment, pretending to check out some necklaces, until Carlson was away from the window.

"That ring my friend was looking at," Janice turned to the sales lady. "I don't have Zercowan money."

"Do you have something to trade?" The lady said.

Janice pulled out her security wallet. She kept a small amount of jewelry in there: A necklace her mom gave her, a ring that was an heirloom, and a few sets of earrings. One of the first things she was warned about on a Navy ship was to keep your important stuff at home or on your person. If you have to abandon ship it will always be with you. She pulled out some solid gold earrings and handed it to the lady.

"Will this be enough?" Janice said.

The lady looked them over carefully. "Gold?"

"Yes, solid gold," Janice didn't remember where she got those earrings. They were simple in design. She only kept them because they matched the necklace, which she never wore.

"None of your people want to part with gold." The sales lady took the ring and handed it to Janice. "Thank you."

Janice tucked the ring in her wallet where the earrings had been. She thanked the sales lady and walked out. Carlson was standing at the corner.

"Took you long enough," Carlson said. "Can we go eat now?"

Chapter 35

Carlson and Janice were called to meet with the Major as soon as their shift ended. They waded through the crowds on the ship. The Zercowans were still everywhere helping with repairs. It made things a bit more crowded.

Carlson made his way into the Security Forces section of the ship.

"I hope this doesn't take too long. I am supposed to meet with Willard soon," Janice said.

Carlson checked the office, but Major Nelson wasn't there.

"Ah, Corporal. Over here," Nelson called out. He waved them over to the patrol briefing room. A Zercowan female was sitting inside. "Corporal, Officer, let me introduce Vistarina Biczen of the Derik's Royal Police. She is one of the Commanders of the police force on the station that controls these space docks. The information she shared with me seems to concern you two more."

"It's nice to meet you," Janice said.

Vistarina was one of the better-looking Zercowans Carlson had seen. She was average height and build, compared to a human anyway.

"So, what information do you have for us?" Carlson asked.

"We have several undercover officers on the station. We use them to catch smugglers mostly. One of the undercover officers recently heard that a human was looking for a Zercowan hitman to kill your Captain."

"Do we have a name or face for this person?" Janice asked.

"Really, we only have a rumor at this point. A contact of my officer told him, because he is believed to be a hitman. Many smugglers try to kill their competition."

"Perhaps we can pass word to set up a meeting with this crewman. Once your undercover gets enough information, we'll take him down," Carlson said.

"We've already started the process. I thought it was best to inform the Major beforehand." Vistarina pulled out a chip. She put it in the center display of the briefing room. A three-dimensional image came up. "This is the meeting place. It is a restaurant used by humans and Zercowans on the station. I hope this will mean you two won't stand out."

"Wait. *Us?*" Janice said.

"This is a protective services matter. I told Vistarina that you'd be helping her on this," the Major said.

Vistarina continued. "There are two exits, here and here. I think it is best if we have two Royal Police and two Security Forces officers at each exit. We'll be sitting inside," Vistarina pointed to a table. "When we get the signal we will move to take him down. The door teams will seal the exits. Of course, we'll take down the undercover officer too."

"When is the meeting?" Carlson said.

"Tomorrow morning."

Carlson looked at Janice. "So much for the short meeting."

* * *

Janice sat at the table with Biczen and Carlson. Every now and then she would laugh when she heard them laughing, but she wasn't paying attention. Janice didn't have many civilian clothes around, she had managed to dig out this V-neck T-shirt and some jeans. She kept her L-pistol concealed in an otherwise empty black purse.

Janice saw a medium-skinned man sit at the table. She nodded to Carlson. He raised a glass to his mouth to hide his communications with the teams. Janice listened to her earpiece.

"So, are you here to make a deal?" the undercover said.

"If you can handle it. My target won't be easy."

"I'm the best you're going to find. Who is your friend?"

"What's your price?"

"My price depends on the friend. If you don't want me to meet your friend, then just say so now."

"And how do I know you are not playing me for a fool? Your Royal Police are everywhere on this station."

"And how do I know you are not one of those Security Forces? A militaristic police force could pull all types of tricks." There was a long pause. "You've talked to Ramuzel, I am sure he made you aware I haven't been caught yet. I am the best you will find."

"Fine. We need our Captain taken care of."

"We? I thought I was working for you. Is this a game to you?" The undercover's voice started to rise. "I am not a person you want to play with."

"Calm down," the suspect looked around the room. "I work for an organization that has certain issues with our Captain. You will work for me."

"It will be expensive. Your Captain is well protected."

"This is why I asked for the best."

"And how do I know you are good for the money?"

"My group has money, and power. You fuck this up and you get nothing. But if you can succeed, you will have a fortune."

"Silver. The jewelers here are paying top dollar for it. Give me 50 ounces of your silver and another five thousand Zercowan dollars."

"That is hefty."

"Take it or leave it."

"Deal."

Janice watched the undercover stretch his back; the sign to move in. Janice pulled out her L-pistol slowly, while Carlson radioed the teams. They were within feet of the suspect when he noticed them.

"Earth Security Forces, get down on the ground!" Janice called out.

The suspect was out of the chair and making a run for the back exit. The teams were moving in on him from the exit. He turned for a large mirror and ran toward it.

"Janice, the mirror," Carlson shouted as he ran after the suspect.

The man flung the mirror off the wall, revealing a passageway. Carlson and Janice chased him through the halls. He knocked over several pieces of scrap wood.

The passage way came to a dead end, but the suspect ran through the wall as if it was made of paper. They continued after him through the torn wallpaper and into the small casino. They chased after him out the front door. Janice wasn't too far behind the man now, and Carlson was just ahead of her.

They chased him up a flight of stairs to a hallway that overlooked the plaza. Carlson was just about to catch the suspect when he suddenly turned around. Janice saw the electro-knife, but Carlson blocked her for a clean shot. He leaned his right shoulder back, avoiding the knife thrusting at him, then swung his arm up, knocking the knife away.

The man took off again. This time Janice was close behind, and Carlson was just behind her. He rounded a corner. Janice came around just in time to see Biczen's knee collide with the suspect's stomach.

He fell to the floor. Janice pushed him flat on the floor and restrained him.

Carlson leaned over and rested his hands on his knees. "Where did you come from?"

"I know a shortcut," Vistarina said with just the hint of a smile.

* * *

Janice downed another cup of water. Carlson laughed.

"How many cups of water you going to drink?" He nudged her arm, causing the water to spill down her chin and cleavage.

"Damn it, Mike." Janice sat on the thin plastic bench along the back wall of the station's police department lobby.

"Come on, its water not wine."

Carlson sat across from her near a bulletin board. Finally Vistarina came out.

"Sorry about the delays. They should be bringing him out soon. We don't process humans, so it takes time."

"I understand." Carlson stood and shook her hand. "This joint operation went well."

"I'd agree. I must admit I have been studying the tactics of police on your planet, so working with you was a pleasure."

The crewman was hauled out of the station from somewhere. One of the other Security Forces officers who would be escorting the suspect pulled out his scanner. Janice looked over his shoulder as he scanned the crewman's neck.

"Crewman Thompson. This isn't your first run-in with Security Forces," Janice said as the officer scrolled through the list.

"You keep identification in your necks?" Vistarina said with a bit of shock.

"Yeah, we get these chips implanted at birth." Janice took the scanner from the officer and slipped out a pen. "We just update them as needed. Just sign in the box for the transfer."

Vistarina signed and handed the scanner back. "I hope we work together real soon. If you are ever in the area and need something, give me a call."

Chapter 36

"We've talked to everyone he knew," Carlson told the Captain. "No one will admit to knowing anything."

Carlson wasn't exaggerating, they had talked to any person who had even the slightest bit of connection with Thompson. He hadn't turned up anything. Those that knew Thompson couldn't provide any leads to what organization he might have been a part of.

"Is it possible they are covering for him?" Serenity took a bite of her lunch.

"I am almost certain some of them are," Janice said.

"Problem is, we can't just haul them in for interrogations without proof. With nothing to arrest them on, we're kind of stuck." Carlson shrugged his shoulders. "Unless something changes, I'm afraid we are at a dead end."

Serenity tossed down her fork. Carlson recognized the disgust on her face. He didn't like it anymore than she did. But there was little he could do about it. He and Janice spent a week turning up every stone they could possibly find.

Carlson watched Serenity rub her face. She sighed again.

"Well, Mike, this is getting old fast," Serenity said.

"I wish I knew why you were targeted." Carlson tossed the rest of his sandwich away.

"I've almost gotten used to that. As sad as that is. I mean this," Serenity gestured between the two of them. She lowered her voice. "I'd like one real date with you."

"I think a date might raise a few eyebrows," Janice laughed. When no one laughed back, she cut it off.

"What if we just happened to take shore leave at the same time?" Serenity said. "I'll go on your next rotation and you and I can meet somewhere off the beaten path."

"It is really risky," Carlson said.

"Now is the time to take that risk. We won't be returning home anytime soon with repairs and travel time. Besides, who would know?" Serenity gave Carlson that irresistible flirtatious smile.

Carlson had to admit, Zercowan space was the best place to take that risk. There had to be a good restaurant away from everybody else.

"You're on duty protection," Carlson said. "I don't think they'd keep the secret."

"I can't bring an armed force onto Zercowa unless I am on official business. This is shore leave," Serenity said. Carlson didn't like it and it must have shown on his face because Serenity said, "I know you don't like it, but don't you want something resembling a relationship?"

"More than anything." Carlson's face lit up. "I'll set it up and let you know where."

* * *

Janice stood by the elevators waiting for Carlson. She had gotten a call from a crew member who worked with Thompson. Janice talked to him, his name was Crewman Long. He said he has more information than what he shared originally.

Carlson came out of the elevator. He glanced over at Janice. "Did he say what he knows?"

"Only that he would talk to us in person, and only in person." Janice walked down the hall to the Crewman's quarters.

"I don't like this. Something doesn't seem right about it." Carlson put his hand on his weapon.

Janice gave the door a firm knock. A man yelled inside, but Janice couldn't understand him. She glanced at Carlson, who only shook his head.

"Long, it's Security Forces. Open the door," Janice called.

Another noise came from inside, this one clearly distressed. Carlson already had his L-pistol drawn. Janice took hers out and tried the door. It was unlocked.

Carlson slowly twisted the handle, then flung the door open. Janice went in first, scanning the room. She saw no one inside. Then she heard a muffled sound. She pointed to the bathroom.

Carlson tried the door, it was locked. He took one swift kick and the door flung open. Janice saw Long lying on the floor, tied up, a sock in his mouth. Janice pulled the sock out.

"Behind you!" Long said.

Janice swung around to see a woman and man trying to sneak out the bedroom door. They were almost out of the quarters when two Security Forces officers approached it. Janice caught a glimpse of an L-pistol in the man's left hand. He was holding it to the woman's back. Janice stayed low in the bathroom.

"All right, I hold the cards here." The man said, backing into the far corner.

"Okay, what do you want?" Carlson asked.

The man fumbled in his pocket for a moment before retrieving a small remote.

"I have explosives in here, let me out or I blow them."

"You'll kill a lot of innocent people, including yourself," Carlson said. "Is that what you want?"

"Fuck you!" The man was now in the corner of the room. "Let me leave, this is your last chance."

"He will do it," Long whispered to Janice.

Janice lay flat on the bathroom floor. She lined up her shot, prayed her marksmanship hadn't gotten rusty, and pulled the trigger. The shot hit the man square in the right shoulder, causing the remote to fall from his grip.

The woman ran to the awaiting patrol officers. The man raised his weapon. Janice pulled the trigger again. He fell back into the corner and slid down.

"What the hell is going on, Long?" Janice pulled him up. They moved out of the quarters so the bomb specialists could have a look.

"That was the reason I didn't talk before. He threatened to kill me if I said a word."

Janice got into the safe area and sat Long down. She began removing his ties. "Who is he and what does he want?"

"Walker, Thompson worked for him," Long said. "Thompson was my friend, but I think he was into something bigger than just smuggling drugs onto the ship."

"And what about you, how do you play into all this?"

"Thompson was just my friend." Long rubbed his wrists. "I mean, I knew he was running drugs, but I'm not a snitch. But treason? No, I'm not hiding that."

Carlson came over and pulled Janice aside. "No explosives in the room."

"Long doesn't know much. At least not yet. I'm gonna have him brought in," Janice said. "What about the girl?"

"Walker's girlfriend," Carlson said. "She's going to talk, but she wants certain assurances first. I think her boyfriend threatening to blow her up may have made her see the light. She has already implied there are secret files on his tablet."

* * *

Carlson watched Willard work on the tablet. Janice seemed to watch her a little more closely. Carlson had looked through everything he could find in Walker's quarters. There hadn't been much, but Walker's girlfriend already told them that.

Willard looked up at Janice and smiled. "Right where she said it would be. Two encoded files."

"Two?" Janice leaned in closer.

"One is a disintegration file, should wipe the tablet clean if I accessed the other file," Willard said. "But, I worked around it. It's a video message."

Carlson got up and walked over to Willard's other shoulder. Willard started the message. A picture of that damned painting with apple covering a man's face came up.

"Not this again." Carlson shook his head. "I thought that was just something the Admiral did."

"It's not done well." Willard clicked some things on the tablet.

The painting vanished. Instead a man from the neck down in the red Martian Navy uniform could be seen. He had several medals on his breast pockets. The rank insignia on his shirt was that of a Naval Captain.

"Clever enough not to show his face anyway," Janice said.

"Go ahead play it," Carlson said.

A disguised voice spoke. "W, the Martian Navy is happy you have accepted our offer. Surely our pay will compensate you for your loss. You've done well for the Society and we hope you can succeed for us."

"I've been told this is a mission that benefits both of us." Walker's voice could be heard. "The Society and the Martians."

"The Martian Navy doesn't care about your brotherhood, W. However, your Captain has become a sort of mutual enemy to us both. We want her dead. She has become a source of inspiration and confidence for the Earth government."

"Killing her won't be easy. Security Forces stays close to her now," Walker said. "We've been trying on our own for some time now."

"I don't care how hard it is. That is why we are paying you well," the Martian Captain said. "Get it done and report it to the Society. Then I will arrange to compensate you."

The screen went black.

"That's all there is," Willard said. "I'm not sure I can crack the voice security on this one. But, I will try."

"Thanks," Carlson said. "Send us a still of this Captain. Maybe we can use what we see here to get something together on who he is."

"And what the hell is the Society?" Janice asked.

"They are a criminal organization of drug runners," Carlson said. "I don't know much about them, but we used to pick up their dealers from time to time when I patrolled in Seattle. But murder-for-hire has never been much of their thing. At least that I know of."

"Maybe they are expanding," Janice said. "Or the Captain stopped one of their drug shipments?"

"The Australia did become a real thorn in their side while we patrolled near Earth," Carlson said.

"Thanks, Francesca." Janice turned to walk away, but then turned back. "Hey, you want to go hang out on shore leave tomorrow?"

* * *

The weather couldn't have been nicer for his first real date with Christina. Carlson smiled as the light breeze blew through her hair. He opened the restaurant door for her then followed her inside. He chose it because it was the nicest restaurant and the farthest away from where most everyone else took their shore leave.

A covered patio went out over the violet river. All the tables had Zercowans sitting at them, except one of the patio tables, which was empty. The host ran over to them quickly.

"Sir, please come this way. I have your table ready. It is the best one in the house."

The host walked away after they sat. Carlson admired the beauty of the river as he watched the wildlife swimming underneath, two dusty brown, almost orange, moons reflected on the water.

He turned his gaze to his girlfriend. It felt right to call her that now that they were having a date. The beautiful light blue dress she wore had a sweeping V-neckline that accentuated her breasts. The dress clung to her slim frame in all the right spots.

Serenity turned her gaze from the river to Mike. She smiled. Her eyes reflected the flickering candle light. Carlson couldn't help but smile back.

"You are so striking. I haven't ever seen you more beautiful," Carlson said.

Serenity blushed slightly. "Thank you, Mike. How did you ever find this place? And find a table waiting for us?"

Carlson had spent a lot of money to hold the table. It took some persuasion to get the Manager to agree, but Carlson wanted this to be the best first date. He didn't know when he might get another.

"It was nothing."

The waiter came. They didn't know how to read the menu so they ordered the recommendations he made. When he left, Carlson found he didn't know what to talk about. The silence was awkward. He had already learned so much about Serenity when they had their nightly card games. What was he supposed to discuss on a first date?

"It's hard to imagine this is our first date," Serenity said. "I mean, to already be in love with you and now we are dating."

"I..." Carlson paused. "I suppose we did it backwards."

Serenity laughed. "Mike, perhaps we are making this a bit hard on ourselves."

* * *

Janice laughed at Willard's joke, nearly spitting out her soda. She'd only managed to eat half her sandwich and a few fries before the conversation took over their dinner.

Despite how easy they were talking, there was still a strange feeling deep inside Janice. She felt something for Francesca, something a bit stronger than she felt for any of her friends. But, she only dated men. This wasn't a date, this was hanging out with a friend.

Friends. That was the best way to think of this. She wasn't even sure how to tell if Francesca had any romantic interest in her.

* * *

Carlson looked out at the river as he held Christina in front of him on its banks. Carlson ignored the wisps of her hair brushing his face with each breeze. They hadn't talked much since they finished dinner. Silently they both knew time was running out and they needed to cherish the moment.

Serenity stared up at him. Carlson looked down and kissed her. He held still for a moment before passion took over and their kiss took on its own momentum. Slowly Carlson pulled away and a small grin crept onto his face.

Serenity took him by the arm and led him down the river. She let go of his hand and took off in a fast walk toward some trees and bushes. She glanced over her shoulder, a playful smirk on her face. Carlson chased after her. She disappeared behind the thick brush.

When Carlson came around the corner, Serenity took hold of him. Playfully she pulled him down into the grass. She kissed him passionately again. This time their emotions won over and slowly Carlson felt her undo the buttons on his shirt.

* * *

Janice sat with Francesca at the park bench. It was the same park she had been to with Mike, only this time she really marveled at how nice it was.

"This is a great place. I can't think of any place like it on Earth," Willard said. "I mean, we are in a major city and yet I can clearly see the stars."

Janice glanced up at the sky. She hardly noticed them anymore. Was she already jaded to their beauty?

"Funny how something so beautiful can be right in front of you, and you never even notice," Janice said, focusing on Willard. "You know, I had a lot of fun tonight."

"It was great." Willard met Janice's stare. "Janice, are you flirting with me?"

Janice felt warmth flood her cheeks, she was flirting with her. She let out a nervous laugh. "I think I was."

Willard just smiled back. "Come on, let's go shopping."

Willard jumped up from the bench. Janice walked next to her. She saw a familiar face across the park, going the opposite way. It took her a moment to recognize that it was Commander Zimmerman.

"Is that the Commander?" Janice stated.

Willard was already waving. The Commander waved back and continued on his way. She had never gone that way, the best she knew it was the way out of town. Janice turned her attention back to Willard.

* * *

Carlson lay there watching Serenity slip back into her dress. She winked. Carlson buttoned his shirt up and tucked it back in.

They kissed for several moments before Serenity pulled away. "We need to get back to the shuttle. I'm afraid it turns into a pumpkin at midnight."

Carlson walked out from behind the bushes holding Serenity's hand. They stopped on the edge of the river. He pulled her in for one more passionate kiss, the last one he might get in a long time. He felt relaxed as their lips met.

"Captain?"

Carlson broke the kiss immediately. The two spun around in an instant to meet face-to-face with Commander Zimmerman. His face equally matched his shocked voice. Carlson swallowed the lump in his throat.

Chapter 37

Serenity sat on the bridge going over the finalized repair reports. The Zercowans had outfitted their ship with a better communications system, they improved the targeting systems for the cannons, and increased the engine's power and maneuverability. She easily had the most advanced ship in the fleet. Best of all, they got it all done two days before the Churchill was expected to arrive.

But, Serenity was nervous. Zimmerman hadn't said more than two words to her in the two days since he caught her with Carlson. In fact, he only said, "It's a nice river," and then walked away. She was sure he had contacted Naval Command and was avoiding her because he thought she would be angry.

Serenity couldn't be angry with Zimmerman for reporting her. It was his duty. She should have done the same. She didn't expect the Admiral would remove her from command, but she was certain that Mike would be moved to the Churchill when they arrived.

She felt tears well up in her eyes. She blinked them away, unsuccessfully, then swallowed the growing lump in her throat. She didn't want to lose Mike. She could request a transfer to an Earth assignment, but the Navy wouldn't likely accept that now. She still had a lot of time on her service period, so getting out wasn't an option.

She'd just have to get over him. In fact, she had already made some distance between them, having said just as little to Mike as Zimmerman had said to her. She loved him, but some relationships don't last even with all the love in the world. It wasn't the first time she had her heart broken.

Emotions overwhelmed her. She stood up and went to her office. She gestured for Carlson and Kanter to wait outside.

She went inside, locked the door, and cried. For several minutes, the flood of emotions was too much to stop. There was a knock on the door.

Serenity's voice shook. "Now is not a good time."

"Captain, I'd really like to talk to you," Zimmerman's voice said through the door.

So now he wants to talk. Serenity shook her head, she may as well talk to him. At least she would know what to expect.

She sat up and composed herself. She dabbed at her eyes to mop up the tears. As she got up to unlock the door, she checked her appearance in the mirror. Her eyes were swollen red.

She unlocked the door and opened it. "If you must talk to me, come in."

Zimmerman didn't look at her as he walked in. He walked over to the couch and stood there. Once Serenity closed the door, he faced her.

"I couldn't help but notice you were upset," Zimmerman said.

Of course I am upset, Serenity thought, but instead said, "That obvious, huh?"

"I think we need to talk about what happened on the surface," Zimmerman said. "I'm supposed to have reported this right away."

Had he not reported it yet? What was he waiting for? Serenity sat down on the couch.

"Sit," Serenity said. "I was under the impression you already had."

"I still may," Zimmerman said, taking a seat. "I have been struggling with it for the past two days. First, I thought I needed to figure it out on my own. That talking to you would only cloud my judgment. But, now I feel I simply can't do it without talking to you."

"Okay," Serenity said. She reached for a pitcher of water and poured herself a glass. "What do you want to know?"

"Was this a one time indiscretion?"

Serenity took a drink of water to buy her some time to think. Was he willing to let a little slip up go? She could easily tell him it was a one time thing. *Human nature got the better of me, it won't happen again.*

"No." Serenity felt it was time to be honest with Zimmerman. Trying to figure out his motives could only complicate things. "I'm in love with Mike. That was our first real date. But, when he was on nights we played cards for hours while we talked. That has been more recently, months now. But I've been attracted to him for a lot longer."

"You could have reported this earlier on and kept it from developing into this. Why didn't you?" Zimmerman asked.

"I..." Serenity thought for a moment. "I don't really know for sure. I've had the argument with myself many times. First, I made up excuses that it wasn't what I thought it was. We were friends. But then it snowballed on me, and now—Well, I love him and to force myself to get him reassigned is an almost impossible task."

"I suppose that is why we are supposed to say something early on," Zimmerman said. "Why didn't you tell me?"

"I didn't even tell Mike for the longest time." Serenity took another drink. "I haven't told anyone. Janice knows, but I don't know if it was because Mike told her or because she was around us enough to know. It was left unsaid. But, I didn't tell you because—well, look at us now. I was afraid of this conversation. Afraid you would say something. I knew what I was doing was wrong, and I couldn't help but hide it."

"Wrong isn't the right word, Captain. It was against the rules, sure. But love isn't wrong." Zimmerman put a hand on Serenity's shoulder. "Rules can be interpreted two ways: By the letter of the rule, and by the spirit of the rule. I've always preferred the spirit." Zimmerman let that familiar smile come back to his face. "This relationship rule was put in place to keep officers from clouding their judgment and ability to lead. I don't see either one here."

Serenity thought for a moment. "Are you saying you don't plan to say anything?"

Zimmerman shook his head. "No, I am not going to report this to Naval Command. Not now, at least. But, if this begins to affect your ability to command this ship, I will have to say something. Too many lives count on it."

Zimmerman stood up and walked towards the door. Serenity followed him.

"Thank you," Serenity said, with probably a bit too much relief.

"Captain, I hope next time you might come to me for some guidance." Zimmerman opened the door. "I'm your right hand man, you can trust me."

* * *

As soon as Janice and Carlson finished their shift with the Captain, Willard was waiting for them outside the bridge. She explained that after trying for so long to get the voice unscrambled she managed to get a small segment unscrambled. Most of what she explained sounded like gibberish to Janice.

They followed her to her quarters. Janice didn't mind the time with Willard, but Carlson didn't seem as excited.

"The odds we know the voice are slim," Carlson said. "Willard, did you run it through for matches yet?"

"No. I thought I'd clue you in first," Willard said. "I can do that when we get there."

"Okay," Carlson said, eyeing Janice.

Janice gave him a nasty look when Francesca turned away. "Thanks for letting us know right away."

"I know for sure it came from the Phobos. The signatures are undeniable once the code was unwrapped. That will be a huge lead in itself for you and the Navy."

They walked into the quarters. Right away, Janice noticed the picture of the Captain from the neck down on the main television. Janice sat on the couch, Carlson just stood. Willard sat next to Janice and picked up her tablet from the coffee table.

"Here, I'll just play it."

Janice listened to the familiar dialogue, only this time the voice was different. Carlson was right, she didn't know who that voice was. The odds were slim. She turned to say something to Mike, but noticed he was pale as he stared at the screen, slack jawed.

"Mike?"

"Janice, get the Captain over here right away. It's urgent."

* * *

Serenity had just gotten settled in at her quarters when Janice called. She didn't have much to say other than Mike insisted she come to Willard's quarters right away. What was he doing in her quarters anyway?

Serenity felt a twinge of jealously, and perhaps that was why she agreed so easily. When she knocked on the door, Willard opened it. Janice and Carlson were talking.

"Damn it, Mike, just tell me what this is—" Janice stopped when she saw the Captain.

"Captain, Ensign Willard unscrambled the transmission. I don't know how, but she did. And well..." Carlson turned to Willard. "Play it again."

Serenity listened to the voice. A chill shot down her spine. Her hip began to ache and she nearly fell. She took hold of the chair in front of her. She could never forget that voice. She heard it in her nightmares. She closed her eyes and for a brief moment she saw its owner. Mathews hovered over her face screaming at her about command codes. She flashed her eyes open.

"Where did it come from?" Serenity asked weakly.

"It came from the Phobos," Willard said.

"What am I missing?" Janice looked from Carlson to Serenity.

"That... is Roger Mathews." Serenity's voice cracked a bit.

"Mathews is locked up on New Alcatraz," Janice said.

"He was. He escaped," Serenity said. No point in hiding it now. "The government has been hiding that fact for months now."

"That is impossible. There is no atmosphere outside the prison," Janice said. "Even the biggest air tanks can't get you to Moon City. You'd have to have help to get that far."

"A crooked Admiral, assistance from the Martian Government and the Society could all provide him the help he needed," Carlson said. "The real question is: What does Mars have to gain from giving him his own ship?"

Chapter 38

Carlson ran down the halls. He could see the suspect starting to get away. Janice was ahead of him. Carlson went around the corner and saw Janice standing outside the doors to the mess hall. Carlson came up. The doors were locked. He nodded to her. She kicked open the door and went inside. The man ran into the kitchen.

Janice ran after him. Carlson heard three shots. He drew his weapon and went in. Janice lay behind one of the counters. She had two wounds in her chest and one in her head. Blood began to run out on the tile. Carlson lunged for the counter. The suspect fired and Carlson slid across the floor right next to Janice's body.

Carlson checked for a pulse and found none. He radioed in. "Officer Down. Mess hall kitchen. Officer down." Carlson peered over the counter and saw the man making his way to an exit. "Freeze! Get your fucking hands up!"

The man stopped and slowly raised his hands. The man spoke. "Come on, Mike, you should be used to losing partners." The man turned around slowly.

For the first time, Carlson saw his face; it was Mathews. Mathews smirked sending a chill down Carlson's spine. Carlson's finger moved to his L-pistols trigger. He squeezed off a shot.

Carlson jumped up from his bed. Janice jumped back and threw her hands up.

"Jesus, Mike! It's me. Relax."

Carlson felt the sweat on his body. His bed was soaked from it. He swung his legs off the bed.

"Damn, Janice, you scared me."

"I scared you?" Janice shook her head. "When you didn't report for duty, I came here looking for you. Then I find you—well, like this. You need to go to sick bay, Mike."

"It was a nightmare." Carlson just then realized what Janice said. "Wait, I'm late?"

Carlson jumped out of bed, ignoring the fact that he was in just his underwear, and ran to the bathroom. Janice followed him, stopping only when he closed the door.

"What kind of a nightmare does that to you?" Janice said through the door.

Carlson splashed cool water over his face. He wasn't about to tell Janice the details. "Let's just say it involved Mathews. I just thought these nightmares were over."

"Well, considering yesterday's news—" Janice paused. "You saw a shrink after that incident, right?"

"Of course. They said it was all a normal reaction to a traumatic experience. They lasted for about a week." Carlson toweled off his face. There wasn't time for a shower. "Can you get my uniform off the couch?"

Janice cracked open the door and handed it to him. "Promise me if they start recurring you will go back."

"I will, I promise," Carlson said.

* * *

Serenity had the news up on the main bridge screen. It was technically not allowed, but the Prime Minister was making an announcement and the Admiral told her to watch it.

The screen turned blue and the seal of the Prime Minister appeared on the screen. That image was replaced by the podium. Carlson watched the bald man walk up to it. He wore a white suit which contrasted with his dark skin. The Prime Minister took a moment before speaking.

"Good Morning, people of Earth. There have been a lot of recent events involving attacks against our armed forces at the hands of groups that seem to have Martian affiliations. The Government of Mars chooses to respond with political games and double speak.

"A ship flying their colors has attacked Earth ships, completely destroying one, without provocation. The Martians refuse to accept, or deny, any association with this ship. We responded with peaceful resolutions while we attempted to get answers of our own. While the resolutions appear to have failed, we did get answers.

"We know now that the Martians are involved in a plot to terrorize the people of Earth. While we cannot say for sure they are directly involved. I can say for certain they are harboring those that are responsible.

"The government of Mars has violated the peace our people have held so dear. We've done all we can to solve this peacefully. And while we are a peace-loving planet, we cannot allow ourselves to be bullied by those that seek to cause us harm.

"The Earth Council and I deliberated for some time and we see no other course of action. We have decided to issue a declaration of war against the Martian government.

"The people of Earth must know this is done with the heaviest of hearts. This will be a swift, decisive military action which seeks to dissolve the corruption in the Martian Government. And, the people of Mars should know we have no conflict with them personally and that we will return to peace quickly."

Serenity felt the deep regret of failure. She had hoped to prevent this from ever happening. She had hoped she could prove the Phobos was rogue and this would never have happened.

Serenity realized it was too late for regrets. She needed to prepare for her own part in this war. She was ready to see the Phobos destroyed, for the benefit of her country and herself.

Chapter 39

Serenity was awaiting the arrival of the primary bridge crew. She had arrived early because she expected to meet the Zercowan ships that would be at the border soon. It felt good to be out in open space again and even better to have another Earth ship with her.

The Churchill was a destroyer, a ship designed to protect the limited direct firepower of aircraft carriers. Her Captain admitted early on that she saw no need for a destroyer around a warship. Serenity had to point out that more guns in a gun fight were never a bad thing.

The bridge crew came on and began taking their stations. Serenity watched Janice and Mike come in after everyone. Carlson talked things over with the night crew as he always did. But, Janice wasn't paying attention. She was watching Ensign Willard.

Not just watching the ensign, Janice was checking her out. Serenity could see that. She wondered why she hadn't noticed before. Perhaps this was something new, or perhaps she had been a bit selfish recently.

She had to admit she thought of Janice as a threat to her and Mike. She was attractive, taller than Serenity, and she got to be around him a whole lot more. Serenity was jealous.

But, she had also learned that Janice was the one that pushed Mike to talk about how he felt for her. Janice had put a lot of focus into helping Mike through so many of his struggles. She was a good friend for Mike. Serenity wished she had a friend like that.

"Officer Kanter, can I speak with you for a moment?" Serenity said.

Janice broke her gaze of Willard and acknowledged Serenity. "Of course, Ma'am."

"Good, in my office." Serenity stood up and headed that way. She turned to Mike. "Wait outside, please."

Serenity closed the door and gestured to a seat. When Janice sat down, so did Serenity.

"Janice, I think I see you becoming distracted by Ensign Willard," Serenity said softly. "If you understand my meaning?"

Janice paused for a moment. "I wouldn't call it a distraction, but I have been hanging out with Francesca a lot more recently."

"So what is on your mind?" Serenity could tell it was a bit more than that.

"I, well..." Janice paused. "Well, I've never dated a woman before. I mean, it has never even crossed my mind until now."

"I see," Serenity said. "Perhaps you have been too focused on what others want and need, that you are forgetting to focus on yourself."

"I don't understand."

"Janice, Mike has told me a lot about what you have done for him. I owe you a lot for your secrecy alone, but the advice and friendship you have given Mike have been more helpful than you know. I want you to understand that. But, what about yourself? Your happiness is important too."

"I am happy with Mike's friendship," Janice said. "I've had a lot of trouble finding love. I worry that I am seeing something in my friendship with Francesca that isn't there, simply because we get along so well."

"Love doesn't know rank, or gender. Either you will fall in love with her, or you won't. But wondering 'what if' won't help you find out," Serenity said.

"Sounds familiar."

Serenity's desk transmitter buzzed. She walked over to it. "Yes."

"The Derik's Eye has arrived. Marshall Korvikan says he has orders to join us and the Churchill," Willard said. "He also has a lead for us to investigate."

"Great, I'll be on the bridge in a moment," Serenity said. The transmission ended. "Talk to her. And soon. I don't need you, or her, distracted."

* * *

Carlson lay on his couch reading his tablet. He hadn't done much recreational reading, but Janice had other plans so he was left alone.

Carlson didn't like the lonely feeling. He always preferred to have friends. He liked to socialize, but oddly enough, he had few close friends. Janice and Serenity were all he really had, and Serenity was a secret to all but four people.

He was glad Zimmerman could be discreet about their relationship, but that didn't exactly open the doors for them. It only meant that the person who had caught them wouldn't tell. Serenity agreed with Mike that they might not be so lucky next time. There wouldn't be any more dates for now.

There was a knock at the door. Carlson sat up and looked at the viewer. It was Janice. "You can just come in."

Janice opened the door. She was dressed in a light blue dress that came down to about her knees. She closed the door and sat down in the chair near where Mike had put his feet back up on the arm of the couch.

"I know you didn't dress up for me," Carlson joked.

Janice gave him a dirty look. "I wouldn't dress up for you anyway. You don't appreciate me."

Carlson shook his head. "So?"

"I just had a date," Janice said. "We had a great time and there will certainly be a second one!"

"Oh yeah?" Mike set the tablet on his stomach. "Who is he?"

"She is more like it." A bit of hesitation came through in her voice.

"Ok, so who is she?" Carlson asked.

"You're not shocked?"

"Janice, will you just tell me who she is?" Carlson asked.

"Francesca."

"Ha! I knew there was something there." Carlson slapped his leg in celebration. "So, tell me about it."

Chapter 40

"**C**onfirm with the Marshall that these are the right coordinates," Serenity said. "We're awfully close to Borvian space."

"Actually, they lay claim to this space already," Zimmerman said. "Though officially it isn't within their borders."

"The Marshall confirms this is where there has been higher than usual ship traffic, including a sighting of the Phobos," Willard said. "I'm not detecting anything."

"Captain, I'll give a power boost to radar and see if we can't increase the range." Morgan keyed away at his console. "There, Willard. That should give you more to see."

"I'm picking up three Borvian vessels on long range radar now," Willard said. "Nothing we have seen before."

"Put us to Battle Stations," Serenity said. "See what Korvikan has to say about those ships."

A few moments passed. Then Korvikan showed up on the screen. "Captain, they are a type of runabout the Borvians typically use to carry supplies out to their various posts and patrols. It is very unusual for them to be out this far."

"What do you think they might be up to? Clearly they are not taking on supplies or dropping any off."

"Captain, I can't say I know. But, with the ship traffic that has been reported in this area, they may have just dropped off or picked something up. I think it is a good lead to pursue."

"Captain, they are starting to move," Willard said. "They are moving away from us."

Serenity nodded to Willard. "Marshall, what can you tell me about their radar?"

"Their sensors are about half of yours."

"Good, we'll follow them from a distance and see if they can take us to our mutual friend," Serenity said. The transmission ended. "Willard, match their speed and course, but keep them as far away as possible."

* * *

Serenity yawned. They had been following the runabout now for almost ten hours. Serenity wasn't about to stand down the fleet. It was just as likely these ships would lead them right into a trap. She had the Churchill stay back to ensure they were not circled.

"Captain, they are slowing down," Willard said. "I'm detecting the Phobos in the vicinity."

"Alert the fleet."

Serenity stood up and paced the floor. She was still certain of a trap, it seemed a bit too easy. She thought about her options.

"Captain, I have a transmission we intercepted," Willard said.

"You Morons!" the speakers said. "There are three vessels following you. Hurry up and dock with us."

"Move to engage them. Scramble the fighters. Don't destroy those shuttles, just harass them to prevent them from docking. Clearly the Phobos wants whatever is on them," Serenity said.

"Captain, there is something odd here," Zimmerman said. "I don't like it."

"I don't, either, but we have our orders," Serenity said. "Move to engage."

"E.S.S. Australia, this is Commander Rikta of the M.S.S Phobos. There is no need for us to bring the war out this far," the speakers said.

"Ignore their transmissions, Ensign," Serenity said.

"Captain, nine new ships arriving. All Borvian," Willard said.

Shit, this was the trap she worried about. "Stay with the Phobos. Have the fleet keep the Borvians off us."

"Captain, we're losing too many fighters," Sanchez said.

Serenity rode out the wave of laser fire. Once the shaking stopped, she spoke. "Damage reports?"

"We have minor hull damage, no breaches. The fleet seems to be engaging the Borvians well; they have lost two ships already. The Phobos is starting to show signs of damage," Morgan said.

There were a couple of loud explosions nearby. Serenity took her seat. "Move us into position between the Borvians and the Phobos. If he runs, it will have to be away from their space."

"Captain, they are starting to show heavy damage."

"The Borvians have lost two more ships, they are turning to flee."

"Captain, there is an asteroid belt not far from here. If the Phobos makes it there we won't be able to spot them," Zimmerman said.

"They are heading that way now, Captain," Willard said. "Should the fleet continue after the Borvians?"

"Once they cross their border, have them return here," Serenity said. "We need to target the engines of the Phobos; I don't want them making it into that asteroid field."

Serenity watched the asteroid field approaching. It was a smaller one. While the Phobos could hide in there they wouldn't be able to leave without being seen on radar. The Phobos moved closer and closer. Then the ship's cannons stopped firing.

"We've lost them in the field," Willard said.

* * *

The fleet had the area surrounded. There was no way to escape without one of the three ships seeing them. It had already been two hours.

"I worry they will be bringing more Borvians," Zimmerman said.

"There was a reason they ran in the first place. I don't think more are coming, though Mathews may be trying to convince them to send more," Serenity said. "Either way, we can't let the Phobos go when we finally have them cornered."

"Captain, the Derik's Eye reports they are receiving a transmission from the Phobos. Directed for them only," Willard said.

"Have them relay it to us," Serenity said.

The speakers turned on. "This is Marshall Korvikan of the Derik's Eye."

"Marshall, my Captain is pleased you've chosen to respond."

"Commander, you seem to do all the talking. Is there a point to this?"

"Your government doesn't have to be involved in our war," Rikta said.

"I don't make the choices for my government."

"We're able to make sure the Borvians leave your people alone, Marshall. We just need a way out of this mess."

"I'm afraid that isn't an option."

"You are making the wrong choice; at least think it over."

"The transmission ended," Willard said.

"They are stalling," Zimmerman said.

"They had to know we would listen in," Morgan said. "They have something up their sleeves."

"But the Borvians would have been back by now," Serenity said.

Serenity thought that over. A huge fleet to crush three ships could be on the way, but it seemed unlikely to her.

"Maybe they are stalling for time. Maybe to finish their repairs," Sanchez said.

"Or for a distraction," Willard said.

"A distraction," Carlson shouted. "That is it!"

Serenity spun around to face him. "What?"

"Tell the fleet to put stronger security teams on their bridges and to search for hidden transmissions. I'd guess that Mathews has made contact with someone in the Society." Carlson was already taking out a laser rifle and handing it to Janice. "That is what he is hoping for."

Serenity knew Mike was right. That was exactly what she concluded when she connected the dots. She turned back in her seat. An internal struggle was exactly what would buy the Phobos enough time to run. "Do what he said, Ensign."

"He knew we'd be listening in. He used our own relay to send a message to this ship," Willard said. "Give me a moment to isolate the transmission."

Willard worked for what seemed like forever. Serenity grew impatient, but she knew Willard was doing her best. Suddenly the display lit up with the familiar apple-faced painting.

"W, we have a change in plans." The voice was disguised. "We need you to gather the rest of our friends and take control of the bridge. I will double your payment and reward the others as well."

The image vanished from the display. Willard looked back.

"That's all there was."

"Captain, if they want a distraction, I say we give them one."

* * *

Serenity hovered in close to her desk transmitter. The bridge was filled with the sound of laser fire.

"This is Captain Serenity. My bridge has been compromised." Serenity put the panic sound in her voice. It wasn't hard even with knowing the laser fire on the bridge was just training weapons. "I need assistance. Please move in and provide support."

A training laser bolt hit over her head, then in her chest. She fell out of view and the transmission was cut off. Serenity stood back up. Though the bolt was no more harmful than a flashlight, it was unnerving to say the least.

"I hope they bought it," Serenity said to Mike as she walked on to the bridge.

"Captain, the Phobos is just coming out of the asteroid field," Willard said. "There is a Borvian fleet, the same ships from earlier, arriving too. But, they are on the opposite side."

"Wait until they are fully clear," Serenity said.

She watched carefully. The Churchill would slip behind the Phobos cutting them off from the asteroids. Serenity would be last to engage.

"Now!" Serenity ordered.

The Australia opened fire on the Phobos. The return fire wasn't strong. The Phobos appeared to be focused on the Derik's Eye.

"The Derik's Eye is taking heavy damage," Morgan said.

"Willard, have them pull back. Get in there and shield them," Serenity said.

There was another huge jolt and a rattle through the hull.

"Hull breach, Deck 6. Forward cannons are damaged," Morgan said.

The Derik's Eye continued to withdraw. The Churchill was raining heavy fire on the aft of the Phobos. Their engines were surely failing.

"Target their bridge," Serenity said.

"Captain, two small contacts are leaving the asteroid field heading for the Borvian fleet. Martian shuttles," Willard said.

That son-of-a-bitch, Serenity thought. She knew right away Mathews was on one of those shuttles. There was no way any of their ships could get to them before they got to the Borvian fleet.

Mike leaned in, Serenity put up her hand. "I know, Corporal."

Mike stood back up. Serenity knew Mathews was sacrificing his entire crew of Martian Navy personnel just so he, and a few others, could get away. And they were following those orders.

Serenity wanted desperately to call off the attack, spare their lives. They weren't to blame for their terrorist traitor of a Captain. But, her orders were to destroy the Phobos. It didn't make it easier.

"Ensign, open a channel to the Phobos," Serenity said. There was no reason to kill them all. "Phobos, stand down and we will spare you. We know your Captain has deserted you. You don't have to die for him."

There was no response. The Phobos continued to fire on them.

Zimmerman leaned in. "They won't surrender; they don't see Mathews the same way we do."

Serenity still didn't like it.

"Captain, the Phobos has multiple hull breaches. They are losing hull integrity," Willard said.

"Hold your fire," Serenity said. She wasn't going to add insult to injury. "They'll implode on themselves in a few moments."

The ship rattled as debris pelted the Australia. The Phobos had been destroyed. Willard jumped out of her seat and hollered. The rest of the bridge staff cheered. Serenity knew they were relieved to know the ship they hunted so long was no more.

"That is enough!" Serenity called out. The bridge fell silent. "Those were humans on that ship, show a little respect."

The crew returned to their stations. Serenity knew she couldn't stop them from celebrating. She couldn't really blame them. But, she wasn't going to watch it.

"Ensign, find out where the Derik's Eye will be heading for repairs. We'll escort them home," Serenity said. "Then notify Naval Command."

Chapter 41

Carlson was bored at his quarters, so he headed over to see Janice. He had hoped to catch her there and see about heading over to the bar. He came in to her quarters; they were dark and it didn't appear anyone was there. He sat down on her couch and figured he would wait. She couldn't be gone too long.

Carlson and Janice didn't get much time to hang out anymore. They had spent hours talking on the night shift—something they lost when Nelson moved them to the day crew. Now, Janice spent a lot of time with Ensign Willard.

Carlson wasn't surprised. Over the years he found he got along with women a lot easier than men. The problem with that was, most women preferred to hang out with the girls. If it wasn't that, it was the jealous boyfriend.

It was a shame that happened with Janice. She was the closest thing he had to a best friend. He had hoped to spend a lot more time with her. Carlson didn't have many close friends; though he got along well with others, he just didn't trust many people. A problem that had gotten much worse after Mathews.

He let out a yawn. Mathews was the reason he was getting a lot less sleep. He had put the issue behind him, until his voice surfaced on those records. Now the nightmares had come back. He tried to keep them under control. He didn't want to return to the shrink.

Mathews was a traitor and he had the connections of the Society at his disposal. Carlson knew he was on one of those shuttles that got away.

Mathews would do something like that.

What Carlson hadn't expected was for him to be so cunning. He managed to not only anticipate that the Australia would be listening in to the transmissions, but to also know they wouldn't fall for it and he needed to escape. And now he was with the Borvians. That bothered Carlson more than knowing he was with the Martians.

Carlson let out another yawn. He decided he would nap on Janice's couch until she got back. He got up and went to the bedroom.

He opened the door to see a naked woman's ass up in the air. Her head buried into Janice, who was spread eagle naked on the bed. Janice shrieked and then the other person spun around. It was Francesca.

"Oh, shit." Carlson turned to leave; only now realizing he had been staring at both of them. "Sorry."

As he got to the front door, Janice called out for him.

"Hold on, Mike." She was still putting on her robe.

Carlson had seen glimpses of Janice's naked body before; she rarely closed her door when she changed around him. But he had never seen it in this way, fully naked and clearly aroused. He felt a little uncomfortable, mostly because of his own arousal.

"Sorry, I didn't think you were here. I was just going to take a nap and wait for you," Carlson stammered. "So, you and Francesca are going well I see?"

"Yeah, we've only just started getting serious though," Janice said. "I haven't had the time to tell you."

"Yeah, not a lot of time for me lately." Carlson bit his tongue.

"What?" Janice didn't sound mad, just confused.

"Never mind, Janice. I'll talk with you later, now isn't the best time." Carlson faked a smile.

"Okay, Mike."

* * *

"The Prime Minister was very pleased with your report." Admiral Kelly was on the Captain's video screen.

"I wish we'd gotten Mathews too." Serenity turned away.

"You don't know that he wasn't on there. Those shuttles could have had any number of items or people on them." Kelly paused. "I know Mathews is a problem for you personally, but to the Earth Navy, and the Prime Minister, the Phobos was the issue."

"We both know that's bullshit." Serenity said, referring to the second half of the Admiral's statement. "Mathews is the real issue for all four governments. I won't deny I have a personal problem with that man, but don't fool yourself into believing he isn't a danger to everyone."

"You may think so, and you may be right, but there are bigger issues here," Kelly said. "It may not seem like it to you, but the war is in full swing out here. Naval skirmishes have been happening almost every time an Earth and Martian ship meet. We've even found a few Borvian ships here and there.

"So far, it has been nothing major. We had one big offensive that took out several Martian surveillance satellites and they retaliated with an attack on one of our remote research stations." Kelly took in a long breath before exhaling slowly. "I don't think the civility of it will last much longer. Anyway, you have the most conflict experience so we need you here."

Serenity nodded. Conflict experience. She almost laughed at that. Not so long ago, she was the youngest Captain and didn't know much of anything. Now she had lost a few naval skirmishes, failed to prevent a war, and destroyed a Martian warship far later than she should have. They called that "conflict experience".

* * *

Janice came back into the bedroom and closed the door. Francesca was laid out on the bed, still covered by the blankets. She sat up and kissed Janice. Janice cut the kiss short.

"What's wrong?"

"I think Mike is mad at me."

"What? Because of us?" Willard said, "I didn't think of Mike as being like that."

"No, no. I don't think he cares one way or the other if I date a man or a woman." Janice lay back on the bed. "I think I've been ignoring him a bit. I've been spending every free moment with you."

"Maybe he is jealous of me."

"No, he is not interested in me that way." Janice wasn't going to tell Francesca why she was so certain. She didn't know about Serenity and Mike's affair, and Janice wasn't going to say anything.

Janice would have loved for a chance to date Mike. He was funny, kind, and a joy to be around. She had even found herself a bit more attracted to him once she got to know him more. But, the Captain was always in his eyes, and Janice couldn't bear to come between them. What kind of friend would she be then?

She hadn't been much of a friend for him now. And with Mathews resurfacing out of the blue, Mike probably needed a friend.

She let out a sigh. "I don't think I've been much of a friend to him recently."

"So, spend some time with him." Francesca leaned up on one elbow to look at Janice. "You need your friends too."

"I suppose you're right."

"Then, you can hook him up with someone and he won't mind so much," Willard laughed.

"I don't think Mike would settle for something that easy."

Chapter 42

There it was. Home. Serenity had seen so little of Earth. It was nice to gaze at its beauty from the docks. The conference room always had the best windows on the ship.

There wasn't a repair dock empty. Serenity had never seen the docks full before. She was just happy they had only a few minor repairs.

The biggest thing for her was her crew compliments. For the first time since she had been in command, the Australia was getting a full crew. She knew that meant a difficult operation for her.

"Full crew, Mike," Serenity said.

"With a shorthanded Navy, that is impressive," Carlson said from the entrance. "I'd be more worried about the Admiral coming to see you in person."

A full crew and the Admiral giving her orders in person was really what made Serenity so nervous. She was about to comment on that when the door opened.

Commander Zimmerman came in; a very short man with a bald head was with him. He had to be the new Lieutenant Commander. He was at least two inches shorter than Serenity.

"Captain, this is Lieutenant Commander Polack," Zimmerman gestured to him.

"Nice to meet you, Ma'am." Polack stuck out his hand. "I'm very honored to be assigned to your ship. I couldn't believe it when they told me I would be serving under *the* Captain Serenity."

Serenity shook his hand. "I'm hardly someone to idolize; just doing my job."

"Well, you are certainly the talk of the Navy. When news came in that your ship had destroyed the Phobos, it was something else." Polack sounded like a kid meeting a sports star. "And if you think the Navy knows your name, the public loves you too. When I told my brother that I was being assigned to the Australia, why he—"

Serenity put up her hand. "Perhaps another time we can chat. For now, let's prepare for the Admiral's arrival."

As if on cue, the door opened again. Kelly walked in with two Security Forces officers behind her. Everyone in the room stood at attention.

"At ease, sit down," Kelly said, already taking a seat. "The mission I have for you is Top Secret. Except for you, no one else will be notified of this mission for three days.

"I am forming a large fleet, which you will be in command of. Our mission will be just part of an operation involving all four branches of the military." Kelly handed over a chip to Serenity. "These are the documents you will need for Operation Reunion. The whole operation rides on your success."

Serenity took the chip. There was no way she was ready to handle an entire fleet in which every other branch was counting on her success.

"The first phase involves all seven warships, including the soon to be completed E.S.S. Africa." The Admiral continued. "Your job will be to destroy all the ships defending Mars, or at least get them cleared out. The close defenses of Mars are limited; most of their more powerful ships are away from the planet.

"Once that is done, transport ships and the aircraft carriers will arrive. You will assist in defending those ships while the Army and Air Force touch down on Mars. Once they are in place and have a base staged and secure, more ships will be arriving.

"There are issues with this, of course. We have a few Zercowan ships in the area, but they will only be providing defense to our borders. The Borvians will likely respond swiftly, but that will give us a month at least. The Army plans to be in good control of things by then. Of course, taking complete control of Mars will take more time. My hope is that I can convince the Zercowans we control Martian space and get them to move in and assist before the Borvians arrive."

"I wish I shared your confidence," Serenity said.

Chapter 43

"**O**ur last shore leave together didn't end well. We got lucky and dodged a bullet," Carlson said.

Serenity had wanted Carlson to come down to the surface and spend some time with her. She had somehow kept Commander Zimmerman from talking. Carlson wasn't going to ask, he might not want to know. But the fact remained he wasn't going to take the chance.

"Then come down to the surface as my protection crew," Serenity protested.

"And how is that fair to Janice?" Carlson shook his head. "To make her spend her shore leave with us, and as a third wheel?"

Serenity turned away from him and stared out the window of her office. "This isn't working out well."

Carlson's heart sank. He had been starting to feel the same way. They didn't see each outside of work. And now her time was spent either making rounds or on the bridge.

He wanted to go back to the night shift but Major Nelson wouldn't allow it. Serenity had no justifiable reason to interfere, either. Carlson could see the millions of reasons for Serenity to end this relationship.

"The Navy isn't what it used to be, Mike," Serenity continued. "I supposed I should have known war was a possibility, but it wasn't the Navy I signed up for. I certainly didn't sign up to be some hero. I just wanted to serve my planet. And now they are about to fight a war that was orchestrated by a madman and this Society."

"You tried your best to prevent this, but it is larger than all of us ever thought." Carlson walked over to her, putting his hand on her shoulder. "It was something you never could have stopped."

"So the planet I love is going to engage in a false war." Serenity looked at him. "And they have the nerve to tell me I can't love who I want to."

"You should worry about the battle ahead, not about us." Carlson hoped he wasn't talking her into ending their secret relationship. "Maybe when things calm down, I'll put in for a patrol post on the planet."

"And I'll see you a few months out of the year, if we're lucky." Serenity went back to staring out the window. "Like I said, this isn't the Navy I signed up with. Maybe I'll get out as soon as they'll let me."

Carlson moved to see her face. She didn't appear sincere. Carlson realized she had been talking herself into this for some time. He smiled at her, she didn't smile back.

"That's not what you want." Carlson saw her face change. "At least not completely."

"As far as the Navy goes, I don't know what I want. I love commanding a ship of my own, it's what I've wanted to do for so long. But, having a psychopath like Mathews after me and this war..." Serenity paused. "And if there is one thing I love more than command, it's you."

"Now isn't the time to be thinking of ending your career." Carlson put his hands on her shoulders and made eye contact. "I love you too. But right now there are seven warships counting on you to lead them. The Admiral won't let you out anytime soon."

"It's just so weird to see you every day, and still miss you so much."

* * *

"I think she wants to end her Naval Career." Carlson was watching the waters of Niagara Falls in the distance. Its roar was much softer at this distance, making it easier to talk to Janice, but its beauty was still just as magnificent. "If she does that for me, I don't know how I can live with myself."

Janice sat back on the bench. Carlson glanced over at her. "Mike, I don't know what to say. If she wants to get out, you can't stop her. It doesn't sound like it's just about you, either."

"I know. I just think it is for the wrong reasons."

"And you told her, right?"

"Yeah."

"Well, that's all you can do." Janice patted Carlson on the knee. "After that, the choice is hers to make. I think she just needs to have something push her one way or the other."

Carlson knew Janice was right and was glad she was available to come to the surface with him. "I'm not keeping you from Francesca, am I?"

"No," Janice said. "It is good to spend some time with you again."

Carlson stood up. He took in the view one more time. "Come on, let's go enjoy the rest of the day."

Chapter 44

Serenity didn't mind the moment of silence. It gave her time to think, something she hadn't had much time for when the fleet was forming. The last hour, while the ships all performed a final check, was a welcoming calm before the inevitable storm.

She could almost see the imaginary line between Earth and Martian space in the distance ahead of them. There wouldn't be a direct flight, but she still didn't like how close they were. The fleet was going to make a lot of maneuvers, but it still seemed they would lose the element of surprise being so close. But the flight plan was orchestrated by Naval Command. Supposedly they knew what they were doing.

Serenity walked back out to the bridge. She took her seat and surveyed the bridge one more time.

"Is the fleet ready to go?" Serenity asked

"All ships are reporting in and ready," Willard said.

"We have a day's flight in front of us." Serenity keyed in some coordinates to her console. She and one other Captain, she didn't know which one, knew these coordinates. The first was in a remote area of Martian space. "Proceed to this area, three-quarter speed."

* * *

Mike was in the elevator with Janice. They had finished their shift and were headed down to the bar to relax before calling it an early night. They'd be arriving at their last checkpoint by morning. From there they would be waiting for word to go.

"No one knows these checkpoints?" Janice said.

"Nope."

Janice heard something on her radio. She turned it up.

"Australia Control to all Officers, shots fired in main engineering, officer down. All available officers respond."

* * *

Serenity was happy to be near the first checkpoint. It wouldn't be long and they could head out of Martian Space. So far, it seemed, the Martians hadn't detected them.

"Captain," Nelson said hesitantly.

"Yes, Major?"

"We've got a situation in main engineering," Nelson said.

"That isn't what I want to hear right now." Serenity turned around to face him. "What is it?"

"Shots fired. We have officers there, but there are hostages."

"We've stopped, Captain," Willard said. "The engines won't respond to my commands."

"They've been cut off from engineering, emergency stop," Morgan said.

"Override it, Lieutenant." Annoyance came from her voice. "We're in the middle of Martian Space, I don't need this now."

"I can't override it from here. I'd have to go down there."

"Then get down there!" Serenity barked. "Major, I want that engineering section back by the time Morgan gets down there."

* * *

Carlson found the Lieutenant in charge of the scene. She was a short woman reading over her tablet while officers and sergeants told her what was going on.

"Samson is still in there, he was shot when he responded to the disturbance call," a sergeant said.

"What about Harding?" the Lieutenant said.

"Still in there too; last I heard, she was concealed rather well."

"So what is the purpose of this? Any reason for the hostages?"

"Obviously they wanted to stop the ship, that's all we know."

"What kind of condition is Samson in?" Carlson interrupted. He got a cold look from the Lieutenant.

"I'd say critical, if he hasn't died already." The sergeant replied.

"We'd better get in there then," Carlson said, more to Janice than anyone else. Janice nodded at him.

"Now hold on, Corporal," the Lieutenant said. "I've got BET on the way."

"We're not going to let that officer die while we wait. We can at least go in there and get 'em out," Janice said.

"I won't allow it."

"Well then write me up when we get back." Carlson turned down the hall to the engineering area's entrance. "Just have a medical team ready."

Carlson made his way down the hall, around one corner and then stopped at the next hallway. He pulled his L-pistol and looked back at Janice. She did the same, then nodded.

Carlson rounded the corner carefully, his weapon aimed down the hall. The massive engineering door was closed, nevertheless, he approached it carefully.

He stopped at the side of the door, Janice went to the other side.

"If I remember correctly, there is a large half-wall about ten feet from this door." Carlson took a breath. "Stay low. I'll cover you to the wall, and then you cover me."

"Got it." Janice keyed in her override code. "Ready?"

Carlson nodded. As soon as the door opened, laser fire flew out. Carlson took a quick peek and saw someone firing at them over a large console. Carlson fired back.

Janice rushed in low and stopped with her back against the wall. The suspect stopped firing. Carlson waited for Janice to get up and ready. Then he made a run for it. No one fired a shot. He stopped and stayed crouched behind the wall. Janice stayed down.

"What did you see?"

"The downed officer is by a large machine of some type, to the left between here and the console the suspect was at," Janice said. "Our suspect ran farther back. Still can't tell if she is alone or not. Medium skin, my height, in a Navy uniform. I lost her behind some more equipment."

"Okay. I'll go to the officer. You cover me." Carlson took a breath. "I'll get him and drag him back here. Then we get out of here and let BET clean the rest up."

"Sounds like a plan."

Carlson checked his battery clip, thumbed the release, letting it fall to the floor. At the same time, he took another from his belt and slapped it in.

"Ready?"

Janice nodded. Carlson went to the end of the wall and peered around the corner. He caught sight of Samson. He wasn't moving much, but Carlson could see a small rise and fall in his chest.

He turned and saw Janice, who then popped over the wall. She made a run for the console the shooter had been at. From there, she could better cover Carlson. When she got there, Carlson ran full speed to the equipment. He slid in behind the machine next to Samson.

"Samson, talk to me. How you doing?"

"I'm weak and tired." The pain was obvious in his voice.

Samson was hit in the stomach. There wasn't a large amount of blood, but Carlson was no doctor, either.

"I'm going to drag you out of here. Just stay awake."

Carlson heard a shot, followed by a sharp sting in his right leg. He started to spin around.

"Drop the gun," a woman said softly but firmly.

Carlson tossed it on the floor. He turned around slowly. He saw the woman Janice described checking around the equipment. She came out in the open walking slowly toward him. Carlson glanced at his leg, he saw no blood, but it still stung.

"This isn't going to work out for you." Carlson tried to hide his fear.

The woman fired a single shot. Carlson rolled to the side, but the bolt still caught him in the left side of his stomach. Carlson clutched it and grunted in pain. He checked the wound; not a lot of blood, which was good.

"In about ten or fifteen minutes, it won't matter to me." The girl's smile was sinister, it froze Carlson in place. "Carlson? Could I be so lucky? Killing you should be an extra bonus."

She pointed her weapon at Carlson's head. Carlson's vision blurred from the pain. He started to think about pleading for his life, but words escaped him. Carlson closed his eyes and heard a single shot.

Slowly, he opened his eyes again; he saw Janice running over. The woman lay slumped on the floor, blood oozing from her head. Janice kicked the gun away from her and then fell to Carlson's side.

"Mike, where are you hit?" Janice keyed her radio. "Get those damn medics in here. The suspect is down."

* * *

Serenity drummed her fingers on the arm of her chair. The whole situation was slowing things down. She didn't like anything about this. It was too much of a coincidence.

She'd put money on the fact that the shooter was one of their new crew members. There were still leaks to be solved in the Navy.

"Captain, the situation is resolved. The suspect was killed. Another Security Forces officer was..." Zimmerman stopped reading the screen.

He walked over to Serenity and sat next to her.

"What is it, Commander?"

He leaned in and spoke in a whisper so only Serenity could hear. "Mike was shot. They don't know his condition."

Serenity immediately felt overwhelming panic. She swallowed the growing lump in her throat. She didn't speak, because she knew that would make her cry. She keyed in the coordinates for the next checkpoint, then looked at Zimmerman.

"Ensign, as soon as the engines respond, head to the provided coordinates," Zimmerman ordered. He leaned in to the Captain. "Go down there. I'll cover for you."

Serenity nodded and stood up. She walked as fast as she could off the bridge. As soon as she entered the elevator, she collapsed into a ball on the floor and wept.

* * *

Serenity looked over Mike; he was asleep now. Janice stood next to her. The Doctor told her it was just a flesh wound in his abdomen and a burn in his leg. It still pained her to watch him lying there.

"I know he'll be fine, but I can't help worrying," Serenity said.

"I'd be worried if you weren't," Janice said. "He was lucky, that is for sure."

"I want to stay with him."

"This mission is important," Janice said. "Shouldn't you be on the bridge?"

"The hell with this damned mission, Janice." Serenity couldn't care less. "Besides, we're on the way to the next point."

"Mike mentioned you might want to get out of the Navy. You're not happy?"

"I don't know. But all of this? A fake war, all these attacks on my ship. Mike getting hurt." Serenity took a breath, and spoke quietly. "Hiding the fact that I love that man. It is all getting to be too much."

"Don't leave on account of him. It is tearing him apart that you might leave the Navy for him." Janice paused. "Do it for yourself, if you must. But I think you are stressed and scared right now. This is hardly the time to be making these choices."

Carlson stirred a bit in his bed, then slowly opened his eyes. His face cringed a bit, then his eyes met Serenity's. She leaned in and whispered to him.

"You gave me quite the scare."

"I'm okay. It's nothing that will keep me down for more than a little bit. I'll be back at it before we start our mission."

Serenity smiled at him. She wanted to kiss him, but that wasn't possible. She cursed having to second guess all her natural moves.

"Don't rush it," Serenity said. She mouthed out the words *I love you.*

"As do I," Carlson said.

Chapter 45

Carlson did rush through his healing. He faked recovery well enough to fool Doctor Farven. He was finishing the last of his tests, trying not to show the pain each downward twist caused his abdomen. He finished that last twist and stood upright.

"What do you think, doctor?" Carlson asked.

Farven said nothing. He just entered some notes into his tablet and walked away. He came back moments later and conducted all the routine checks doctors do.

Farven waited until he had the tongue depressor in Carlson's mouth before he spoke again. "Don't think I don't know what you are doing here, Mike."

Carlson made a garbled reply that sounded more like the mating call of a wild beast. Farven put up a finger signaling Carlson to keep quiet.

"I won't make a big deal about it. I'll return you to duty, but you had better come back here should it get any worse." Farven waited for Carlson to nod before he removed the depressor. He produced a bottle of pills. "These are pain killers, not very strong ones, but they will keep those pains at bay without affecting your judgment."

Carlson took the bottle. "Thank you."

* * *

Serenity wasn't able to sleep all night. She checked her watch. Three hours until they arrived at the last checkpoint and now she was starting to feel nervous. It was one of the few times she knew for sure she was about to be in a major naval conflict. She didn't like knowing ahead of time.

She found herself trying to plan for the all the "what ifs" she could imagine. She knew damn well she couldn't plan for everything. She just couldn't help thinking of the worse case scenarios. She wondered if that made her a pessimist.

Once they arrived, they just needed the go ahead from Naval Command. For all she knew they could find something out that canceled the whole operation. She'd feel better if they did. She wasn't convinced that taking control over Mars was the right answer.

She got out of bed and went to get her uniform. There was no sense in trying to sleep any longer.

Chapter 46

Serenity put the fleet to General Quarters as soon as they arrived at the last checkpoint. She didn't know what to expect when she got there. Since the attack on engineering she expected the Martians were aware of their planned attack.

She was relieved when no one was waiting for them. Most of the crew should be unaware of what they were doing. With the exception of the Captains, no one was made aware of the mission.

"Captain, I have a message for your eyes only," Willard said.

Serenity saw the message come up on her screen.

Christina,

We received your RSVP for the reunion. We are so glad you could make it. The other guests will be coming too. We can't wait to see you there.

That was the go ahead message. Serenity took a breath.

"Ensign, have the fleet form up into a large V. Put us toward the rear," Serenity stated. "Sanchez, all cannons ready."

There was no turning back now, except in retreat. Earth was about to escalate this unpleasant conflict to a full scale war. Serenity stood up. She glanced at Carlson, he gave her a confident nod.

"The fleet is in position," Willard said.

"Proceed to Mars, full speed," Serenity said. Willard looked back at her. "Ensign, is there a problem?"

"No, Ma'am."

From their current location Serenity had five minutes until they arrived. Suddenly her uncertainty faded. She felt right standing there leading the charge.

She could see on the radar they were arriving now. "Enemy contacts?"

"Seven stations, six appear to be space docks. All of them have ships in for repairs. Five other ship contacts, moving on us now," Willard said.

"Have the Antarctica and the North America take out those docks quickly. I don't want those ships leaving them. The Africa, South America and Asia need to intercept those enemy ships. The Europe will follow us on the main station."

"The Martian's are transmitting," Willard said.

"Unless it is surrender, ignore it," Serenity said. "Target the station's bridge. Keep the ship orientated so that the most cannons can fire on them."

Serenity felt the rattle of the laser fire hitting the ship. She widened her stance for the possibility of jolts.

"Only minor damages, Captain," Morgan said. "Willard is keeping the hits spaced out."

"The Europe is taking more of the hits," Willard said. "The North America reports that the space docks are destroyed. A Warship managed to get out of the docks, they are dealing with it now."

"Make sure they finish the job on those damaged ships," Serenity said.

"Captain, the station's bridge is failing," Sanchez reported. "Should we finish the station off?"

"Yes. Circular firing passes."

Serenity couldn't believe it was going so well. She was even starting to worry about it. It really seemed they were completely off guard.

"There isn't much left of the docks," Willard said. "The Asia reports they are having some trouble, they took a hit to their life support system."

A huge jolt rattled the ship. Serenity stumbled a bit. The bolt must have hit close to the bridge.

"Have the North America and Antarctica assist them."

"The station is falling apart," Sanchez said.

"Move us toward the remaining Martian vessels."

"Captain, they're falling apart too," Willard said.

Serenity sat down. She typed out a message to Naval command giving them the go ahead for the second fleet. She sent it.

"Naval Command says the guests are on the way," Willard replied. "They also report that the Martians have called for all ships."

"Have the fleet fall back into formation," Serenity said.

"Captain, two Martian ships are arriving. Two warships and a massive Borvian vessel," Willard said.

"Captain, according to the Zercowan records that is a Borvian qualer. A very powerful ship and it has to be about twice as large as us. I'm reading more about it. There aren't many of them in the Borvian fleet,"

Zimmerman said.

"The Europe and Africa will follow us in to attack that ship," Serenity said. "Have the others take care of the Martian warships."

"Captain, the qualer has launched some type of fighter I haven't seen before," Willard said.

"That's not a fighter," Zimmerman called out. "That is some type of projectile weapon. Don't let it hit the ship, it's highly explosive."

"Sanchez, you heard the Commander. Taking those out is first priority."

Serenity looked on radar as she saw the fighter craft slowly disappearing from the radar. She glanced out a bridge window to see a projectile hit the side of the Antarctica. The explosion pushed them right into the South America. She turned back to the radar and watched the two warships vanish from the system.

"Captain, the Antarctica and the South America are virtually destroyed—the collision was too strong. They lost life support," Willard said.

"All ships have lost their fighters," Sanchez said. "The other warships are having trouble with those projectiles, they are coming out at an alarming rate. Our targeting systems seem to be keeping up, barely."

"Thank God for those Zercowan upgrades," Serenity said.

There was a loud explosion and the ship shook violently, sending everyone from their seats. Serenity tumbled to the floor.

"Captain, we've lost the Asia," Willard said as she climbed back to her station. "The Europe reports engine failures."

Three working warships left. Serenity started to panic, but she took a breath. "What about them?"

"Minimal damage on the qualer. We're doing what we can just to keep those projectiles away. The Martian warships are in bad shape. One is starting to fall apart. The other is making a strong show. The North America is in bad shape, but still fighting."

"Notify Naval Command, I recommend a full retreat," Serenity said.

"Captain, the last of the Martian warships is destroyed." Willard said. "Naval Command denies retreat."

Another projectile exploded. The bridge shook even more violently and Serenity caught her arm on a console as she fell. She shouted from the pain of it, but stood up quickly. She checked her injury, it didn't appear broken. Zimmerman rushed over to her.

"I'm fine," Serenity said. "Those projectiles are way too close. How many of those damn things *are* there?"

"The typical compliment is fifty," Zimmerman said. "They've fired at least seventy."

"Seventy-eight," Sanchez stated. "Now Eighty. Two heading for the North America."

Serenity heard the cannons fire. She could see from the small window two large explosions on the North America. They missed.

They were now being hit with cannon fire. Serenity said a quick prayer thanking the fact that it seemed the qualer was out of these projectiles. Now the ship's cannons could focus on it.

"The Europe has engines online again," Morgan said.

So she had the Europe, the Africa, and her ship. "Damage reports?"

Serenity wasn't going to blindly follow a no retreat order. She would run if it came down to it. There was a creak in the floor underneath her. Then suddenly the floor shifted to the back left of the bridge. Serenity shifted her stance avoiding falling over. She sat down in her seat.

"One of our bridge supports gave out," Morgan said.

"The Borvian ship is turning to run." Willard sounded more than relieved.

"They don't have aft weapons. This is our best chance to destroy that ship. Probably the only one within months of here," Zimmerman said.

"Sanchez, keep firing," Serenity said.

With the concentrated firepower of three warships on the aft of the qualer, they were causing heavy damage. It was very slow and didn't make it far before it was destroyed.

"Move us to a high orbit of Mars," Serenity said. "Damage?"

"Hull damage on seventy percent of the ship, though most of it is not bad. Only three minor breaches. Sixty percent of the cannons are malfunctioning and we have lost a power plant."

Serenity stood up. The bottom of the door to her office was about chest level now. She almost laughed at the sight, but she thought it was inappropriate.

She reached up and opened the door, then pulled herself up into the room. Her arm protested the entire time, her hip hurt more. She got into her office. Carlson and Janice climbed in after her.

Janice closed the door. Serenity undid her pants pulling them down to reveal the large scar on her hip. There didn't appear to be any new injury. She looked over her arm. It was bruised from elbow to wrist. She sent a transmission for a medical crew.

"I think it looks worse than it is," Serenity said to Mike. "I still have all the function of my hand and arm."

"What about your hip?"

"It's fine," Serenity lied. She forced a weak grin at him. "As good as your stomach."

She contacted Naval Command, sending them the full report. Almost instantly, Admiral Kelly was on the line.

"Three ships left," Kelly said.

"And we are all in bad shape," Serenity said. "One more attack before the fleet arrives and we are toast."

The medical crew came in. Serenity waved them over. They began examining her arm, while she listened to what the Admiral had to say.

"Then let us hope no other ships arrive," Kelly said. "We've intercepted and destroyed a number of ships attempting to arrive at Mars. The best we can tell, the next ship that could arrive won't be for three hours. The other guests should be there by then."

"Good."

"The other thing we just discovered, another qualer in the area. Problem is, we don't know for sure where it is."

Serenity slumped on her desk. "That isn't what I need to hear."

"But it is the truth." The transmission ended.

* * *

"Captain, that other qualer is on radar." Willard's voice reflected panic. "They are moving on our position."

"When will the other fleet be here?" Zimmerman asked.

"Any minute now, I hope," Serenity said. "Hold position, let's see what she does when the fleet arrives."

"The destroyers are arriving now," Willard said. "The qualer is holding position."

"Just holding?"

Willard nodded her head.

That was odd. She had only ever seen the Borvians attack, or run. She felt the ache in her hip and sat back down.

"The Carriers and transports have arrived," Willard said.

"Move us in a defensive position to cover the fleet's arrival to the planet. Keep us between the qualer and the arriving fleet."

Serenity watched the radar, it didn't move. The seconds seemed to last forever, giving way to minutes that seemed to last for hours. Serenity didn't realize she was on the edge of her seat.

"Captain." Willard's voice made Serenity jump. "The Fighters are making their way into the Martian atmosphere."

Serenity sat back in her seat.

"Nervous, Captain?" Zimmerman asked just loud enough to be heard.

"I wonder what that ship is waiting for." Serenity paused. "This is out of character for Borvian tactics."

"Maybe they are questioning their involvement, or they are waiting for another fleet." Zimmerman shook his head. "The Borvians have been difficult for me to understand."

"Captain, the transports have touched down," Willard said. "The Borvians still haven't moved. Naval Command says to hold for orders."

Chapter 47

Serenity read over the orders again. They were one of the most foolish orders she had read. The Admiral wanted her to take a shuttle to one of the Carriers, the Pacific, for a meeting between fleet heads and Naval Command.

She sent a transmission back to the Admiral.

When the Admiral's face came up, she appeared angry. "I'm sorry, Admiral, but these orders seem out of place."

"Do you have a problem with them?" Admiral Kelly's anger sounded more the work of stress than Serenity.

"I just don't understand why? I mean, the Borvian ship is right out there. To take—"

The Admiral raised her hand. "I don't see what the Borvians have to do with this. This isn't the time for selfish pride, this is a Naval operation and I feel this is best."

Serenity paused. "If I refuse?"

"Serenity, don't get foolish. We are all under a lot of stress." The Admiral paused. When she got no response from Serenity she spoke again. "If you refuse, I will have you arrested and turn command over to Zimmerman."

"Yes, Ma'am." Serenity ended the transmission.

* * *

Serenity didn't know why she followed the Admiral's orders; it went against all her logic. But, she knew Kelly and she knew there must be a reason for this. Something that couldn't be said over transmissions.

She insisted Mike and Janice come with her. They were exhausted sitting next to her on the shuttle, but she felt better that they were there.

She glanced out the window. The Carrier was getting farther away. She began to panic. *Damn it, these orders were fishy.* She leaned into Mike and whispered. "We're heading away from the Pacific."

Carlson stood up. Janice did too. He pulled his weapon and started to walk up to the Cockpit. Just then the cockpit door slammed down.

"Shit," he cursed. "Well, here is the trap you were worried about."

Janice fidgeted with a console. "I can get up radar, but no communications. The Australia is moving to intercept with the other warships. We're headed for the qualer."

Serenity saw an uncountable volley of the projectiles launching from the Borvian ship. "They'll be destroyed."

"What's that smell?" Carlson asked.

Serenity's eyes got heavy. She watched Janice slump to the floor. Carlson started to run to her before he fell over. Then Serenity couldn't keep her eyes open any longer.

* * *

"Commander, the shuttle has docked with the qualer," Willard said.

"God damn it, Admiral." Zimmerman paused. "They have Christina."

"What the hell was she doing on that damn shuttle anyway?" Kelly said.

"You ordered her to go to the Pacific for a meeting with Naval command." Zimmerman pointed at the Admiral. "And now you've ordered me to keep from saving her."

"Watch it, Commander," Kelly said. "I never gave those orders. I sent instructions for her to turn over fleet operations to the Pacific. Then have the three warships return home for repairs. There was never any mention of leaving the ship."

Zimmerman thought for a moment. "I can still save her."

"Commander, I have three warships left. I am not losing them. Return to Earth for repairs as ordered."

"You're just going to leave her with them?"

"There is no other choice at this point. I'll look into the matter when you return."

"They'll be dead by then!"

"Those are your orders, Commander."

The transmission ended. Willard looked back at the Commander. "Sir?"

"Send the Europe and Africa on their way." Zimmerman watched the qualer as it got farther away. "Make a transmission to the Zercowans, maybe their ships in our space will help."

Zimmerman turned to Major Nelson. He was waiting to have to fight him on this.

"I'm in agreement with you, Commander," Nelson said. "She wouldn't leave any of us behind."

Chapter 48

Mike shook his head as if it would somehow clear the fog in his mind. He wasn't dead, but he still hadn't decided if that was a good thing. He was in a cell, clearly on the Borvian ship. How long had he been here? It felt like he just passed out.

He walked over to the barred doors. "Janice!" He called out. The name bounced off the walls.

Nothing.

"Christina!"

Still nothing.

Carlson went back to the cement platform and sat down. He took stock of what was in the room. A hole in the floor, just small enough to be a toilet, and nothing else.

He checked his uniform. His duty belt was gone, so was everything in his pockets, except for three of the pain pills the Doctor had given him.

There had to be a reason he was still alive. Carlson didn't know what it could be, but there had to be some advantage for him in that.

Two Borvians walked up to his cell. "You, come with us."

Mike stood up. He almost made a smart ass comment, but decided he had better get an idea of his situation first. He didn't see anyone in any of the other cells as they walked along the cell block. They left the room and continued down the ship's corridors.

They were very different than those of the Australia. There weren't any of the finishes that he had seen on other ships. All pipes and metal structure were visible. It was put together for the purpose of war, all luxuries spared.

Carlson tried to remember his path, but after several minutes he realized they were purposely leading him in circles so he couldn't remember where he came from. Carlson gave up and tried to take stock of how many Borvian's he saw. That proved impossible too. Though he did notice most of them were not armed.

They finally stopped at a door. The door opened and they threw Mike in. The door closed behind him. Two other armed Borvians stood by a fireplace that was in a sunken sitting area. There was a table near the back couch with several bottles of liquid. Based on the style of them, Carlson guessed it was liquor. Clearly, no expense was spared for this one room.

A large desk stood in front of him, a large chair sat empty. Carlson started to walk toward it, when someone cleared their throat. Carlson turned to see Roger standing there grinning at him.

"Mike, it has been far too long," Mathews said.

"I knew you slithered away from the Phobos, but working for the Borvians?" Carlson shook his head.

Mathews made his way to the desk. "Mike, look at this. Naval Commanders are practically gods in their eyes." He gestured around the admittedly grand room. "But, I certainly don't work for them. I don't work for anyone."

"Not even the Society?" Carlson made eye contact, despite the fact that he wanted to turn away.

"Work for them? No," Mathews said. "I practically run them. I've orchestrated the biggest weapons trade and key Society members now work for me. This little war is going to make me very rich. Now that they have an Earth Army on their planet, the Martians will be more than willing to pay a lot of money for the weapons we've got."

"Why, Roger? We were partners." Carlson turned away. He was too disgusted by the man he saw. "You were my best friend."

When Carlson looked back, Mathews had turned his back to him. "That's the only reason you're not dead yet. I've been ripping my hair out trying to stop you and that new partner of yours. You've been a problem for me since the beginning."

"That's just it. You threw away your career, your friendships, for this Society. It makes no sense," Carlson said. "But what has bothered me even more is, why the Captain?"

"The Society asked me to do it," Roger said simply. "They paid well for it. I'm afraid she simply interfered far too much in their smuggling rings. They contacted me right after she took down their biggest supply ship. It took a few weeks to find a way to get to her without you around."

Was it that simple? Was that really all that this was about? Carlson couldn't believe that. "So you betrayed your planet, your oath, and the Captain for money."

"Ah, yes. You always did have a special place for the Captain in your heart." Mathews shook his head. "You've thrown away your life protecting someone you love. Someone who will never know you love them. You are wasting your life, your love and your career on that woman. She really isn't worth it."

Carlson couldn't suppress the rage anymore. "You won't win."

"You've been really good at stopping me. I'll give you that. But, I've already won."

"That seems to be undetermined at this point," Carlson said through his clenched jaw.

Mathews shook his head. "I had really hoped you might see the logic in this. Or at least the dollar signs."

"I'm not corruptible, Roger."

"Everyone is corruptible; it's just the price that varies." Mathews stood up.

Carlson watched Mathews walk down to the seating area and say a few words to the guards. Carlson walked up to the couches. The guards pointed their weapons at him. He stopped.

"So I suppose there is no convincing you," Mathews said. "I'll be honest, I don't have the heart to make you watch Serenity die."

Carlson felt weak. Then he suddenly realized Serenity was still alive. He felt his strength return at the hope he could get out of this.

Carlson gestured to the almost full bottle on the table. "A last drink, maybe? Then you can kill me."

Mathews nodded. "Rum was always your favorite."

Mike took a very small swig from the bottle before flinging it straight into the fire. The liquor spraying over the Borvians as it flew past them. The bottle splashed into the flames, sending a fireball on to the Borvian guards.

In the same instant Carlson dived on Mathews, who quickly kicked him square in the abdomen. Carlson crumpled over in pain. As he struggled to get up, Mathews hit Carlson square in the jaw knocking him over.

"You are something else, Mike." Mathews kicked him in the stomach again.

Carlson rolled over. He came face to face with a Borvian weapon lying on the ground. He rolled again to conceal it. He heard the door open again.

"Kill him," Mathews yelled.

Carlson spun over ignoring the screaming pain in his stomach as he managed to fire two shots killing the guards who had entered. He spun toward Roger, and fired as Mathews ran out another door. The shot missed wide.

Carlson struggled to his feet. He fumbled his way to Mathew's desk. Reaching in the pocket for the pain pills, he swallowed two. The console was hard for Carlson to operate, but the text was in English.

Janice was supposed to be four decks down in the cells. Serenity was a deck above in a room of some type. Carlson tried his best to memorize the map. There would be a lot of guards around Serenity if this report was right. He would need Janice's help.

Carlson made his way to the door that he'd come in. It suddenly opened and he quickly shot the two guards who entered. He peered around the corner.

Carlson ran down the clear hall and took a left. Two more guards shot at him. Then a blaring sound came over the ship's speakers followed by a Borvian message. Carlson was able to kill the other two during the distraction.

* * *

"There is definitely laser fire on the ship," Morgan said.

"The Captain?" Zimmerman let a little hope slip from his voice.

"There is no way to know."

"Nelson, you have a BET team ready?"

He nodded. "We've got to stop them."

"Three Zercowan ships have arrived," Willard said.

"Good, move us to engage. We do not destroy that ship until we know Serenity is safe."

* * *

Carlson walked down the cell blocks slowly. His weapon out and ready. He saw a guard outside one cell. He fired once, hitting the guard in the head.

Carlson heard someone. He stopped and peeked into a supply room. A Borvian stood there pointing a gun at Janice.

"Take off your clothes," the guard said.

Carlson flung the door open and fired three times into the guard's back. Janice jumped up and took the guard's gun. She ran over and hugged Carlson.

She pulled back and looked at him. "Where's the Captain?"

"One deck up."

* * *

"The Zercowans are taking a lot of hits from those projectiles, but they seem to have the defenses for that," Sanchez said. "They certainly seem distracted."

"We need the help," Zimmerman said. "Ensign, open a transmission to the qualer."

"It's open."

"Borvian vessel. This is Commander Zimmerman of the E.S.S Australia. You have members of our crew. Release them and we will disengage."

"No response."

"Repeat it until they—" The ship jolted violently, knocking Zimmerman into the Captain's seat. "Morgan, report?"

"That last projectile was destroyed too close to our hull. We've got a huge crater in our lower forward hull. It is about three-quarters of the width of our ship and at least four decks high. I have air locks on it, but we lost a lot of personnel."

"Keep sustained fire on the qualer."

* * *

The ship shook again. Carlson stopped Janice short as a pipe fell in front of them. He fired on two more Borvians that came down the hall. Hitting both of them.

"She should be around this corner."

Carlson peeked around it, but ducked back when three guards fired at him. He fired back.

Janice lay low and peeked again. She fired three shots, then nodded. "Go slowly Mike, I'll cover you."

Carlson got to the doorway, Janice ran up next to him. He opened it slowly. Then he heard a scream.

"Christina!"

Carlson didn't care anymore. He flung open the door and walked down the hall firing on any Borvian he saw. There was nothing else but rage. A whimpered cry came from a room on the right.

He looked in just as Mathews stabbed Serenity in the leg again with a steel blade knife. Carlson fired one wild shot that hit Mathews in the leg at the knee. The skin melted away. He fell to the floor screaming.

Carlson ran to Christina on the bloodstained table. "Christina! Are you okay?" Carlson slowly helped her up. "I wish I would have gotten here sooner."

Serenity tried to stand, but her left leg wouldn't hold any weight. "I can't walk."

"Don't worry love, I'll get you out of here." Carlson pulled Serenity's left arm over his shoulder and helped her up. He turned to Janice, who had been pointing her weapon at Mathews. "Help me get her out of here. He's nothing."

"It's not over, Mike. You haven't won," Mathews said.

Carlson thought about shooting him, but he couldn't do it. "It isn't about winning or losing, Roger. It is about doing what's right."

"Come on, Mike," Janice said. "We have to get out of here."

* * *

Mathews lay on the floor of the room. The pain in his leg blurred his vision. The ship shook violently. He heard another alarm. They were abandoning ship.

This wasn't how this was supposed to end. Why hadn't he killed Serenity from the start? He was a different man then. He had turned a blind eye to a few drug dealers, but he wasn't a killer. But the Society was ready to expose his corruption, unless he was willing to cooperate.

He really wasn't able to kill Serenity. Even just moments ago, as he was face to face with her again, he couldn't do it. Telling others to kill her was just enough separation, but he just couldn't kill her directly. He was weak, and now he would die because of it.

Anger replaced his self-pity. If he could only get off this damn ship he'd show them. He'd end this once and for all, even if it cost him. He tried to move his leg, but he just couldn't get himself up. Pain shot through his leg again. His eyelids felt heavy.

"Roger!"

"Over here." Mathews struggled to call out, his voice raspy.

Rikta came running into the room. She looked around before finding him collapsed on the floor. She knelt by his side. "We've got to get you out of here."

Mathews smiled and put his hand to her face. "You've never looked more beautiful."

Rikta kissed him. "Now I know you're delusional."

She lifted him up. Mathews draped his arm around her for support. They made their way out of the room, each hop made his leg scream in pain.

"This way," Rikta said. "I have a pod waiting for us."

* * *

"Commander!" Willard jumped out of her seat. "It's our shuttle. They're on board."

"Destroy that ship." Zimmerman said. "Get a security team and a medical team to the shuttle bay."

Zimmerman let out a sigh of relief. He was bound to lose his rank and wind up at a desk job, but he was glad for it.

"They are launching escape pods," Willard said. "The ship is falling apart."

Zimmerman watched as the qualer was destroyed. "Leave them to die in space. Take us home."

Chapter 49

Serenity walked down the halls of the Naval Command. She walked with a limp in her left leg and used a cane for support. Every now and then the left leg gave out, but the Doctor expected her to recover with therapy.

Carlson argued with her about even leaving the ship, let alone walking around. But she had to see the Admiral in person. He was worried she might not walk the same again, and Serenity knew he was right to worry.

She knew now that the Admiral's orders were faked and it was a misunderstanding that caused her to leave her ship. But, that wasn't what had her blood boiling.

Serenity walked around a corner and right toward the office door.

A lieutenant at the desk yelled after her. "Captain! You can't go in there unannounced."

Serenity flung the door open and stormed across the Earth Navy seal on the floor. Admiral Kelly stood up. Her two Protective Services officers started to pull their weapons. Serenity was sure Carlson was doing the same behind her.

"Stop," one of them said.

Kelly put up a hand. "It's okay."

Serenity, who never broke stride, stopped at her desk. She slammed her fist down on the Admiral's desk. "God damn it, Tracy! What the hell are you doing to my ship?"

"Calm down, Captain," Kelly said. "Your ship is being repaired."

"I'm talking about Commander Zimmerman! That man is a hero and you're going to demote him?"

"He disobeyed an order. As a result, I have to perform extensive repairs on that ship, all the lives lost—that man should be in New Alcatraz or, at the least, sitting at a desk somewhere. I spared him that."

"I'd be dead if he didn't act!"

"And the lives of three is worth the nearly six hundred that died?" Kelly asked. "It's the sad fact of things, Christina. It would have been easier to replace you than what we have to do now. Listen, as your friend I am thrilled you're alive. But, as the Commander of the Navy, discipline had to be enforced."

"You have to know he did the right thing!" Serenity was still yelling.

One of the officers protecting the Admiral spoke to Carlson. "This is getting out of hand."

Carlson whispered in Serenity's ear. "You can't change it and you're only likely to get yourself in trouble. You might wind up locked up yourself."

Serenity nodded.

"I'm sorry for my outburst. It's been an emotional event for me," Serenity lied. "I had assumed I was speaking to the Tracy Kelly I knew. But, if I may say one thing.

"Suppose Zimmerman had followed your orders. Suppose the Borvians—or worse, Mathews—saw that they could capture naval officers without a response from the Navy, then what? Imagine the bloodshed then. Imagine the military secrets that would be revealed. Capturing high ranking Earth military members can't be just accepted.

"Zimmerman may have sacrificed the ship and some of the crew, but he gave a strong message that this won't be tolerated by the Navy."

Serenity turned and walked out of the room. She moved as fast as she could. She wanted out of this building and she ignored the protests of her leg. It gave way and her cane wasn't ready. She crashed to the hallway floor.

Mike and Janice ran over to help her up. She pushed them away. "I am fine. Just angry."

A tear rolled down her cheek.

"I know." Carlson still helped her up. He said nothing until they were out at the shuttle. "You can't change it. You can either get out now, or stay in. But it won't be long for Zimmerman to get his rank back. Everyone knows he did the right thing."

She climbed into the shuttle. She glanced at Willard, the only one she trusted enough to fly her down here.

"Didn't go well, Ma'am?" Willard asked.

"Let's just head back to the ship."

* * *

Zimmerman was more worried that Serenity would get herself demoted than he was about his own punishment. He appreciated the Captain's support, but she wasn't in the mood for talking with the Admiral. To him, any punishment was worth it. He didn't really care.

They were tied up in space dock, and would likely be for a while. Zimmerman heard some alarms sound.

"Urgent message from Naval Command."

"Play it."

"All Earth vessels, border ships have spotted a large Borvian fleet entering Earth space. The ships are heading for Earth. All ships in the area are to head for Earth at maximum speed to protect our planet."

Zimmerman analyzed the data. Fifty Borvian ships were headed their way. How did they get here so fast? How did no one know about a fleet this size?

"Get a hold of the Captain."

* * *

Serenity had asked Francesca to make a flight over the Niagara Falls. They were pretty and she wished she had time to see them. She could probably take leave, but she needed to be on her ship. As disgusted as she was with the Navy, the Australia was still hers to command.

"Captain, urgent message from Zimmerman," Willard said.

Serenity used a console to bring up Zimmerman's face. He wasn't smiling.

"There is a large Borvian fleet headed *here* any minute. We are working to get out of the docks as fast as we can. We are not in much shape to fight, but we have to try."

"I agree."

"I talked with a Zercowan Marshall here. He says he has seen this type of formation and tactic before. He says it is likely a hit-and-run operation. They have several key targets in mind, likely our stations at the moon and here; they will fly in and hit the target hard and flee."

"They have to know of our planetary defense cannons. You're probably right. I'll be up soon. Get in position to protect the station."

The transmission ended. Willard had already pulled them up into space. They were just getting out when Willard spoke.

"Captain, they are already here."

Serenity moved to the front of the ship and sat next to Willard. She peered out the front window. Carlson and Kanter crowded the cockpit door.

"They aren't even slowing down," Serenity said, mostly to herself.

Suddenly, the space in front of them erupted in cannon fire as the planetary defense cannons and ships opened fire. Willard keyed some buttons.

Serenity watched as the Borvian fleet unleashed a rapid volley of laser fire, and several projectiles at the Australia. In the next instant there was a bright flash. Serenity turned away and then back.

The Australia was gone. The Borvian fleet was gone.

"Captain, I saved a transmission that was sent and broadcasted all over the Australia just before she was destroyed," Willard said.

Serenity was still in shock. She only nodded.

An image of Mathews appeared on the screen. "Mike, I told you this wasn't over. Well, now it is."

ACKNOWLEDGEMENTS

I am probably one of the few people that always reads the acknowledgements section of a novel. This is something that I've done long before I ever considered writing a book of my own. It has always fascinated me to think that behind the words on the page there is an author. And behind that author is a group of people that supported them.

The irony behind this is that I never gave my own acknowledgements section much thought. Don't get me wrong, I've always thought about the people that have propelled my writing forward. I knew I would thank them for everything they did, but I just never really figured out how I'd say it. It wasn't until I'd nearly finished the final layout of this book, that I finally wrote this.

This book was a long journey, one that I have stopped and started more than once. It started from 2003 to 2004 with the original manuscript for the first book, along with the manuscript for one and half more books. I only wrote them for fun, a little bit of stress release. I stopped writing until late 2010 when I felt the need to do it again. I had stories to tell and I needed to tell them. I wrote several shorts, but it wasn't until late 2011 when I returned to this manuscript. It took a complete rewrite, and several long editing sessions, but here we are, nearly another year later with the finished book you have now.

I didn't do it alone. I have a lot of people who supported me along the way.

My wife Amy is the first person I have to thank. When I first wrote this manuscript I was still a newlywed. I spent many late nights in bed typing madly on my laptop rather than doing those things that newlyweds do. She put up with it. And years later when I picked up writing again, she didn't complain. And sometimes not complaining is better than encouragement. She has listened to every idea I've had. And she has offered an opinion, even when they weren't solicited. I love you, Amy. Thanks.

My three kids, to which I dedicated this book, are a large reason why I returned to the craft of writing and with more seriousness than before. There was a time I dreamt, imagined, and loved in a way only a child can. When these three boys were born, each one of them brought back my dream of writing a novel and the imagination I needed to do it. It is because of them that I pursue my dreams, in a hope that they will always chase after theirs.

My oldest son Richard, better known as Cinco, one time said to both his mother and me out of nowhere, "I don't want to be stuck on Earth my whole time." Cinco, keep your imagination active, your dreams alive, and your desires strong and you'll never be stuck anywhere. With your love to read, you'll travel to places far and wide.

Jango, my middle child, has been a never ending supply of one-liners. Jango, just at the moments when I take life too seriously, you have reminded me that in the grand scheme of things, it doesn't really matter. Your candid humor has always brought a smile to my face, even the impression you do of me when I am mad.

My youngest, Kirk is just beginning to show us what his personality has to offer. When I am working on these writing projects, Kirk has never been afraid to run into the room and ask, "What you do, Daddy?" Kirk, thanks for reminding me that life is not all work.

While many writers have told me that family doesn't usually provide much support when it comes to their craft, my Mom has been the opposite of that. She has made sure everyone she sees knows of her son "the writer" and ensures they all know where to find my works both long and short. Thank you Mom, I am lucky to have a fan like you.

My Dad is one of two people I've known with such a massive collection of Science Fiction books. I remember my Dad's books taking over the walls of his bedroom. I would look at those books, sometimes when I should have been listening to him, and be fascinated by their covers and the worlds they held in their pages. I vaguely remember, as he boxed them all up for storage, thinking what if my name was on one of those books. Thanks in large part to my Dad; I have my name on a book cover that holds its own world inside its pages.

There is one person who I always remember holding a book. This is my Aunt Phyllis Hallack. She is also the other person I knew with a big collection of science fiction books. She inspired me to read, if simply because I always saw her interest in books. Unfortunately, she didn't live long enough to see this novel published. But when I started working on this project again, I felt she was near. And something tells me that she'll find a way to read this novel even in the afterlife.

Curt Espinoza has been my best friend since I was in the third grade. We grew up watching every great science fiction movie and TV show of the late 80s and the 90s together. Though we have our own families now, not many people can claim they are still great friends with someone for so long.

I have to thank Robert Wilson, my editor and friend. I met Robert through a writers group. I read his novel *Shining in Crimson* before it was ready for print. And while I may have helped him a little, he has helped me a great deal. Seeing his novel succeed inspired me to finally finish mine. He showed me that getting your novel published could be done, if you're willing to put in the work. And without his editing, this story would have been a fraction of what it is today. Thank you for helping me *look* at my mistakes and *smile* at them.

The folks over at the Hatrack Writers Group deserve a big thank you.

When I returned to writing, they welcomed me into their group. They helped me refine many of my short stories, and they have taught me so much. For every question I've had, they pooled their resources together to help me with an answer. There is a collection of great minds over there, both established in the craft and yet to be discovered. The knowledge they continue to share with me has allowed me to grow as a writer and a person.

Though I have never met Jeffrey A. Carver, his free website www.writesf.com was the first thing I read when I began my study of writing science fiction in 2010. He took a moment to respond to my email as well. The resources he has put together are a phenomenal help to writers.

I have to thank *Liquid Imagination Online* for my first short story sale. I felt validated as a writer the day I got that acceptance letter, and the rest has been history. Of course, I thank all the other publications that have purchased my stories. Each one has brought me new fans.

My experiences in life have brought a lot to my writing. My plots, my characters, and my worlds are all based on those. I've also been fortunate enough to make some great friends along the way. I can't possibly name you all here, but I appreciate you all a lot.

Last but not least, I have to thank you, the reader. Storytellers tell their tales to be heard. And I can only hope you enjoyed this story. And thank you for reading the acknowledgements to see the people behind this author.

ABOUT THE AUTHOR

Richard Flores IV is a writer of Speculative Fiction living in Washington State. He has had several short stories in publications such as *Liquid Imagination Online*, *Cygnus Journal of Speculative Fiction*, and *InfectiveInk.com*. This is his debut novel, though he now has three others published and two more in progress. Richard is the Editor-in-Chief for Factor Four Magazine. Richard fits writing around raising his three boys, watching hockey (go Sharks), streaming on Twitch, and working a day job. He also tries hard to blog regularly about writing, life, and how the two mix together. For more information about Richard Flores IV, or to contact him, visit: www.floresfactor.com